PRAISE FOR *Little Indiscretions*

"[Posadas provides] a sprinkling of endearingly kooky characters. . . . [*Little Indiscretions*] is all so . . . *charming* that it makes you think about psychopathic killers with renewed affection." —*Time Out New York*

"A perfectly plotted novel to gladden the hearts of all amateur detectives . . . [Carmen Posadas] is a joyous writer." —*Le Monde* (France)

"The joy in reading *Little Indiscretions* becomes how Posadas weaves each character's story, each with its single thread that threatens to unravel his or her life." —*Columbus Dispatch*

"*Little Indiscretions* gives us a close-up view of a glittering Madrid high society that is rotten to the core." —*La Vanguardia* (Spain)

"The action proceeds with all the inevitability of a Greek tragedy to a denouement both hilarious and horrifying." —*Publishers Weekly*

"Posadas invents clever devices for delivering each suspect. . . . There's murder in the air." —*San Francisco Chronicle*

Little Indiscretions

Little Indiscretions

A NOVEL

CARMEN POSADAS

TRANSLATED BY

Christopher Andrews

RANDOM HOUSE TRADE PAPERBACKS / NEW YORK

2005 Random House Trade Paperback Edition

Published in the United States by Random House Trade Paperbacks, an imprint of The Random House Publishing Group, a division of Random House, Inc., New York.

RANDOM HOUSE TRADE PAPERBACKS and colophon are trademarks of Random House, Inc.

Originally published in hardcover in the United States by Random House, an imprint of The Random House Publishing Group, a division of Random House, Inc., in 2003.

This work was originally published in Spanish as *Pequeñas Infamias* by Editorial Planeta SA, Barcelona, Spain, in 1998. Copyright © 1998 by Carmen Posadas

Library of Congress Cataloging-in-Publicaton Data

Posadas, Carmen.
[Pequeñas infamias. English]
Little indiscretions / Carmen Posadas.
p.   cm.
ISBN 0-8129-6631-7
I. Title.

PQ8520.26.O72P4813 2003

863'.64—dc21   2003043105

Printed in the United States of America
Random House website address: www.randomhouse.com

2 4 6 8 9 7 5 3

Book design by JoAnne Metsch

For Mariano

Part One

TWENTY DEGREES BELOW ZERO

Be lion-mettled, proud, and take no care

Who chafes, who frets, or where conspirers are:

Macbeth shall never vanquished be until

Great Birnam wood to high Dunsinane hill

Shall come against him.

SHAKESPEARE, *Macbeth*, Act 4, Scene 1

1

NESTOR, THE COOK

Sunday, twenty-ninth of March (in the small hours)

His mustache was stiffer than ever, so stiff a fly could have stepped out to the end, like a prisoner walking the plank on a pirate ship. Except that flies can't survive in a cool room at twenty below zero, and neither could the owner of the blond, frozen mustache: Nestor Chaffino, chef and pastry cook, renowned for his masterful way with a chocolate fondant. And that's how he was found hours later: eyes wide open in astonishment, but with a certain dignity still in his bearing. True, his fingernails were scratching at the door, but there was a dishcloth tucked into the string of his apron as usual, though looking smart is hardly a major preoccupation when the door of a 1980s-model Westinghouse cool room, two meters by one and a half, has just shut automatically behind you with a *click*.

And *click* was the last sound he heard before congratulating himself on his luck, Bloody brilliant, but it can't be true, since incredulity often precedes fear, and then: Jesus, why now of all times? The housekeepers even warned me about it before leaving, and there's a notice in three languages posted prominently in the kitchen, stressing the importance of not forgetting to take certain boring precautions like lifting the bolt so the door doesn't accidentally swing shut behind you. You can never be too careful with these old models. But Christ almighty, I can't have been in here more than two minutes, three at the most, stacking away these boxes of chocolate truffles. No doubt about it, though, the door went *click*. You must have done something to upset it, Nestor, and *click* it went. Now what? He looked at his watch: four in the morning, said the phosphorescent hands—*click*—and there he was in the pitch dark, inside the spacious cool room of a country house, almost empty now after a dinner party at which maybe thirty guests had assembled. . . . But think, think, for God's sake. Who's staying the night?

Let's see: the owners of the house, naturally. And Serafin Tous, one of their old friends, who arrived at the last minute. As it happened, Nestor had made his acquaintance a few weeks earlier, briefly though, very briefly. Then there were the two employees of Nestor's catering company, Mulberry & Mistletoe, whom he had asked to stay on and help him clean up in the morning: his good friend Carlos Garcia and the new one (he never could remember his name). Karel? Koral? Yes, it's Karel, the Czech boy who does weights and is so handy around the place, beating egg whites to a stiff peak and unloading a hundred boxes of Coke without working up a sweat, all the while singing "Lágrimas negras," a Caribbean *son,* with his rather unfortunate Bratislava accent.

Who would hear him shouting and kicking the door, again and again, bang bang bang, each blow resounding in his skull as if he were on the receiving end? Bloody *brilliant.* Thirty years in the trade and not one accident, now this. Just great! Who would have thought disasters could pile up like this, Nestor? A couple of months back you were diagnosed with lung cancer, and just when you're starting to get over the shock and accept it, you end up locked in a pitch-black cool room. Dying of cancer is unfortunate, but it happens to about one in five people. Freezing to death on the Costa del Sol is just ridiculous.

Keep calm; it's going to be all right. Nestor knew that American technology, even the most dated, was designed to handle all eventualities. Somewhere, maybe near the door frame, there had to be an alarm button that would ring a bell in the kitchen, and someone would hear it. The thing was to stay calm and think clearly. How long can a man in a short white jacket and checked cotton trousers survive at twenty below zero? Longer than you'd think; come on, pull yourself together. His hand started to feel its way quite calmly (under the circumstances) along the wall, up a little, down a little. No! Not to the left—careful, Nestor. His fingers had just encountered something prickly and ice-cold. Holy Mary! There's always some sort of dead animal in these cool rooms, a hare or a rabbit with its bristling whiskers . . .

Suddenly, stupidly, Nestor thought of the owner of the

house, Mr. Teldi. He pictured him not as he had seen him a few hours ago but as he remembered him from twenty or twenty-five years back. Not that Ernesto Teldi's famous mustache resembled a rabbit's long, sparse whiskers, then or now. It was smooth and elegantly trimmed, like Errol Flynn's. And it hadn't so much as twitched when he had seen Nestor reappear in his sitting room. Total indifference. But then perhaps that was to be expected; a gentleman like Ernesto Teldi has little reason to trouble himself with the domestic staff, so why would he remember a cook he had seen just once, ages ago now, back in the seventies, in the course of an afternoon fraught with such terrible emotions.

NESTOR'S HAND WAS feeling its way across another section of the wall. A little to the left now . . . but always trying not to wander too far from the door . . . this way. The lifesaving button must be over this way. Everyone knows Americans are practical people—there's no way they'd put the alarm bell where it can't be found. Let's see . . . but his hand seemed to be delving into an even darker abyss, so Nestor decided to give up the methodical search and go back to banging: six, seven, eight (thousand) kicks against the stubborn door. Holy Virgin of Loreto, Merciful Mother of God, Santa Maria Goretti, and Don Bosco . . . please make someone wake up and come down to the kitchen looking for something to eat. There must be one insomniac among them. Adela maybe. Oh yes, dear God, please make Adela come down.

LITTLE INDISCRETIONS 7

LITTLE INDISCRETIONS 7

ADELA WAS MR. TELDI's wife. A banal thought ran through
Nestor's mind (it can happen even in desperate circumstances):
Time is so unkind to beautiful faces. Adela must have been
about thirty when Nestor met her in South America. Such
smooth skin . . . He stretched out his hand . . . Jesus! Those
bloody dead hares again. There they were—yes, it was them,
with their furry bodies and little white teeth glowing in the
dark in defiance of the laws of physics—but what about
Adela?

No. She hadn't recognized him either, apparently, when
they'd met to finalize the details of the evening, and that was
much more surprising. Their paths had crossed on various occasions, at her house too, but of course that was all many years
ago. More than once she had come in and found him chatting
with Antonio Reig, the family cook, in that house of theirs in
faraway Buenos Aires. "Ah, so it's you, Nestor, back again?"
she would say, or simply, "Good evening, Nestor." She always
called him by his first name. Yes, that's what Adela used to say
to him back then—"Good evening, Nestor"—and sometimes
she would even add: "How are you? . . . Well?" before disappearing from the kitchen, trailing the unmistakable fragrance
of Eau de Patou while the two cooks went on gossiping, swapping stories about her, as even the most discreet people are
bound to do when someone vanishes leaving such a delectable
trace.

A sound from outside made Nestor perk up and listen. He

could have sworn he'd heard a noise coming from the other side of the door. And for someone with his long experience of kitchen sounds, there could be no doubt: it was the fizz of a soda siphon. Except that soda siphons disappeared from kitchens years ago, and, anyway, you wouldn't hear a quiet little sound like that through the reinforced door of a cool room. Santa Gemma Galgani, Blessed Virgin Mary, Mother of God, he begged, don't let the cold make me stupid. No nonsense, no hallucinations. I've got to stay calm to find this damn button that's going to save me. If this weren't a summer place in the off-season, there'd be a light in this bloody cool room for sure, and none of this would be happening to me.

But of course a blown bulb isn't going to be replaced in a house occupied for most of the year by an old couple whose idea of housekeeping is a halfhearted look around now and then to check that there hasn't been a burglary. People are so inefficient and sloppy in their work these days, Nestor thought. It's just plain irresponsible. But, no, he couldn't let the cold or panic cloud his thoughts. He had to go on feeling his way in the dark. The button couldn't be far away; that much was certain. The housekeepers might be chronically slack, but the alarm wasn't up to them. It must have been built into the system, and no self-respecting American engineer would design a cool room where a man could freeze to death like a sorbet . . .

Nestor heard the soda siphon again. He told himself it couldn't be, it was completely impossible, although it did remind him of a place in Madrid where those contraptions were still in use, along with all sorts of other gadgets: chewing gum dispensers, old cash registers, gramophones playing teenybopper hits from the fifties and sixties . . . Old-time toys for men with certain tastes and gorgeous boys—all the boys who work in those bars are exquisite creatures, and they're always accompanied by obliging gentlemen who are only too happy to buy them a fruit soda . . . But it's best not to talk about such things. *Silence* and *discretion* have always been his watchwords. Fruit soda, that's Serafin Tous's favorite drink, thought Nestor, although he had a glass of sherry this evening and spilled most of it on his trousers when he saw me. Such a respectable widower. No, no one needed to be informed of Nestor's little discovery. Least of all Adela and Ernesto Teldi: close friends are always the last to know the things that really matter, that's the truth. Not like you, old boy, he thought. All the little secrets you know about so many people—like Serafin, for instance. But that's hardly surprising when you've been in the trade for thirty-odd years, working in so many different places. You hear a few things. Nestor believed that knowledge was power, as long as it was never put to use. Or, rather, as long as you stayed in the background, listening and keeping it all under your hat, which was easy enough for him, since no one pays much attention to domestic staff, especially not to a professional cook who doesn't go in for gossip. But that didn't stop the stories from filtering into the kitchen, where they were blended with the meringues and set like nougat.

Serafin . . . what an appropriate name, he thought, suddenly remembering his first encounter with the seraphic Mr. Tous, and the second, and both memories made him smile. It was the last thing he should have been thinking about, but he couldn't help it. Fate has a weird sense of humor: *Serafín* . . . as in the holy, as if that harmless-looking gentleman had been fated to finish his days surrounded by cherubim.

A laugh. A clearly audible laugh on the other side of the door. Impossible. He was imagining things; it must have been the cold, seeping in now through his ears, his mouth, his nose. It felt like a fine drill trying to penetrate each orifice of his body, boring into his brain to knock out the neurons one by one. And the last thing Nestor needed right now was cold-deadened neurons. That's how people die in the mountains, numbed by the freezing temperatures, smiling stupidly. No, you fool, it's not a smile, it's a *grimace,* everyone knows that. But so what? Soon you won't even be able to think straight, you'll go completely off the rails.

That's enough. Let's think this through. Try to think methodically: Who else is in the house? Who else could save me? There's my assistant, Carlos Garcia—one in a million, that boy—and there's Karel or Koral or whatever the hell he's called. And Chloe, his girlfriend, who insisted on coming along in case we needed an extra hand. Any one of them would do. Someone's bound to come along in the next few minutes, thought Nestor, for he was certain that with all his banging he must have pressed the alarm button at some stage—God bless the Westinghouse engineers! Surely one of those kicks or punches had set off the lifesaving alarm. It was just a matter of time. The door would open. But meanwhile he had to do *something* to stop his neurons freezing or he'd lose it completely. If you stop thinking straight, you can behave like an absolute

moron. He'd seen a television documentary once on Arctic explorers that said they've been known to take off all their
clothes and go running around stark naked like lunatics in the
desert. Careful, Nestor, don't be silly, no stripping off, and
don't even think of moving from the door. You have to keep
banging on the door and shouting. Don't move away, even a
few centimeters, or before you know it, you'll have lost your
bearings and you won't know which way's which. The darkness can be treacherous. Don't budge, Nestor, and don't let up.
But the problem was the cold, seeping in through his mouth,
his nose, his ears . . . *that* was what would kill him. It would
drive him mad, Santa Madonna de Alexandria.

He looked at his watch. The luminous hands indicated
four past four. How slowly, how terribly slowly, time passes.
And then he had an idea: he could block off his orifices, all of
them . . . well, not the nose, of course, but the ears for instance.
What with? With the only thing handy: paper. You mean from
your little black book, Nestor? Obviously from the little black
book, you dumb fool! And destroy an irreplaceable collection
of dessert recipes from all the countries of the world and the
great houses of Europe? Worse still, you'd be destroying all the
secret details of . . . Now there's proof your neurons are freezing up, you old fool. What use is all that to you now? So Nestor
extracted a thick notebook covered with moleskin from the
inside pocket of his white jacket. Block out the cold, hang on
a bit longer, and it'll be okay, his intuition told him, and his
intuition had never failed him yet.

He heard a noise on the other side of the door. And another.

The alarm button had worked! At last someone had heard him, and soon they would open the door. He was saved! It would teach him to work late in the kitchen on his own and go marching into an old cool room in a strange house without taking precautions. But it's over now, it's over. The door's about to open . . . *click*. And again, *click*.

And not a moment too soon: just when the cold was getting to him, filling his head with stupid thoughts and fears.

2

KAREL, THE CZECH
BODYBUILDER

*I*T WAS KAREL, the Czech boy, who found him, but much later, at about four minutes to seven in the morning.

Karel was in the habit of getting up at dawn, so the hours people keep in Spain, and especially the hour they go to bed, struck him as obscene. "It's *obscennie,* Nestor, truly" (when he got worked up, his accent was especially thick). "It's really bad for you to go to bed so late. It gives you no time to recover."

It was difficult for someone like Karel to change his morning routine after so many years—to forget the discipline of rising early that had been drilled into him in Moscow, where, like so many other boys from the Eastern-bloc countries who showed sporting promise, he had been adopted by the great military family and trained, first in a "pioneer camp," then in the Lefortovo barracks, in the southeast of the city. At Lefortovo, he was known as Karel 4563-C, an up-and-coming weight lifter, a future Communist star, chosen by destiny (and by the Julius Fucik Committee for Czech-Soviet Friendship) to outshine all others at the Atlanta Olympic Games, which were to take place ten years later, the very same month that Karel would turn eighteen.

However, many unexpected things were to happen before the long-awaited month of July 1996, most important the fall of the Berlin Wall in '89, an event that temporarily prevented Karel from returning to his country (after all, an investment's an investment, even if it takes the form of an athlete and is part of a disinterested exchange between two kindred nations like the Soviet Union and Czechoslovakia). But curiously, just a few months later, when the Russians began to be faced with more urgent problems than winning Olympic medals, they were only too glad to cut costs, so they allowed and even politely ordered Karel and other Czech, as well as Romanian and Polish, sportsmen to go home. Karel was just twelve years old when he went back to Prague at the beginning of the nineties, so it wasn't hard for him to make the transition from weight lifting to a vocation more in tune with the new era that was about to dawn. "Bodybuilders"—that was what they were called, apparently, in the West, and according to his new classmates at the Sportovni Skola in Prague, the capitalist countries held major competitions and awarded prizes for the finest biceps and the most sculptured calves. And there was even the chance of getting your photo in the muscle magazines, which paid well, *splendidnie* even, although, according to his friends from the Sportovni Skola—aspiring bodybuilders like himself—real professionals were few and far between, and they didn't make much of a living.

Even so, what could be finer in life, sighed all those young dreamers, than the pursuit of the perfect body?

⟶

FOR KAREL, ONLY one thing measured up to bodybuilding: cultivating the magical sounds of the human voice. And this was to be the other focus of the young Karlicek's adolescent enthusiasms before his departure for the West.

It all began with the last gasp of Czech-Cuban fraternity (Anno Lenini 1992), when Karel was invited to compete for the José Martí Medal for young sportsmen at the XXth Spartacus Games, a sporting event of great revolutionary value, held that year in Camaguey, Cuba. It was there, among his comrades from the Most Beautiful Land (i.e., Cuba), that Karel succumbed, at the tender age of fourteen, to the rhythms of Latin music: the *son,* the cha-cha-cha, the bolero, and the conga. The spell was so strong that from the moment he returned to the Sportovni Skola in Prague, his burning ambition was no longer to be a weight lifter, or even a bodybuilder, but to become a member someday of the magnificent Cuban *son* band, famous throughout Eastern Europe, that rejoiced (and still does) in the name of Los Bongoseros de Bratislava.

Sadly, since destiny is not in the habit of granting every wish, his musical vocation had to go on hold. Three more years went by: 1993, 1994, 1995 . . . and then, one fine day, an opportunity came up to emigrate to the West. First to Germany, a natural destination for Czechs, but things weren't easy there. So Karel flew a little farther south, to France (where things

were no easier), and then farther south again, ending up in
Spain, where he couldn't find work as a bodybuilder, and certainly not as a cha-cha singer, and had to make do with a job
helping out and running errands on a motorcycle for a catering
company called Mulberry & Mistletoe.

$$\backsim$$

SOME ADOLESCENT OBSESSIONS, however, leave indelible
traces. Which explains why that morning, many miles from
Bratislava, and many more from Camaguey, when Karel
emerged from his room in the Teldis' house and went down to
the kitchen in search of Häagen-Dazs ice cream to help him
get going at that ungodly hour, he was singing and moving to
the rhythm of the well-known tune "El son montuno."

$$\backsim$$

THE SONG FROZE on his lips at the sight of Nestor inside the
cool room, eyes wide open and his left hand still scratching at
the door, or so it seemed. There was a scrap of paper in his
right hand, but Karel barely noticed it: there were far more urgent things to do, like finding out whether his friend was dead
or if there was still some hope of bringing him back.

The long years of military training that all elite sportsmen
underwent in the former Soviet Union can come in handy in a
situation like this. Trainees learned how to respond to all sorts
of accidents. Karel Pligh had learned, for instance, that freezing does not always cause immediate death but sometimes in-
duces a kind of lethargy, similar to hibernation, from which
the victim may be revived by a relatively simply procedure,

which he applied as best he could for a good ten minutes after dragging Nestor out of the cool room. First he gave him heart massage, pressing down rhythmically with his fists as required by the so-called Boris technique, then he tried mouth-to-mouth resuscitation, over and over, and not until the eleventh or twelfth attempt did he finally give up. Only then did he notice the piece of paper in Nestor's right hand.

Although Karel had been thoroughly trained in first aid, his education in television and film had, by contrast, been sadly neglected. Otherwise he would have known, like everyone else, that you don't touch anything at the scene of an accident. "Be careful, leave things exactly as they are until the police get here. . . . Remember that anything, even the most insignificant detail, could turn out to be some kind of clue . . ."

We know the cautionary words so well. But as soon as it was clear that Nestor was dead, Karel's priority was to notify the other people in the house. So without giving it much thought, he pulled the scrap of paper from the cook's clenched fist. It had torn in Nestor's tightening grip, and all he could decipher was fragments of a list of desserts:

> *especially delicious with cappucci*
> *lso be served with a raspberry coul*
> *which prevents the mering*
> *not to be confused with frozen chocolate*
> *but rather with iced lemon*

Poor, poor Nestor, poor dear friend, thought Karel, pondering death's curious habit of visiting the conscientious when they are absorbed in their work. A true chef, right up to the last, he said to himself as he took the piece of paper. And then he removed the dishcloth tucked into Nestor's apron string: a little quirk that death had underlined. The most respectful thing to do, he thought, was to ensure that these objects were properly laid to rest, now that their owner was sleeping eternally. And so, with great tenderness (and some difficulty), Karel managed to fold the frozen dishcloth. As to the list of desserts he had removed from the deceased's hand, he thought the most appropriate thing would be to put it in a cookbook, and it just so happened that over on the marble benchtop lay a copy of Brillat-Savarin's *Physiology of Taste,* Nestor Chaffino's bible and constant companion through thirty busy years in the profession. Karel slipped the piece of paper between the pages of the book, shut it, and placed the folded dishcloth on top, making a neat little pile. Only then did he go back to the door of the cool room.

With the light shining in from the outside, he had no trouble finding the alarm button that Nestor had been searching for. He pressed it. Nothing. He'd have to find some other way of waking up the others. Ringing the bell at the service door, for instance. But Karel's faith in electronic devices had been shaken. A good shout would be much more effective. So Karel Pligh shouted. He shouted with all the force of his well-trained lungs.

3

THE SHOUT

*F*IVE PEOPLE HEARD Karel Pligh's shout in the early hours of the morning on the twenty-ninth of March.

Serafin Tous, a friend of the family

When you haven't had a wink of sleep all night, the sound of a man shouting can have a decidedly odd effect on your mind. Serafin Tous thought it was a factory siren, and since he was a respectable independent magistrate with no links at all to industry, he rolled over and made the best of his last chance to catch a little sleep after a night of merciless insomnia.

He had spent hours worrying about that man. Was it Nestor? Yes, that was the fellow's name, according to his friend Adela. It didn't ring a bell at all, but there was no mistaking that mustache, even if he had seen it only twice, and briefly both times. The first time was the worst, about three weeks back, at a club called Freshman's. And just as he always did when he remembered that discreet establishment, which he had discovered quite by chance—he just happened to be passing by, God knows he wasn't looking for the place—Serafin Tous tried to focus his thoughts on his late wife. Nora, he said to himself, and he even pronounced her name out loud, counting on the calming effect of those two syllables. Nora darling, why did you have to leave me so soon?

In the course of that terrible night at the Teldis', which was almost over now, Serafin Tous had told himself a thousand times: If Nora were still alive, I would never have even thought of visiting an establishment like Freshman's. And he would never have seen that gossip-mongering chef appear in the kitchen doorway, preceded by his mustache, or heard him chatting with the owner of the club (it sounded like they'd both been knocking around in the hospitality business for years). And if he had never encountered the proud owner of that mustache, he would have been sleeping peacefully instead of suffering the effects of that terrible insomnia.

⁓

05:31, *CLICK* . . . 05:32, *click* . . . While Serafin lay there worrying, his alarm clock, a rather old-fashioned model, showed the time with square, phosphorescent numbers that flipped over like the pages of a calendar. Minute by minute. Like the artful drip-drop of Chinese water torture.

Forty-three years! Forty-three long years, perhaps not years of happiness exactly, but years of peace at least. That is what Nora had given him: more than half a life together, just the two of them. No children with whom to share their affection, no nephews or nieces, no adolescents. A long, peaceful stretch of entirely adult life, from his distant student days when, to pay his way through a law degree, he'd worked as a piano teacher in a school run by the Christian Brothers, up till that afternoon when Nestor had seen him at Freshman's. Forty-three years of perfect respectability: more than enough to make up for a moment of weakness. Forty-three years since his last glimpse of that unforgettable boy with his blue eyes and his crew cut (where could he be now? what could have become of that body, so thin for a fourteen-year-old, and those downy blond knees?) up till the ill-fated moment when he crossed the threshold of that private club.

After a brief welcome and a few questions from the owner, he was shown to a room that smelled of erasers and chalk dust. Perhaps there were other rooms at Freshman's with other sorts of décor. Glancing into one on the left as he passed, he thought he could make out an old American gramophone and a soda fountain, but the room to which he had been taken was more like a classroom, and it did indeed smell of chalk and erasers, and of colored-pencil shavings too. The worst thing, though, was the upright piano against the far wall. He couldn't resist. He went over to the instrument and even dared to lift the lid and caress the keys. They were so beautifully smooth, as if someone had been playing on them continuously for the last forty-three years. Dear God, so many impulses that he had thought were dead and gone had been simply lying dormant, for there he was, in a little room at Freshman's, caressing a piano and gazing at the owner, who, to cap it off, looked for all the world like an arts-and-crafts teacher.

"This way, sir, if you please. Perhaps it would be best to start by having a look through our photograph albums. The boys have been hard at work this year making them up, and they've done a lovely job, as you'll see."

The classroom with its smell of colored pencils . . . the piano . . . and that man going on and on, holding two large albums bound in red leather.

"We are very proud of our boys. Why don't you have a look? Go on, there's absolutely no need to worry, everything's aboveboard here. None of the lads are underage, I assure you."

The way the photos were set out, it was like an old school album: row after row of diligent pupils. A large range of adolescent faces for Serafin Tous to admire: blond boys and dark ones, some smiling broadly with braces on their teeth to make them look younger than they really were.

"Take your time, sir," said the arts-and-crafts teacher. "Take as much time as you like. We're in no hurry, me and the boys."

More photos of bright-eyed lads, some wearing knee-length shorts, like his pupils back in the old days when he used to give piano lessons all those years ago before Nora's love (and her money) had come to shelter him from harm.

"What do you think, sir? Perhaps you'd like to be left alone for a minute? It's often easier to think that way. While you're doing that, I'll go and chat with a friend of mine, a colleague who's dropped in to see me. I'll be back in a moment."

Serafin felt calmer on his own, flipping through the pages, and was able to concentrate on the multitude of young faces before him. Some boys were wearing spotless white sports gear. Three or four were dressed as explorers, and he flicked back to the pictures of muscular youths with dirty faces, dressed as commandos. Page after page of faces, until the click of the door almost made him slam the album shut: the arts-and-crafts teacher had returned.

"No hurry, sir, please keep looking. Can I bring you something? Fruit juice with soda water, perhaps? It's very nice the way we make it here. You'll see, just like the old days . . ."

And suddenly, just like the old days, there it was, that face. Well, perhaps it wasn't exactly the same as the face he had loved. Serafin sat back in the chair. It couldn't be . . . but how could anyone resist those eyes, that limpid gaze, that blond crew cut? You couldn't see his hands in the photo, but Serafin was sure the fingers would be nervous, like the fingers that had once entwined with his on the keyboard as he taught them to play a simple sonata. He preferred not to remember what had happened next, that day and so many others throughout the course of a whole ruinous year. Serafin shook his head. No, no. There are memories that should remain securely locked away.

"How are we doing? May I take a look, sir, if you don't mind? So Julian has caught your eye, has he?" he heard the owner of the establishment saying. "Excellent. I'll go and call him."

And he disappeared before Serafin could say a word.

We'll just have a drink together, he promised himself as he sat there waiting, when out of some dark nook in his subconscious came the imperious urge to bite the nail of his index finger. What would his wife have thought if she could have seen

him? Just a couple of drinks, I swear, Nora, he thought, mentally trying to reassure her. I'll have a fruit juice with soda
water, like in the old days, and I guess he'll have a Coke.

And that was exactly what happened. He bought the boy a
drink, and that was it. So that fellow with the pointy mustache,
Nestor or whatever the hell he was called, had no right to be
spying on him from the kitchen door as if he were some kind
of criminal. Serafin Tous had a clear conscience.

But now that they had run into each other again, what if the
chef were to reveal the circumstances of their first encounter?
What if this Nestor fellow took it upon himself to tell Ernesto
or Adela or one of their friends? It's a sad fact, thought Serafin
Tous, that what actually happens in life doesn't matter half as
much as what people say about it, and it's safe to assume that
they rarely err on the side of generosity.

06:05, *click* . . . 06:06, *click*. Every time the numbers flipped
over, it was like a reminder or a warning: he was that much
closer to the moment when he'd have no alternative but to confront that loathsome man with his pointy mustache. No one
gossips like a cook. What a squalid profession it is: scurrying
around among pots and pans, they remind me of cockroaches,
thought Serafin with a bitterness quite out of keeping with
his normally mild personality. They're like insects creeping in
through cracks, turning up everywhere, going from house to
house as they please, carrying filth, and that's how they end up
knowing all about other people's private lives.

All we did was have a drink together, Nora. I had a fruit
soda and he had a Coke. I swear by all our years of happily
married life, you have to believe me. Those forty-three years

were a new life for me, without the music I once loved so much, without the memory of childish fingers on piano keys. I haven't touched a piano since then. You changed my life, darling, and I let you do it. We were so safe in our grown-up world, Nora, a world without temptation, where a grown man has little likelihood of coming across a boy in flannel shorts and with a crew cut. But then Serafin stopped. What are you saying, Nora dear? Something about my visit to that tarot reader the other day, the famous Madame Longstaffe? Please, don't think I'm looking for . . . you're wrong, I swear you're wrong. It's just that I'm so lonely . . . Look, he added, no longer sounding quite so contrite. I don't mean to be reproachful, darling. I know I should be grateful for all the years of peace you gave me. But really, with all the unpleasant people there are in the world, all the horrible individuals who would be better off dead and buried, why did you, my love, you of all people, have to go and die so soon?

Chloe Trias, the kitchen hand

Chloe also heard Karel's shout from the kitchen, but after a few seconds she was sleeping again, like the little girl she still was at heart. She reached across to the side of the bed where her lover should have been, but instead of Karel Pligh she found a reassuringly familiar hand, one that for many years had kept her company at night. Then she rolled over and went back to sleep, with her chestnut brown hair, cut in a bob, falling across her face.

Seeing her half-asleep like that, you wouldn't have thought

she was almost twenty-two, especially when she curled up with that invisible hand, which was in fact nothing more than a lump in the sheets. Other nights, a corner of the bedspread or a pillowcase would do the trick: a strong enough longing can easily transform cotton or linen into human skin. So holding the imaginary hand of her brother, Eddie, Chloe lapsed again into a deep and innocent slumber, as if outside it were still the black of night.

Sometimes, like that morning of the twenty-ninth of March at the Teldis', she dreamt that Eddie was coming to take her to visit Neverland. But Neverland, that island haven for boys who refuse to grow up, has changed a good deal since the days of Peter Pan and Wendy, of Mr. Smee and Captain Hook: no more crocodiles going tick-tock or pirates stealing Lost Boys. No, these days visitors to the island may find themselves unpleasantly surprised, as if, before landing, they had been dosed with an evil drug. True, the coastline is still skull-shaped; it is, after all, the same island lost in time that she used to visit as a child, flying off after her brother's shadow. And yet, for some time, or to be more precise since Chloe had met Karel and Nestor Chaffino, a treacherous wind had been blowing her off course, so that she never quite knew where she would end up.

And on this occasion, the visit to Neverland was completely wrecked by Karel Pligh's second cry for help from the kitchen.

Cries from the real world have a regrettable tendency to distort the dreams they infiltrate. Some can even turn peaceful idylls into nightmares, and so this second shout, though it did not succeed in waking Chloe, dredged up a mass of memories she would have preferred to leave undisturbed. She pulled her hair across her face, trying to shake off the bad dreams, and this strategy did give her a moment of relief. A relatively inoffensive childhood memory came back to her: a banal scene, at least for a start. "But, darling," said a voice, "what extraordinary names to have chosen for your children. Oedipus and Chloe, truly! . . . Another one of your *caro sposo*'s whims, no doubt. Psychiatrists do come up with the strangest ideas. It might seem amusing at first, but what about later on, when they grow up? Imagine going through life with a name like Oedipus. Just as well it didn't occur to your *caro sposo* to call the girl Electra while he was at it."

Amalia Rossi, better known as Carosposo, was one of those neighbors who obligingly inform a child of all his or her family's darkest secrets. As far back as Chloe could remember, Amalia had always been in and out of the house: a fat blond woman, quite a bit older than her mother, divorced three times, the last time from an Italian actor who had left her his surname as well as an exasperating tendency to make light of truly serious matters.

It was Amalia, wicked witch that she was, who, some years later, had taken Chloe to the bottom of her Italian garden and told her that her brother, Eddie, had just died. And in her dream she suddenly saw the whole scene again, every detail intact: Amalia Rossi's ring-laden fingers running through her brown hair, snagging every time, while Chloe, absolutely numb, pulled leaf after leaf off the box hedge, thinking: It isn't true, it *can't* be true. Get me out of here . . . somebody help me!

Thankfully, in the dream, that horrible hand could suddenly be transformed into its opposite: the beloved hand that snatched Chloe out of the Italian garden and took her flying, flying away to Neverland, or anywhere else, anywhere at all, as long as it was away from there.

Come on, Chloe, fly with me a little while longer, said the hand, while down there in the garden Carosposo's voice seemed to choke on its own disgusting words of commiseration, like a myopic boa constrictor strangling itself in its tremendous grip for want of prey. Higher, Chloe, come on, up we go . . .

When she flew away with her brother in a dream, she could believe it was all a lie. Everything that had happened on the nineteenth of February seven years before. It wasn't true that Eddie had borrowed his father's Suzuki 1100 to try it out on a straight stretch of La Coruña highway. And the biggest lie of all was that he had lost control of the bike going around a bend, just where the twenty-two-kilometer marker happened to be waiting. Twenty-two: his age then, the age Chloe was now about to reach. But Eddie, like Peter Pan, would never be a minute older: forever young, forever identical to the photo Chloe had carried with her since the day he had died, although she never looked at it. It's good to carry around pictures of the dead but best not to look at them; it hurts too much.

For a moment she thought she could see Eddie's face on the bedside table. But no, it couldn't be. She must have been imagining it. The photo was in its usual place, in her bag, hidden away in a little red leather case, somewhere under her sports gear and the Led Zeppelin and Pearl Jam CDs. Chloe never took it from its case, but she knew every detail by heart. She

had taken it herself. They'd been laughing and Eddie looked
so handsome on that afternoon of the nineteenth of February,
just before he went away forever. Every one of her brother's
features, so similar to her own, was fixed in her memory: only
their eyes were different. Eddie's were very dark, almost black,
while hers were blue, but apart from that, his hair, cut short,
was the same color as Chloe's, the lips were the same, and the
shape of the face. Everything about the photo reminded her of
that last day, even the clothes he was wearing: his father's motorcycle leathers, peeled off down to the waist. It was an incongruous sight: a boy with sensitive, almost feminine, features
disguised as a biker. That was what they had been laughing
about.

"And where do you think you're going, Eddie?"

Her brother had never been especially keen on motorbikes
(or anything else to do with his father) and yet that day . . .

So it's easy to understand why Chloe preferred not to look at
the photo of her brother. Luckily, there were other images filed
away in her memory, more faithful reflections of his true personality. Eddie looking very serious with the tip of a pencil in
his mouth, for instance, and she only had to concentrate on this
image to make it expand and come alive like a film in Cine-
mascope. Then she could see Eddie writing something on one
of those old-fashioned computers. She could see the short hair
on the back of his neck, and those lively eyes that sparkled
whenever he got onto his favorite topic: literature.

"Are you writing a novel, Eddie? What is it? I bet it's a story
with adventures and romance and crime and stuff, isn't it?"

But Eddie didn't let her see what he was writing.

"Not yet, Clo-Clo. I'll let you read the next one, I promise you."

(Chloe hated that nickname: it made her sound like a chicken. But Eddie was her brother, and he could call her what he liked, even Clo-Clo.)

"One day I'll let you read what I've written, but not this; it's garbage. I've still got a long way to go. The problem is," he said, sucking the pencil point as if that might help him solve it, "first of all, you need to find a good story to tell."

"Oh come on, Eddie, I bet you can think up something really good, something brilliant . . ."

Eddie kept running his hand through his hair, over and over, as if he might find the secret in there, the key to a good story. But then he ran out of patience.

"Well, there's no point racking my brains, Clo. I guess there's only one way to come up with a really good story, and that's to have tons of experiences, get drunk, fuck hundreds of girls, kill someone or something—live fast, on the edge, and look death in the face. But it's just a matter of time. I'll get there someday, Clo, you'll see. I promise you . . ."

"And what happens to a writer if he doesn't have any interesting experiences?" asked Chloe, who, like a lot of thirteen- and fourteen-year-olds, was always on the lookout for some patient soul to bombard with rhetorical questions: And what if this happens? And what if that doesn't? . . . "And what if you don't get to fuck hundreds of girls or live fast and look death in the face? What if it turns out you don't like getting drunk and you don't have the guts to be a killer, Eddie?"

"Well, then I'll just have to steal someone else's story, won't I?" he replied, sick of her stupid questions.

They never got to talk about it again. Of all the experiences he had wanted to have, Eddie was granted one, at least: living fast and looking death in the face. More's the pity, because there at the edge of La Coruña highway, the twenty-two-kilometer post was waiting to send him off to Neverland.

"COME ON, CHLOE, come fly with me . . . let's fly higher, let's dream again." But . . .

A RACKET OF voices from the stairway burst into her dream. Startled, she let go of Eddie's hand. What the fuck? Jesus!

Eddie wouldn't have liked to hear her speak like that. He wouldn't have liked her new haircut either—a short bob, shaved up the back of the neck—or her clothes, and he certainly wouldn't have approved of her pierced tongue and lower lip, not to mention her left nipple (and various tattoos). In fact, there were a lot of things he wouldn't have liked about the new Chloe, who was almost twenty-two now, like him. Only he was gone. He had left her alone with her psychiatrist father and her uncaring mother. . . . He had gone and he only came back from time to time, at night, to take her by the hand and whisk her away through the window, although she knew those nocturnal escapades were no more than a dream, so why pretend? Neverland doesn't exist. It's a story for little children, and stupid little children at that. All she knew for sure was that

Eddie had died seven years ago and the world had gone on without him.

So how come the photo of her brother was sitting on the bedside table? Chloe was certain she hadn't taken it out of its red case, she never did, and yet there he was, her brother, Eddie, looking at her with that smile she had tried to imitate so often in front of the mirror. Eddie standing there silently in his father's leathers with the sleeves tied around his waist, as if he were Michael Doohan, smiling, not knowing he had only minutes left to live.

"Tell me a story, Eddie. Don't go; stay with me." That's what she should have said that afternoon, but she didn't say anything, and Eddie jumped onto the Suzuki 1100 and went off in search of stories, because he was only twenty-two years old and nothing worth writing about had happened to him yet.

"And what if you get old and you still haven't had any experiences worth turning into literature? What then, Eddie?"

"Well, Clo-Clo, then I'll just have to kill someone or steal their story, won't I?" he said, and off he went, for good.

⁓

FROM THE STAIRWAY came a clamor of voices and general confusion. Chloe decided to get out of bed and see what was happening, but she took her time. No point in hurrying, she thought. Nothing ever happens anyway. And that was the truth. Since that nineteenth of February seven years before, nothing had happened. Abso-fucking-lutely nothing.

Ernesto Teldi, the owner of the house

They say you end up getting used to anything. You even get used to nightmares if they come back night after night, relentlessly, for twenty years. Maybe it was even longer—1976 to 1998: twenty-two years. A whole lifetime, for some.

Karel Pligh's shout from the kitchen didn't wake Ernesto Teldi but unobtrusively took its place among the other shouts that inhabited his dreams, one among many and not the most terrible.

Just as he had learned to live with his nightmares, Ernesto Teldi knew that the persecution would cease the minute he managed to wake up. It was really quite a reasonable arrangement—calm days in return for troubled nights—and that was how it had always been, both when he lived in Argentina as a young man and since his definitive return to Europe several years ago. Not once in all that time had he been bothered by an unpleasant thought or a fright during his waking hours, not even now that he had to travel quite often to Buenos Aires to look after some new business. Occasionally on his trips he would hear that someone suffering from nightmares similar to his own had finally talked. Some had written books, while others opted for prime-time television, like that bald, sweaty army officer called Serenghetti or something like that, whose public confession Teldi had happened to see one afternoon in the Hotel Plaza. The fellow had multiple chins and reminded him of those shar-pei dogs with their folds of cinnamon-colored flesh. He hung his big bald head and explained to the interviewer that the worst thing was simply walking down the street, "Because, you see, there are all those young people, and you can't help looking at their faces."

Having said that, he wiped his canine jowls with a fat, trembling hand as if belatedly trying to stop the words from coming out of his mouth.

"What I mean is, well, say I go out for a walk," he continued with difficulty, "and I'm minding my own business, walking down the Calle Corrientes for example, and suddenly I realize I can't look at anyone under twenty-five without thinking, That boy or that girl, that gorgeous blonde, maybe she was one of . . . just the right age, you see." Then Serenghetti paused and turned to the interviewer, who was looking at him with a highly professional and screen-friendly air of disgust. "And then," he said, switching at this point to the second person in a hopeless bid for compassion, "you remember what you did to their parents when they were just babies, the age their own kids are now, and you hear the motors of the Hercules drowning out their shouts, not completely, though. You can still hear them, and you can't forget the terrible look in their eyes, and you can see that look in the faces of the boys and girls on the Calle Corrientes or Posadas or whatever. You see what I mean? They're looking at you, and you're trying to keep calm and wondering what they know. What's behind those eyes? But they don't know anything. They were just babies when we went around and gave them out. And the way I saw it back then, well, it was the most humane thing to do. Poor kids. Anyway, now they have other parents who love them, who brought them up and sent them to school and wiped their noses and comforted them in the first months when they cried at night for their real mothers. But by then their real mothers," said Serenghetti, sniffing and breathing noisily through his shar-pei nose, "were at the bottom of the river under several meters of dirty water, and that's where they are still, down at the bottom, dead but not buried, and there you are walking down Corrientes thinking you can see their eyes every time one of those kids looks at you."

Serenghetti wiped his own nose after coming out with all this on prime-time television. A moment of silence. A couple of coughs. The interviewer seized the climactic moment and wrapped up the show with a truly professional blend of sorrow and loathing, and the fat guy probably went home thinking now he could breathe a bit more easily having publicly confessed his sins. True, many people would despise him after what he'd said, but they already did, before they knew the whole truth. And now maybe a couple would feel sorry for him. Why not? Deep down, in some dark corner of our souls, we are all comforted to find out that our little cruelties pale into insignificance beside what others have done.

⁓

ERNESTO TELDI, HOWEVER, was of quite a different mind. A public confession was certainly not on his agenda. In any case, what did he have to confess? Nothing. His situation was completely different. He'd done a little deal and it was all over in a night. No one could honestly say he had collaborated with the army or had anything to do with those stupid assholes. His only sin—if you could call it that—was to have maintained polite but distant relations with the colonel in charge of the barracks near the town of Don Torcuato. They had known each other for a good while, almost since Teldi had arrived in Argentina. Minelli always called him Teldi the Spaniard, with a certain respect. Teldi, for his part, thought the colonel was a good sort. One night, just that one night, mind you, it must have been in '76 or thereabouts, not long after the generals took power, anyway, Minelli asked him a favor: he wanted to borrow Teldi's light plane.

That was all he knew. At the time, anyway.

"Look, Teldi," said Minelli. "Best not to ask any questions. You do a bit of trading on the black market, don't you? You bring tobacco back from Colonia and land in the field just across the way. It's a good little business and you wouldn't want it messed up, would you? We really don't give a damn what you do. Listen, here's the deal: I turn a blind eye, you don't ask any questions. Got it?"

So Teldi the Spaniard asked no questions, because in those days nobody did.

He only started asking two or three years later, very quietly, very timidly at first, when rumors began to spread in the towns along the estuary, rumors about planes that were loaded up when they flew out over that part of the Río de la Plata but always came back empty. There was talk about what happened out there, and screams in the night, but it was better to forget all that or at least push it to the back of one's mind so it didn't get in the way, because Minelli was a good sort after all. He kept his word and always turned a blind eye to the smuggling. In return, Teldi kept his side of the deal; he didn't ask any questions.

So now Ernesto Teldi could go for a walk on Calle Corrientes or Posadas without a worry in the world, because he hadn't asked any questions. Not then, not later, when it was all over, when he had given up smuggling cigarettes and had used his already considerable fortune to embark on a new career as an art dealer in Buenos Aires. It all worked out for the best.

And yet, two years after his little conversation with Minelli, when he was still trading on the black market, something happened one night. Something truly strange, although it was probably no more than a figment of his imagination. In any case, one night as he was flying his plane across the river to Colonia, he thought he heard a shout coming up from the water, then another and another. It was crazy, it couldn't be . . . With the noise of the engines you can't hear a thing, especially flying at that altitude. He looked down. The black waters of the river were as quiet as ever: no movement, not a sign of life. "Impossible," he said to himself, lighting a cigarette to smoke the fright away, and he didn't give it a second thought. But those shouts took up residence in his dreams. And they were still there twenty-two years later; very reasonable guests really, since they never bothered him during the day and only made their presence felt at night. Fortunately, you can get used to anything in the end, even living with ghosts.

That is why the shout coming from the kitchen of Teldi's country house that morning seemed to be just one of the many that inhabited his dreams. He didn't wake up until Adela came in from the bedroom next door to get him. She had to shake him repeatedly before he opened his bleary eyes, dazed by the light of the real world. The first thing they registered was a letter lying on the bedside table. There it was, a fat envelope addressed to "Teldi the Spaniard," his name written in green ink. It had arrived the night before, in the mail, without a sender's name or address. Before looking at Adela, Ernesto stared at that little paper packet that, logically, should never have emerged from the world of his dreams. Shit, he thought, it's still there. I'd almost convinced myself it was just another nightmare.

Adela Teldi, the model hostess

As soon as Mrs. Teldi heard Karel Pligh's shout, she thought something irrevocable had happened. And if it was irrevocable, why hurry? Adela didn't leap out of bed or rush into the corridor screaming. She had never been able to understand what it was that impelled people to go running around when they found out about something over which they had absolutely no control: a patient in a hospital whose brain scan has gone flat . . . a drowned child floating in the sea . . . They start rushing around, as if by getting in a flap they could outrun death and rewind the film, back through those crucial minutes. Back to when the brain scan was still showing signs of life and the child was safe at the top of the cliff, under his mother's watchful eye, a few seconds before he gave her the slip for good and she went running, flying, hurling herself at a small body that she knew was irreparably broken.

Since the previous night, Adela had known that something was going to happen. There was no specific reason for her hunch except that strange tingling sensation in her fingers.

"By the pricking of my thumbs, something wicked this way comes . . ." Adela was not a great reader of Shakespeare's tragedies, but those lines had provided the title of a novel she remembered from her Agatha Christie phase. She had enjoyed that one, and it was true, too, about the pricking. Just before something awful happened, she could always feel it in her thumbs. For Shakespeare, of course, and Agatha Christie, only the worst kind of witches had prescient thumbs, but what did that matter? she told herself. Life isn't a novel in which everyone has to play a predetermined role and stick to it. In real life, you end up playing all the roles. Sometimes you're the victim. Sometimes you're the hero. Or the schemer, or an extra. And so on, right through the cast.

Now it's your turn to play the witch, Adela, she said, gazing at herself in the mirror. She certainly looked the part. Fifty-two years of narrowing her eyes in that charming way. More than half a century of smiling broadly to display her faultless teeth. The sun of a thousand beaches, too. A moderate amount of whiskey. Many sleepless or almost sleepless nights (not to mention countless personal setbacks, which she had borne with serenity, aided by Camus' philosophy of indifference). All this amply accounted for the dreadful Hecate-like apparition in her bathroom mirror. Slowly, Adela's hand moved over that scene of devastation, her face, then down to her neck and chest. She decided to put on one of her bathrobes, the finest, smoothest one. She didn't intend to get properly dressed but only to conceal her true appearance as best she could, so that when she went running out into the corridor or down the stairs to see what Karel Pligh was shouting about, she would look like a mature but, my word, still very good-looking woman, caught unawares, charmingly *déshabillée*. She brushed her hair a little, not too much, then came forward and peered at herself in the mirror with her blue, shortsighted eyes, absently stroking her cheek with three fingers and her neck with another, as if she were looking for something . . . but there was a good deal of deft and subtle repair work to be done if she was to achieve the desired effect, so on this occasion her touch did not revive the memory of that boy's kisses, kisses that had, in the last two weeks, turned her whole world upside down.

And yet every one of Carlos Garcia's caresses was there, deeply imprinted on her skin, on her temples, on the unflattering creases near the corners of her mouth, which had resisted the expertise of her plastic surgeon. A cyclone leaves a trace of its passage even on the hardest rock, and a beach hit by a tornado will never resume its former shape. Something similar had happened to Adela's face: since the unleashing of that passion, it was the same as before yet somehow very different.

For heaven's sake, Adelita—that old Nat King Cole song had taught her how to laugh at herself and her name, which was so much at odds with her personality—for heaven's sake, my dear, anyone would think you'd never had a lover before. She laughed. The mirror on the wall kindly reflected what was still a quite lovely smile. Dear oh dear, Adela, she added, a veteran like you, with a service record—to use a military metaphor, and what could be more appropriate?—that would have impressed even good old Nat King Cole. A boy young enough to be your son comes along, and look at you: head over heels! There was no denying it: the encounter with Carlos had turned her world upside down. It had been overwhelming, absolutely *devastating*, she might have said, if she hadn't been allergic to self-dramatization. Yet devastation had been wrought: every last trace of her former loves had been swept away. All gone. She looked at herself long and hard in the mirror, but nowhere on her seasoned, worldly skin could she find the tiniest memento of those other affairs, even the truly scandalous ones. Those secret affairs, including one that had done terrible damage, and after that, brief, passionate escapades and various bits of fun: all completely wiped from her memory. Looking at herself in the mirror, the only thing Adela could remember was an inexperienced hand trembling as it touched her body, as if it were venturing into unexplored territory. A hand that was slightly moist and that had the sweet smell of very young skin. That was all.

Adela Teldi contemplated the little hollow at the base of her neck. No doubt one of his kisses had left a trace of love's perfume in that fragile, wrinkled little cup: witch's flesh, old skin, like all the skin on her body; but strangely, its texture had never seemed to bother him, not even that afternoon when they first met.

The way it had all begun was truly odd. She had been planning a party for some friends at her country house, so on one of her visits to Madrid, she decided to visit a catering firm that had been recommended to her. But when she arrived at Mulberry & Mistletoe, she was annoyed to discover that the owner, a certain Mr. Chaffino, was out, so she had no choice but to deal with his assistant. Which turned out to be more than satisfactory. The assistant was a charming, conscientious young fellow. They started talking about broccoli flans, then they considered various wines to accompany the dishes, discussed the finer points of goat's cheese on salad leaves, and what about some vol-au-vents with meat or fish maybe? Then they came back to the question of the wines . . . but soon Adela realized that with all that talk about food and drink, she was feeling ravenous and parched, so she asked the charming young fellow if there was "a place nearby where perhaps we could finalize the details of the dinner over a drink . . . I'm sorry, I've forgotten your name. What did you say it was?"

After repeating his name, Carlos suggested the Embassy, which was nearby. When they got there, they ordered two tomato juices and a few chicken sandwiches and went on talking food: whether it would be better to have two sea bass on the buffet or a salmon and a sea bass; yes, yes, definitely a salmon with dill as well as the sea bass with tartar sauce . . . And so the conversation continued, accompanied by more sandwiches, smoked trout this time (the Embassy does a very fine smoked trout sandwich), and they talked on and on, still about catering, even after they had paid and left and were walking together toward the Plaza Colón, at which point they realized that they hadn't even considered dessert.

There was nothing for it; dessert would have to be discussed. And they can't have quite sated their appetites at the Embassy, because soon they were heading for the Phoenix Hotel to have a last drink.

⌐

IN THE BAR at the Phoenix, the tomato juices became Bloody
Marys (not one but three, and strong) and Adela wasn't looking at her watch anymore. What did it matter what time it
was? To hell with meeting her husband at such and such a
time. To hell with the party at her country house on the Costa
del Sol and her thirty guests. To hell with everything, because
by this stage Adela couldn't even remember how she had ended
up in a room at the Phoenix Hotel, where, as she sat on the bed
taking off her stockings, she couldn't help recalling a scene
from *The Graduate.* When she had seen that film for the first
time at the end of the sixties, Anne Bancroft had struck her as
mature, to say the least, almost an old woman. And there she
was thirty years later, in an unfamiliar hotel room, taking off
her black Woolford stockings, first one leg . . . then the other,
just like Anne Bancroft—*"Coo-coo-cachoo, Mrs. Robinson, Jesus
loves you more than you will know . . ."*—and it was hard to know
what the boy was thinking as he watched her, but he was certainly better looking than Dustin Hoffman, by a long shot, and
younger too: Adela suspected her graduate was not even
twenty-two years old; twenty-three at most.

STANDING IN FRONT of her dresser, Adela applied the sub-
tlest touch of eyeliner, putting some depth back into her
gaze. Now all she needed was a layer of powder and the effect
would be perfect, without it looking like she was wearing any
makeup at all: that's it, just about right. How much time had
passed since she heard Karel Pligh's shout? Five minutes per-

haps, no more. In fast forward, memories tumble past in no time at all . . . but maybe it was longer, ten or even twelve minutes, for suddenly Mrs. Teldi heard another shout. Had it come from her husband's room? Ernesto Teldi often cried out in his sleep. She knew what caused his nightmares. Although they never discussed his past, it held no secrets for Adela. Likewise, they never talked about that other incident, her own dark secret, something that had happened a few years after she and Ernesto had gotten married and moved from Madrid to Argentina. When was that again? In 1981, or maybe '82? Adela had tried to forget, but the best she could do was to muddle the dates. Suddenly, stupidly, she started singing: "If Adelita went off with another man." In the mirror, her eyes had a feverish look, which was quite unusual, since their mistress was not inclined to let them betray any sign of weakness. Self-control was the key, the self-control she had maintained for more than seventeen years, ever since the day her sister Soledad died.

If Adelita went off . . . but Adelita never did. That was her punishment. As well as knowing that the price of an unblemished reputation is silence. Or death. But now you're getting all melodramatic, my dear, she thought, doing a final check of her arms and hands, applying the finishing touches to her artful look of early-morning informality. It's sheer melodrama to suppose that all your problems, past and present, could be solved by a death. Highly unlikely, too; impossible, in fact, despite the strange tingling in your thumbs, you old witch. Time to get moving; you'd better go out and see what's happened, can't put it off much longer . . . but first, my God, I nearly forgot. I have to go in next door and tell Ernesto. What's the bet he's sleeping like a log.

Carlos Garcia, the waiter

From the servants' quarters on the top floor, Carlos Garcia could hear Karel shouting in the kitchen. But he didn't mistake the shout for a factory siren, as Serafin Tous had done. He didn't ignore it, like young Chloe, or think it was part of his nightmare, like Ernesto Teldi. Like Adela on the next floor down, Carlos got out of bed when he heard the shouts, but rather than indulging in some leisurely morning grooming, he headed for the door, hesitating only for a moment to look at the deep hollow left in his pillow by the head that had rested next to his.

He couldn't remember when Adela Teldi had left his room; it must have been a good while ago, certainly before dawn, but . . . Come on, hurry up. It was urgent from the sound of it—you can worry about that later. Better get down there and see what's going on.

Which is what he did.

There was no one in the kitchen except Karel, and Nestor's body stretched out on the floor. The room seemed perfectly tidy; there was nothing to indicate what might have happened. Without asking questions, Carlos knelt for a moment beside the body of his friend. He felt no pain or sorrow or even incredulity—it was just strange. There was something impersonal about the whole scene, as if that corpse had never been Nestor. The corpse of a friend is already a stranger, identical to any other corpse. Who had said that? It was all too true. But it wasn't the moment to be probing his memory.

Nevertheless, during those long minutes of confusion, before the others came bursting into kitchen, with only Karel there, impassive as a ventriloquist's dummy awaiting manipulation now that he had accomplished his mission and raised the alarm, Carlos Garcia did have time to remember many scenes in which his dead friend had played a part. And he relived those scenes: things they had been through together, shared secrets, laughter, little mysteries, and the odd premonition, beginning with the time, two weeks back, when they had gone to see a certain fortune-teller. And yes, maybe that was where it all began: the chain of events that would lead to Nestor's death.

4

I. A VISIT TO MADAME LONGSTAFFE'S HOUSE

A PARROT OR perhaps a lorikeet with red and blue plumage, a green breast, and a very tatty tail looked at them with one eye. The other eye, also asquint, was looking up at the ceiling, contemplating a corner miraculously free of decorations or knick-knacks of any sort.

They shut the front door. Nobody had opened it for them, but a sign saying COME IN AND WAIT YOUR TURN IN THE LITTLE AQUAMARINE SITTING ROOM, THANK YOU directed them to the second door on the left. They went in, greeted the three people in the room, and sat down to wait with the patience required of those who frequent such establishments.

After a little while, Carlos Garcia looked at Nestor as if to say: Do you think I could take a newspaper from this, um . . . magazine rack? And his friend's mustache, which fitted in perfectly with the décor of the house, replied: Of course. Carlos was about to delve into that multicolored plaster imitation of a doctor's bag and make his choice among the glossy magazines and newspapers when he noticed the head of a Roman tribune peeping out. He promptly withdrew his hand and decided to look around the room instead.

He had heard about fortune-tellers' houses: they were always weird. Some, no doubt, were decorated in the Chinese manner, with little colored lamps, and yins and yangs everywhere, even on the bathroom tiles. And Cuban faith healers, all the rage recently, probably had their places done up like Bacardi ads, with bongo drums and seashells everywhere, and statues of Babalú Ayé and Shangó and the Blessed Saint Barbara. But Madame Longstaffe, the famous clairvoyant, was Brazilian. She hailed from the peerless city of Bahia, and her house defied the imagination: the natural reaction to such surroundings was flight.

"Let's go."

"*Cazzo* Carlitos," said Nestor (*cazzo* was his favorite word, and Carlos still hadn't worked out if it had an affectionate overtone or was just an insult, since his boss used it in every imaginable situation). "*Cazzo* Carlitos, you're the one who insisted on coming, and now that we're here, we're going to stay."

⁓

ASIDE FROM THE novelty magazine rack, the most disturbing decorative feature in the room was a stuffed white Maltese terrier perched on an alabaster column. But it didn't seem to be bothering any of the other clients waiting their turn. There was an elegantly dressed woman occupying the sofa on the right (threadbare Aubusson tapestry with little Indian cushions), a Rastafarian cleaning his fingernails with a large knife, leaning against a Japanese screen, and a very nervous woman in sunglasses trying to look as unobtrusive as possible, who had chosen a seat in front of the window so you could see only her silhouette, like Fedora in the Billy Wilder film. None of them seemed the least bit surprised by the presence of a mummified dog on top of a column. Carlos observed that the animal had its ears pricked and its little pink tongue hanging out, as if it were smiling. On one side of the column, a bronze plaque provided an explanation: "Dear Fru-Fru, you will always be in my thoughts. Day and night I will remember the patter of your little paws following my weary footsteps."

"Let's get out of here," said Carlos, with the natural impulsiveness of a twenty-one-year-old but also, truth be told, a superstitious fear of what he might discover about himself and his future. Yet if he didn't want to find out, why had he asked Nestor to come with him to the clairvoyant's house? His friend was right.

"Eh, *cazzo,* it was your idea to come and find out about your imaginary lover, and if you think you can back down now, after pestering me for days about it at Mulberry and Mistletoe, you can forget it."

II. FROM MULBERRY & MISTLETOE TO
MADAME LONGSTAFFE

THERE IS SOMETHING about stoves and ovens that makes people confess their secrets. Take a young man, put him in front of a pan full of simmering syrup with orange blossom and pieces of pumpkin and other such flotsam in it. Next thing you know, he'll be baring his soul to a friend or mentor, whoever happens to be present, like a young bard confessing himself to a druid. Not that there was anything bardlike about Carlos Garcia—slack first-year law student turned part-time waiter—and far from being the green homeland of the Celts, Mulberry & Mistletoe was a very exclusive catering business, owned by Nestor Chaffino. HOME AND BUSINESS CATERING, said the card. DINNER PARTIES, COCKTAIL PARTIES, AND OTHER SOCIAL OCCASIONS. WE SPECIALIZE IN DESSERTS. VISIT US FOR A FREE QUOTE. As for Nestor, well, maybe there was something druidlike about him: not so much his appearance (an Italo-Argentine cook with a pointy blond mustache is hardly the spitting image of Panoramix), but there was a certain wizardry to the way he stirred his pots and pans, and somehow it made people feel like opening their hearts to him.

And that was why, in the course of a long winter afternoon, while helping to prepare large quantities of morello cherries soaked in cognac for one of Nestor's famous desserts, Carlos had timidly begun to reveal his secret.

It all started with a casual remark, one of his philosophical observations on a subject that would never even occur to most people, let alone a waiter rushed off his feet with not a moment to spare for idle speculation.

And yet it had occurred to him.

"No, honestly, it's something I've noticed time and again, Nestor: when you're working as a waiter, you reach a point when you realize that people have lost their heads," he confessed as they were making syrup to keep themselves busy while waiting for customers. "Don't get me wrong. It's not that you start thinking they're all crazy, though there's that too," he added, laughing. "No, there you are, busy serving the wine, and all you can see are the details, like they're not whole people anymore, just *bits* of people."

"Pass me the cognac, will you, Carletto," said Nestor, interrupting, "and stop eating the cherries."

Carlos, who didn't drink, was discovering the magic effect of cherries soaked in cognac, which bring out secrets even more effectively than the stirring of pots.

He went on to explain to his friend how, since he had started working at Mulberry & Mistletoe, he had discovered a whole new way of looking at the world: the way you see things when you're carrying a tray full of glasses. "And from that vantage point," he said, "it turns out people have no faces. No, seriously, it's true: when you're serving drinks, you don't look into their eyes to see who asked for whiskey and who asked for grapefruit juice. There are other ways of telling. And when you're out there taking orders and they're milling around you and making a racket, you can only recognize people by very specific bodily features. Do you see what I'm getting at?"

Nestor said he hadn't the foggiest idea, and Carlos had to make a special effort to explain something that can only be understood fully by people who are constantly having to deal with large groups of strangers.

"What I mean, if you'll listen for a minute instead of looking at me like I'm a lunatic, what I mean is that however important these people you're serving are, when you're trying to remember who's who, you don't remember their faces or their names, not even if they're film stars or government ministers. What you end up doing is telling them apart by some insignificant detail: a gold tooth, a telltale scar left by one too many visits to the plastic surgeon, whatever . . . sometimes it's a piece of jewelry—an old cameo, for instance. It's not as if you're looking for these details, but something just catches your eye. And if you happen to see one of them in the street later on, you won't recognize their face but you'll find yourself thinking: Look, there goes the woman with the arthritic fingers and bloodred nails who only drinks vodka and lemon . . . And that fat man with a wart on his neck? He's the one who asked me for matches to light his cigar—those moist lips were made for smoking big cigars. Do you see what I mean now, Nestor? For me, people come in pieces, eye-catching details that sum up their personalities. It's one of the things you discover as a waiter, and then of course the habit carries over into your private life too. I guess that's why I've started thinking about her again . . ."

Nestor pricked up his ears at the last words and stopped stirring. "Her?"

And Carlos went on. He wasn't really conscious of sharing

a secret with his friend; it was more like he was talking to himself.

"Not that I ever stopped. I mean, I used to think about her every day before, but the problem is now, since starting this job, when I look at a woman's hands, I keep thinking they're *her* hands, or I notice the neckline of some woman I've never seen before because it looks like *her* neckline. Haven't I ever told you about the woman in the painting?" he asked. "No, I guess not. I haven't told you or anyone else, and I'm not going to start now. There's no point in telling anyone about her."

Nestor said nothing. He kept stirring the syrup, but one more cherry soaked in cognac was all the prompting Carlos needed to launch into the story of a very old secret, a secret that went right back to his childhood.

5

I. THE WOMAN IN THE PAINTING

"CAN YOU IMAGINE," said Carlos, feeling he had found the perfect introduction to his story, "can you imagine spending your whole life looking at mouths and lips, hoping to find a smile you've never seen? And if I told you I spent my time at work, and the rest of my time, for that matter, searching for things like a shadow falling across a woman's neck or the curve of an earlobe, you'd think I was crazy, wouldn't you? But everywhere I go, I'm on the lookout for details like that."

Nestor's response to this curious effusion was to say: "Come on, Carletto. It's all right; don't be ashamed. Some of the things that go through our minds seem completely crazy, but there's not a lot of nonsense in the book of fate, if you see what I mean, Carletto."

Carletto didn't see at all, and he didn't understand why Nestor's curious accent kept coming and going, shifting from

Spanish to Neapolitan and back again, depending on his mood and what he was saying. But on that fateful afternoon, alone with Nestor in the kitchen at Mulberry & Mistletoe, having finally resolved to tell his story, Carlos didn't give a hoot (as Nestor would have put it) about his friend's wandering accent. It could roam the whole world over for all he cared. He was busy trying to find the words to tell the story of an old obsession, one that went back almost to his birth.

He went on to explain why for many years now, but especially in the last few months, he had been haunted by the image of a woman and why a pair of adolescent lips could have such a hypnotic effect on him—he'd stop whatever he was doing and follow their curve, or perhaps it wasn't so much the lips themselves as the smile that lingered on them, for the mouth that obsessed him was always smiling. In his mind's eye he could also see a pair of rather inexpressive blue eyes, neither cold nor still, just absent. Then the hair, platinum blond, tied back so you could just make out the shape of an ear and tell that it was unadorned. And, farther down, the shoulders, where his gaze could have lingered a lifetime had it not been drawn immediately to the hands, so different from each other: the serene right hand, fingers slightly apart, as if they were about to alight gracefully on a veranda rail, while the left was holding something close to her chest: a little sphere, a jewel or some sort of cameo, intensely green in color.

It was, of course, a portrait he was describing. A painting of a girl about whom Carlos knew nothing: a painting that had always been in his grandmother's apartment in Madrid. He had been there only twice before he had inherited the apartment, two or three months earlier. And the third time he had gone to visit his new property, not long before joining Nestor's staff, a mass of childhood memories had come flooding back.

⁓

WHEN NO ONE IS left to tell what happened, family histories keep their secrets. Only the walls could have explained, for instance, why Carlos's grandmother and his father hardly ever spoke to each other. Father and son lived far from Madrid, in a small town near the Portuguese border. The father, Ricardo, was a quiet, unambitious GP, who had been through life without causing any disturbance apart from the flutter inevitably provoked by a handsome body in a doctor's white coat. The grandmother, Teresa, was his wife's mother. And his wife, Carlos's mother, was called Soledad. She had been dead for many years.

Carlos had not yet turned four when his mother died, and that was so long ago now that all he could remember of her was the *ching ching* her bangles made, a sound that should have been cheerful but wasn't. In his memory it was accompanied by words that he couldn't be sure he had actually heard, since they might have been part of that store of early memories fabricated retrospectively from what other people had told him. In any case, he associated the *ching ching* of the bracelets with a voice whispering in his ear: "Carlitos, give your mother another kiss. She's going on a trip. Another kiss, darling." That was all. His memory had not retained a single feature of her face. Soledad was faceless, although it would have been simple enough for the obliging fabricator of false memories who lives in all of us to restore those features, one by one, since Carlos kept several framed photographs of his mother in his sitting room. Some of the frames were wooden; others, imitation silver. And on each frame a name, a date, and a place were inscribed: Soledad, San Sebastián, 1976 . . . Soledad, Galicia, 1977 . . . and so on, up to the most recent: Soledad at her parents' house, 1978. She always had the same smile, and the face that Carlos discovered in those photos was not at all like his own, since his mother's hair was very dark and her straight but pretty eyebrows were darker still. Some of the photos showed Ricardo Garcia as well (although he wasn't mentioned in the inscriptions), always sitting or standing close to his wife. In those, Soledad had a calm expression. "Soledad, San Sebastián, 1976," for example, showed them in summer clothes, sharing a beer in the Paseo de la Concha, while in "Soledad, Galicia, 1977," they were laughing, arm in arm, ignoring a woman to their right, who looked like she was trying to get out of the picture. Any one of these images could have provided him with a false memory, or at least a face to go with the tinkling of the bangles or the more doubtful recollection of a voice asking for a kiss, in spite of which all he could remember were sounds, a voice perhaps, but no face.

⌒

APART FROM THE sitting room with its reverently displayed photographs, the house in which Carlos had lived with his father had all the virtues and vices of an exclusively masculine habitat. When the father of a young child loses his wife, he usually looks for some way to fill the gap she has left. Either he marries again or, sooner or later, he ends up delegating the more tedious domestic tasks to a female relative—a sister or a second cousin, who looks after the day-to-day running of the household and occasionally revives the memory of the departed, sometimes speaking of her fondly, sometimes quite the opposite. So the dead mother lives on in her house, with the help of her female successor. But that is not what happened in the Garcia household.

It was clear from the start that Ricardo Garcia was not going to follow the pattern. He never showed the slightest desire to remarry (although he did become almost conjugally fond of eau-de-vie and, later, anisette) and was quick to reject the offers of two distant cousins who would have been only too happy to help him out. He mourned for Soledad in a very private and unspectacular way: by building up a collection of framed photographs.

In the end, the housekeeping problems were solved quite simply by hiring help. As soon as Carlos was old enough, he was packed off to boarding school, and the chores were done by local girls who came in now and then to cook, change the sheets, and give the living room and the bedrooms a quick dust. They hadn't known Soledad; they just did the work. So little by little, all things feminine disappeared from the house and from Carlos's life, including the living memory of his mother. The dead are all too easily reduced to anonymous photographs growing dim in their frames on the mantelpiece unless love or hate keeps them alive.

∽

QUITE A DIFFERENT fate, however, awaited the girl with long fingers and blond hair, whose portrait hung in his grandmother's flat. Perhaps because this girl, unlike his mother, did have a face. Carlos remembered very clearly how he had discovered her. What is more, he could relive every detail of the scene. It was his earliest childhood memory, and there could be no doubt that it was genuine. It could not have been made up afterward from the stories that others had told him. It must have happened just as he remembered, because no adult would have bothered to tell him about it. Only children are interested in such things.

He was sitting on the floor, playing with something or just tracing the arabesques in the carpet with his finger, when unfamiliar feet approached suddenly and a pair of hands put a painting down against the wall beside him: an oil painting of a young woman with blond hair. A few moments later, the same hands put another picture next to the portrait, but it was much less interesting: a drawing of what appeared to be a tree, or maybe several trees. In any case, it disappeared from view soon afterward. It was lifted up and hung where the blond lady had been, high up on the wall, so high that Carlos had never seen her before.

But he had come face-to-face with her now . . . and those blue, indifferent eyes were smiling at him. He could have put out his hand and touched that deliciously white hand, delicately grasping something in its fingers. His contemplation was interrupted by murmuring voices engaged in a long, unintelligible conversation. He looked up briefly but paid no attention to the voices, fascinated as he was by the strange apparition down at his level, on the carpet, in the child's world where young women with long fingers and smiling blue eyes are unknown and only the seamy underside of the adult world is visible: chair and table legs, heating pipes, a cobweb beyond the reach of the fussiest feather duster, and the feet of those who move in the grown-up world above, disdainful feet that seemed to be gesturing at the picture of the girl, and women's shoes standing on tiptoe as if to stress a point, or so it seemed. Meanwhile there she was, with her curious smile and her look of indifference. It didn't seem to bother her at all being down there on the ground, a talking point for so many opinionated feet.

A few minutes later they made her vanish. This time four arms and as many unfamiliar hands—such strong, such lucky, hands—reached down to the young lady and lifted her up into the adult world, out of his sight.

⁓

IF CARLOS WAS eventually able to determine that he had first seen the portrait in February 1982, it was because a few days later something else had happened, something which, unlike that fateful meeting, had since been overlaid with a multitude of false memories: he learned of his mother's death. Despite the gravity of the event, he could not remember it clearly or visualize the scene, because Soledad had died unexpectedly, a long way away, during a trip to South America. So there was no painful sickness to remember, no corpse to kiss good-bye, not even a funeral, or if there had been one, someone had decided it would be better for such a young child not to be present.

That sensitive soul, whoever he or she was, had spared him the sight of his mother disappearing under a pile of white flowers and spadefuls of earth thumping on the wood of the coffin. And the Our Fathers. And the Hail Marys. He had been spared all those memories.

Carlos could, however, remember the following days. That short space of time seemed more like a century, it was so crammed with memories, some true, some false, none of them pleasant. Moist kisses from lots of people he didn't know and anonymous, pitying voices saying, "Poor thing." Such a weight of tears, laments, and sighs. Then the trip back to the village, just him and his father: it was the end of an era. For Carlos, who was not yet four years old, it seemed like the end of childhood. Thinking of his cousins, whom he had met briefly at his grandmother's apartment during the days of mourning, and his friends from the village, he supposed he must be an adult now, because nothing so grown-up had happened to any of them.

Years went by before his second encounter with the woman in the painting, though just how many was hard to say. All Carlos knew was that it happened during Holy Week, but was he seven, eight, nine, or ten when he went to Madrid for the holidays? He did not know. What he did know was that his father was overseas at the time, and that was why he'd had to spend a couple of weeks at his grandmother's apartment. His father hardly ever left the village; it must have been the first time he'd gone away since his ill-fated trip to South America with Soledad. For the first few years after her death, when Carlos was younger, Ricardo never mentioned the long journey that had taken him and his wife to Uruguay, Argentina, and Chile, but suddenly, around the time of Carlos's second visit to his grandmother's apartment, he began to talk about it often, especially when he had exceeded his habitual dose of spirits. On such occasions (Carlos particularly remembered a long conversation on the train to Madrid), Ricardo would go over everything he and Soledad had done in Buenos Aires: the places they had visited together, how happy she'd been, and so on, in great detail, all recounted and relived with a strange, almost pedantic insistence that Carlos would only begin to understand many years later, when he had grown up and learned to deal with his own unwelcome memories. He realized then that his father's insistence had been motivated by a secret desire to wear out that painful part of his past, as if he were compulsively putting on the same article of clothing day after day, unconsciously hoping it would fall apart sooner rather than later, at which point he would be able to relegate it to a box and forget it forever without qualms.

AS TO THE exact dates of Carlos's second visit to his grandmother's apartment, if he had asked his father (which he had not done and could not do now), perhaps he would have been told that the visit had taken place in April 1986, when he was eight years old. Eight: the age of exploration, of ghosts and secret forays; the age at which a mystery lurks behind every curtain and every armoire opens into a magical world, which you may enter at any time, but who knows when you will return?

His grandmother's apartment was especially rich in mysteries.

It was only many years later that Carlos would come to wonder why his father had not been allowed to cross the threshold when they had arrived that day, and why, instead of kissing her son-in-law, Grandma Teresa had rather coldly touched his arm. But that was grown-up stuff, and he was busy with mysteries of his own.

There were so many things to discover in that apartment.

For a start, you could see right away that it belonged to someone rich, as opposed to all the houses Carlos had known until then: his father's desolate residence and the homes of his friends, which smelled of boiled vegetables and could all have done with a fresh coat of paint. Nothing like this light-filled apartment with its high ceilings: Number 38 Calle de Almagro. Number 38, his grandmother used to call it, speaking of the apartment as if it were a person.

"Be good, Carlos. I'll come and pick you up as soon as I get back."

"Yes, Dad."

"Eat all your food and try to get up a bit earlier on Sunday."

"Yes, Dad. Of course, Dad."

"Listen to your grandmother and do what she tells you . . ."

Addressing herself directly to Carlos and ignoring his father, his grandmother said: "Let's get one thing straight, young man: at Number 38, you'll have a siesta every afternoon," at which point Carlos looked her in the eyes for the first time.

And then he thought, or rather, a thought began to form

that would develop over the few days they spent together: Grandma Teresa was like her apartment, full of corners. Both were large and angular; both had unexpected nooks and crannies. People are a lot like their houses, at least from a child's point of view, so Carlos soon came to identify his grandmother's moods with the various rooms at Number 38, which varied in appearance depending on whether the doors to the hallway were open or shut and whether it was raining or dark outside. Some sunny mornings, for instance, Grandma Teresa seemed to resemble her dressing room, and when you came to think of it, they both smelled of lavender. His grandmother seemed so fragile then, the deep darkness of her eyes offset by the almost metallic blondness of her hair. And the dressing room made the same impression: its walls were painted a very pale ocher, contrasting with the darkness of the two windows, which were always shut. But at night a hard gleam came into his grandmother's eyes, banishing any hint of fragility, and then Carlos thought she was like the entrance hall: a damask-hung tunnel, predominantly red. Yet all these childish impressions were like sketches for the definitive picture: Grandma Teresa in perfect harmony with the décor of her yellow sitting room.

Teresa spent most of her time in that almost circular room, with its one window opening onto a balcony and a stretch of sky, not always blue. She never entertained any visitors there but sat alone, a vague smile on her face as she played solitaire in front of the fireplace, ignoring Carlos and hardly even glancing up from her cards when he came in to give her a kiss. Rather than look at him, she would lose herself, or so it

seemed, in the contemplation of an utterly uninteresting painting hanging on the opposite wall—a landscape with a tree—
while with her elongated fingers she placed a jack on a queen,
then an eight on a seven . . . all the while saying not a word to
her grandson. But that, as Carlos soon discovered, was the best
thing about his grandmother and her yellow room: most of
the time both of them were distantly kind. Only around three
o'clock did they liven up briefly: the room was illuminated by
watery afternoon sunlight and Grandma Teresa, without fail
or variation, intoned her stern refrain: "As you well know,
young man, here at Number 38, you have a siesta."

And it was during the siesta one day, as Carlos was investigating the contents of a room at the back of the apartment, that
he encountered the young lady in the painting once again, only
to be caught a few minutes later by a maid called Nelly. The
siesta was an ideal time for escapades and secret exploration,
and Carlos had been making the best of it for several afternoons when, quite by chance, he came upon that portrait of a
lady, which he remembered only too well from his first visit
to the house after his mother's death. But now the painting
wasn't in the sitting room, or in any other room, and Carlos
would never have found it had he not heard Nelly's steps
approaching and tried to hide in an armoire. There it was,
among various dusty bits and pieces, barely visible, half covered by a blanket. Just then Nelly opened the door of the
cursed armoire, but she could scold him and yell at him all she
liked. Filled with a strange new emotion, he was busy removing the blanket to reveal the lady's bust. Before Nelly could extract him forcibly—"Naughty boy! Get out of there, you little

devil!"—and get hold of his ear—"Don't you think you can run away from me"—he managed to reach out and stroke that dust-covered neck. His fingers slid down to the neckline of the black-and-white dress, a little farther down, and then to the right to touch those long, slender fingers holding a green-ish sphere. "Just you wait till your grandmother finds out what you've been doing during siesta time, you stupid child," shouted Nelly. While he was being told off, the lady in the painting seemed to be watching him with her blue eyes, as if she were heartily amused by it all. And that's what gave him the courage to stand up to Nelly, stick out his tongue, and yell with a fearless insolence: "Stupid? You're the stupid one, Nelly. Stupid Nelly! Smelly Nelly! I haven't done anything wrong."

All the same, what he had done must have been very wrong indeed, because from that day on, the door of the room at the back of the apartment was kept securely locked and his grand-mother wouldn't hear a word about the portrait, not even when he came into the yellow room and found her smiling at the successful conclusion of a game of solitaire. Are you listen-ing, Grandma? Please, Grandma . . . But the most he managed to get out of her one day was: "You're mistaken, young man. A woman in an armoire? What *are* you talking about? There's no such thing in this apartment." And she smiled again at an ace of hearts, or maybe it was a king of clubs, but the smile disappeared as she added: "If you keep on about these bad dreams, I'll have to tell Nelly not to give you stew at lunchtime. Besides, with this lovely warm weather we're having, it's time for summer food, salads and so on."

That was the only time Carlos ever heard his grandmother give instructions about the running of the household, except regarding the siesta, which continued to be obligatory at Number 38, and curiously, it was thanks to that much resented nap that Carlos, after finding the portrait, was to make a second great discovery. He learned that during the siesta, a boy may be visited by a peculiar sort of dream from which he wakes all hot and bothered, breathing heavily, with a strange warm feeling between his thighs, which is over too soon, gone like the fleeting image of three long, very white fingers, holding what? Carlos didn't know, but perhaps he would be able to glimpse it in his next dream, and perhaps he might be able to caress that blond hair too, which sometimes reminded him vaguely of someone else's hair, but whose? Was it Nelly's? His grandmother's? There were so many mysteries, too many, and yet, at the age of eight, there were also important lessons to be learned.

Such as how to keep your mouth shut.

FIFTEEN YEARS LATER, his grandmother was dead. The deep-red entrance hall, the ocher dressing room, the yellow sitting room, and everything at Number 38 now belonged to him. He didn't inherit any money, not a cent; those years of playing solitaire and keeping up appearances must have eaten up all her savings. Since that Easter holiday long ago, Carlos had turned into the sort of young man he had shown signs of becoming as a child: more interested in dreams than in reality, more often to be found at the movies than in class (although, in his own way, he was an assiduous student: he repeated his first year of law three times). In fifteen years, he had grown as tall as his father and had developed the same dark, slightly wasted look, as if fate had used him for an experiment: take the look and bearing of a typical nineteenth-century hero and add a pair of Levi's. He had curly hair, long sideburns, and skin so pale you could see blue veins on his temples. One day Marijose, his father's nurse, had said to him: "If you'd been born last century, you'd have made a great hussar." She might not have known much about military history, but she had watched a lot of historical romances on television and at the movies. Marijose, however, had moved on; her services were no longer required. It would have eased Dr. Garcia's mind to know that Teresa had left the apartment in Madrid to him and his son, but he had been dead ten months when the will was read.

All Carlos had to do now was move to Madrid and take possession of Number 38. How he wished his father could have been there; he wouldn't have had to stay outside this time or face an icy welcome and a halfhearted touch on the arm. But Carlos left the village on his own. When he got to Madrid, he discovered that his inheritance was in a sadder state than he had anticipated. Everything was covered with white sheets: the old beds, all the furniture and fittings he remembered from his last visit. In all those years, no one had bothered to change a thing. Not even the ashtrays had moved; it was as if they were held in place by the will of the departed, as if the whole house were a derelict tomb. Carlos, however, was not bothered about the furniture. Like a little boy loose at siesta time again, armed with his grandmother's bunch of keys, he went looking for the forbidden door, and then the armoire, and there she was, just as before, the girl in the painting, among piles of useless junk. Carlos lifted up the portrait as a pair of anonymous hands had done almost twenty years before, took it to the yellow room, and returned it to its rightful place, usurped for so long by that landscape with trees that his grandmother liked to contemplate while playing cards. It was only then that he fully realized what the inheritance meant. Number 38 was his, all his. There didn't seem to be anything very valuable in the apartment, but that didn't matter: after the sale he would have far more money at his disposal than ever before in his life. Until then, he said to himself, it was just a matter of being careful and finding a part-time job that wasn't too demanding so that he would have time to continue with his law degree (that was the theory, at least). And while he was looking for a buyer, he could live in the apartment and discover its secrets.

⁓

"SO LET ME get this straight, *cazzo* Carlitos," said Nestor, interrupting his employee at this point in the story while a copper pan full of cherry syrup came perilously close to boiling over in the kitchen at Mulberry & Mistletoe. Carlos's confession had been so long that Nestor felt he was losing the thread, and he had to stir the syrup backward, which is something you should never do, unless you don't mind your morello cherries turning into sour cherries.

"So let me see if I've got this straight. You have just moved to Madrid because you inherited an apartment, but there's no way you can afford to maintain it. And just to make things complicated, you don't know anyone here, but you're having a romance with a lady who lives in an armoire. Is that it?"

"Oh come on, Nestor!"

"What I'm hearing is an unexpected inheritance, a child-hood dream, a great romance . . . you sound like the typical wide-eyed country kid who's just arrived in the big city. Seri-ously, next you'll be telling me that one day you're going to meet this mysterious girl walking a little dog in the Retiro or eating a hamburger at McDonald's. The vapors from that cherry syrup must have gone to your head, eh, Carlitos?"

"I know I'll never meet her—I'm not that stupid. But I keep finding *pieces* of her everywhere, I swear," said Carlos.

And then he had to explain all over again that since joining Mulberry & Mistletoe, he had realized that working as a waiter allowed him to gather the scattered parts of his lost love: one woman's marvelous smile, the ivory skin revealed by another's low-cut dress . . . and that was enough for him. After all, he didn't know who the girl in the painting was, when she had lived, whether she was a real person or just the painter's ideal image. For Carlos, these were insoluble mysteries.

Alcohol, however, was working its old magic, and Nestor, who was normally so careful, was feeling its effects as well. Once he reached a certain degree of tipsiness, the chef's atti-tude changed unexpectedly. "This business with your ideal woman," he said in an impetuous rush. "I'll let you sort that out for yourself, but there are such things as omens, and that's the bit I'm interested in: the twists and turns of destiny." Then, lowering his voice as if he were about to pronounce a strange spell, he added: "Come on, Carlos, don't tell me you wouldn't like to find out who that girl was. Why don't we try? It's all very romantic, this searching for her features in other women, but don't you think it's silly when you could be looking for the real thing?"

"I actually *see* her features," said Carlos, who was just as drunk as his boss. "Don't forget I own her now, the woman in the painting, and I can look at her every day if I want to, even if I'll never know who she is or why she is holding that green jewel."

Nestor, however, had something more practical in mind than adoring a picture. So he told his friend what it was and finished off with a little pat on the shoulder, as if to say something like: *Forza,* Carletto, we've had a bit of cognac and a few cherries, sure, but that story of yours is a beauty. So listen, don't you worry: I know a way of finding out family secrets when there's no one left to ask . . .

II. THE GENTLEMAN WITH A CREW CUT

"I GOT ONE question for you, man—and don't you be lying to me now. What time you seeing Madame Longstaffe?"

The Rastafarian, who had been leaning against the Japanese screen cleaning his nails for hours, eyed Nestor suspiciously while Carlos, startled, emerged from his daydream.

"Wouldn't be five, would it?" he asked with a menacing air. " 'Cause I'm telling you now: that's when she's seeing *me*."

As he said "me," he pointed to his chest, visible in the opening of his skintight shirt, with one long fingernail. Carlos seized upon that anatomical detail with his waiter's eye, schooled over the last few months. Had he seen this character again in the street, he might not have recognized his dreadlocks or his teeth, which were disconcertingly white given the general squalor of his appearance, but he would certainly have remembered that one long fingernail.

"At five, it's my turn, man. Five o'clock on the dot."

Nestor beamed him a charming smile and told him not to worry, it was quite all right, their appointment was for five-thirty and they were happy to wait. No problem, man.

The Rasta-man smiled back and was about to resume his position in front of the Japanese screen when his path was blocked by a very nervous gentleman, who, on emerging from Madame Longstaffe's room, had gone past the door that opened onto the street and come into the waiting room by mistake.

He stopped. He looked to his right and left, first at the lady on the tapestry-covered sofa, then at the lady by the window. He seemed relieved not to recognize either one of them. The presence of the Rastafarian didn't bother him, but he was noticeably taken aback when he saw Nestor sitting on the sofa. The cook simply said, "Good-bye, Mr. Tous," as if he knew him vaguely, but the man beat such a hasty retreat that all Carlos could remember about him was an air of respectability and his gray crew cut.

"Be patient, Carlitos," said Nestor with a sigh, referring not to the fleeting apparition of that shorthaired gentleman, obviously, but to the leisurely pace at which Madame Longstaffe was exercising her divinatory skills. It was a quarter to six and there were still three clients ahead of them in line, including their Rastafarian friend. "We'll just have to be patient," he said before lapsing again into the tranquil silence he had observed since entering the clairvoyant's house. So Carlos went back to thinking about what his friend had said to him while the cherry syrup was simmering:

"Yes, yes, this story of yours is a-very romantico" (Nestor's accent seemed to become more Italian with each liqueur-soaked cherry) "but like I tell you: getting nostalgic about some woman who doesn't exist, falling in love with a ghost, and looking for traces of her in other women, this is a-crazy, Carlos, and impractical. I tell you my theory, Carletto. It's much more logical. Obsessions like this are always an anticipation of something that is going to happen, you see what I mean? That girl in the picture isn't a real girl, and even if she is, what do you care, because she's probably dead, or if she's alive she's an old woman by now. But if you're so fascinated by this picture, it must mean that somewhere there's a girl just like her, exactly the same, and we'll find her!" shouted Nestor, who was quite worked up at this point.

Then he declared that he knew a way to discover old family secrets and summon the creatures of childhood fantasy. It was very simple, he said. All they had to do to solve the mystery was pay a visit to Madame Longstaffe, the famous clairvoyant.

Yet as soon as he had made this declaration, and in spite of his inebriated state, Nestor Chaffino started backpedaling, as if fear had suddenly sobered him up.

"You know I'm joking, don't you, Carlos? It's a silly idea, consulting a clairvoyant. All that stuff about the spirit world, it's a load of rubbish . . . just forget I ever mentioned it, all right? You're not going to tell me you believe in witches now as well as ghosts, are you? Look, no spell has ever been able to turn a fantasy woman like yours into living flesh and blood, honestly . . . No, there's no point in insisting. I'm not coming with you. It's a scam, the whole thing. I don't believe in spells. They're fakes and con artists, all those clairvoyants . . . but what makes it really dangerous is they're also devilishly *cunning*. And Madame Longstaffe is the worst of all, believe me . . ."

MAYBE THE CHERRIES were to blame. Maybe it's just that there's something irresistible about a good romance. Or maybe there was another reason for Nestor's capitulation, one that can't be revealed at this point in the story. In any event, Carlos finally managed to overcome his friend's reluctance. So there they were, the two of them, waiting their turn in the little aquamarine room. And that was why Nestor had been so hard on Carlos when they arrived.

"*Cazzo* Carlitos, you're the one who insisted on coming to see this witch, so that's what we're going to do, but be warned: I take no responsibility for whatever happens as a result."

6

WHAT THE CLAIRVOYANT SAW

MADAME LONGSTAFFE, lying flopped on a chaise longue, addressed them in her thick Brazilian accent: "I'm so tired, young man, completely *exowsted*." Naturally: it was past eight-thirty and she had been drawing on all her reserves of human and esoteric energy to light the way for four very hard cases (especially the mysterious woman who remained by the window, a truly *exowsting* client), and all that effort had knocked her flat, as Nestor and Carlos could see from where they stood in the doorway, not daring to enter. Only her legs were visible, wrapped in fine green muslin, resting delicately crossed on the chaise, while her feet, encased in slippers that would have provoked the envy of a Venetian doge, quivered intermittently.

"What a frightful afternoon! Come in, gentlemen. I'll see to you in a few moments."

But she didn't stir. Carlos and Nestor went in and sat down on two chairs at the back of the room, next to the desk where the fortune-teller plied her trade. An imposing pair of thrones they were; the short-legged Nestor was left with his feet dangling. Just as well: a few seconds later, a small fluffy white dog appeared and began to manifest a lively interest in the chef's ankles. Quite a fixation, to judge from the way he was barking and trying to get at them, while Nestor, having recoiled into the chair, didn't know whether it was better to wait out the siege or shut the mutt up with a well-aimed kick.

"Fri-fri, tais-toi," said Madame Longstaffe from the chaise longue, then "Sit!" and *"Raus!"* Her polyglot performance would no doubt have greatly impressed the two friends had they not been busy giving each other knowing looks, telepathically united in their pity for the little dog, conducting a silent dialogue that might have run something like this: "Nestor, did you hear what she called the fluff ball?" "I'm afraid I did: Fri-Fri, son of Fru-Fru, no doubt." "Poor creature! Thank God animals have no idea of the awful things going on around them . . . I mean, can you imagine?" "I agree, I agree, don't start me: just the thought of having one of my relatives (my father, maybe) mummified and stuck on top of an alabaster column with a nameplate . . ." "And knowing you might end up like that yourself one day." "It's terrible." "Isn't it just?"

And they concluded their telepathic conversation with a mutual shudder.

The memory of the stuffed Maltese terrier in the aquamarine waiting room prompted them to look around and discover that the room they had entered was a splendid example of the inimitable Longstaffe style of interior decoration. It was dimly lit by a single Bloomsbury lamp, but what little light

there was permitted them to make out various motionless animals, watching them with blind, glass eyes from a series of display cases: one or two large iguanas, what appeared to be an
owl over on the right, a vixen with a glaucous stare, and no
doubt other witnesses to Madame's love affair with taxidermy.
But before they had a chance to scrutinize the rest of the cases
from which yet more immobile creatures peered, their inspection was cut short by the clairvoyant, who rose (not without a
good deal of effort) from her divan and came toward them,
holding out her hand.

"Good evening, gentlemen."

The most interesting thing about the famous fortune-teller
was not her impressive mass of blond hair or the tunic of trans-
parent green muslin in which she was wrapped or even her
height, nearly six feet, but another characteristic altogether,
one that neither of them noticed right away.

"It's up to you," she said in a lilting Brazilian accent completely
at odds with her distinctly Germanic appearance. "What would
you like: the shells, tarot cards, or the crystal ball?" And as
she said "crystal ball," she turned her head around, and seeing her head-on for the first time, Carlos noticed how much
she resembled the Marbella socialite Countess Gunilla von Bismarck.

"So, what's it to be?" she asked impatiently, tired perhaps of
how her appearance always made strangers gawp. "I don't
have all night, you know, and I'm too *exowsted* for the shells, so
take your pick, mister: tarot or crystal ball."

Then, seeing Carlos hesitate, she added less abruptly: "All
the ways of fortune-telling are pretty much the same in the

end, you know. I've developed an eclectic method, so you can choose whichever you prefer, only don't take too long about it."

"I just don't know . . ." Carlos said slowly. "Maybe the cards . . ."

But he didn't get to finish the sentence, because Nestor, who had decided to take matters in hand, launched into a concise and reasonably accurate summary of the story of the girl in the picture, to which Madame Longstaffe listened in attentive silence, interrupting only now and then to say, "What a lovely story!" or, "How delightful!" or sometimes, *Que beleza.* She had picked up the Maltese terrier and put it on her lap. She stroked its head as the story unfolded, and when Nestor was through, she sighed and twisted around to the left as if she were looking for something in one of the desk drawers.

As she did this, Carlos noticed something very odd about the fortune-teller, a quality unique among human beings: Madame Longstaffe's face had two completely different aspects. Now, for example, looking down, with her hair pulled back, she no longer resembled Gunilla von Bismarck. A sudden and unaccountable metamorphosis had transformed her into the spitting image of Malcolm McDowell: a nasty shock for Carlos, who had recently seen *A Clockwork Orange* on television. He did a double take and stared incredulously, but there it was, that terrifying face—all that was missing were the stiletto and the single false eyelash under the left eye—and it belonged to Madame Longstaffe, who was rummaging intently through the drawers of her desk. Then she found what she was looking for (a pile of well-worn cards), and turned back to face them: Gunilla von Bismarck again, a much more restful sight.

"To cut a long story short, madame," said Nestor, who had broken the awkward silence by repeating the end of his little speech, "that's why we came to see you. Like I said, the boy doesn't really need a tarot reading to find out about his future. What he needs is a love potion, you know what I mean, some kind of spell that will help him find a girl like the one in the picture, or as much like her as possible. I know it sounds crazy, but I've been told you can work wonders, madame."

"Have you now? What exactly have you been told?" said the clairvoyant, interrupting him sharply, and a look of fear flashed across her Barbie doll face (if you can imagine an aging Germanic Barbie doll). "You seem to know a great deal about all sorts of people. Too much, if you ask me . . ."

Nestor smiled, reaching out across the desk to touch the soothsayer's arm, flattering her all the while. But then his grip tightened, as if to express something that good manners prevented him from putting into words.

"All right, all right, as you wish," replied Madame Longstaffe, caught off guard and unaccustomed to such treatment from her clients. "Forgive me, I don't want to be a busybody, but . . . but," she added, suddenly more animated, turning her head so that she looked like Malcolm McDowell again, "there's something I want to tell you. It won't take long. Forget about the boy for a minute. Let's talk about you: I think I can see something that will happen to you, something you should know about."

Before Nestor's menacing grip could tighten again on the

fortune-teller's arm, she continued in the same tone of voice: "You're suffering from an incurable disease. It's been diagnosed, hasn't it . . . cancer, yes? Well, you'll be glad to know that you're not going to die of . . ."

At this point Nestor began tapping firmly on Madame Longstaffe's arm, as if he were sending a threatening message in Morse code, and it must have read something like this: "For God's sake shut up, you old witch, not another word," because she pulled her arm away in surprise, as if one of her stuffed birds had pecked at it. Yet only a few seconds later, like a Boy Scout, honor-bound to tell the truth in all circumstances, the two-faced fortune-teller added:

"At least let me warn you, sir. Are you sure you wouldn't like to have a little chat about the state of your lungs or the dangers of cool rooms and chocolate truffles? And dessert recipes? And what about a little moleskin notebook? No? You're not curious about that, either?"

The old bat's totally lost the plot, thought Carlos, but of course he didn't say a word.

If Nestor sent another message in Morse code, Carlos missed it, because Fri-Fri's yapping and licking distracted him and the next thing he heard, a few seconds later, was: "Very well, there's no point in trying to help someone who simply refuses to listen. Anyway," and again she seemed very tired, "*isso não é comigo*—why should I care? It's getting late, so let's get on with it and wrap this up. Let's see, what can I give this young man?" Then she began delving in her drawers again with an air of professional authority.

This time Carlos didn't find the metamorphosis so striking.

He must have been mistaken before, when he thought the old woman could change faces simply by leaning forward or turning her head, because now, with the tip of her tongue peeping out between her lips to show how hard she was concentrating, Madame Longstaffe still looked exactly like the Countess von Bismarck—not a trace of clockwork orange. Just as well.

"Here it is," she said, rising from the depths of her drawers, enveloped in a cloud of dust that was anything but magic. *"Esta bom,"* she added as she sat up straight and set on the table a tubular bottle the size of a little finger, which she then handed over to Carlos, saying, "Listen carefully, *filhinho,"* and instructing him to drink four drops every night of the full moon until the bottle was empty.

"And by the time you've finished the treatment, young man, things will be looking up: the spell will have taken effect. It's child's play, this one."

"Really? Have you had a lot of cases like this?" asked Carlos.

Wearily, Madame Longstaffe waved her green sleeves at him. "You know, sweetie, if there's one thing I hate about this job, it's the monotony. It's so boring these days. When clients come with love problems, it's for a spell to help them find the perfect match or to hold on to someone who's trying to escape. Of course every now and then something unusual does come up. Like someone who wants to blot out the memory of a terrible passion or an unspeakable desire," said Madame Longstaffe with an absent look, as if she were not talking to her clients but thinking aloud about the day's events. "Did you see that very proper looking gentleman who left just now, the one with his hair cut like a German soldier in the First World War? Well, *he* was one out of the bag. He wants to rid his heart of an unwelcome urge," she added (this inexcusable lapse of discretion can only have been caused by extreme fatigue) while stroking the fur on Fri-Fri's little head into the shape of a crew cut, before realizing what she had said and pulling herself up short. "Enough of that, Marlene." (Marlene? Was that the famous clairvoyant's name: Marlene Longstaffe?) "All I meant to say is that there's not a lot of variety with these love problems, because, you see, searching for the living image of your ideal woman, well, it's hardly very original, is it? But if that's what you want, honey, here it is: that'll be fifteen thousand pesetas, and now, if you don't mind, let's call it a night."

That said, Madame Longstaffe rose from behind the desk with a good deal more agility than before and flopped back into her chaise longue, muttering something that was not so much a good-bye as an articulated sigh: "Santa Maria, it's been a long, long day."

But to judge from the slight Yoruba accent, she may have been addressing her faithful Fri-Fri rather than her clients.

Their visit had disturbed the mystic quiet of the fortune-teller's room. Its ambience had been upset by the noise of rummaging in those drawers full of tiny, secret bottles like the one Carlos had taken away. Yet once Madame was comfortably ensconced again in her chaise longue, everything was just as it had been before.

⌒

THE DIM LIGHT of the Bloomsbury lamp . . . the glassy eyes of the animals . . . it was all so cozy. To linger there after the appointment would have been like profaning a church. But there's nothing quite so tempting as a little profanation, and Nestor just couldn't resist. He put a finger to his lips to stop his friend from speaking.

"Just a couple of minutes," he whispered urgently, "then we'll go, Carletto. It's not every day you get to observe a witch in her den, I'm telling you."

"Hang on. You're the one who didn't want anything to have to do with her prophecies."

"That's right, I don't. I'm just curious to find out what witches do when no one is watching them. She'll probably pull out a cell phone, and I bet she won't be calling the spirit world."

Then the cook put his finger to his lips again and the two friends went back to the place where they had hesitated on the way in.

"Shhh," he said. "Just a couple more minutes."

⌒

ON THE OTHER side of the room, Fri-Fri had leapt up and made a hollow for himself in the folds of his mistress's tunic: it was a charming scene. Madame had stretched herself out, and just as before, all they could see were the fortune-teller's legs, or to be more precise, her right foot, which, bare inside its slipper, was bobbing up and down in time with some imaginary music. That was the only movement. Her slipper, rubbing against the edge of the chaise longue, looked as if it might fall onto the carpet at any moment.

"Come on, let's go," whispered Carlos. "This place is starting to give me the creeps. What are we waiting for, anyway?"

But just then they saw Madame Longstaffe reach over to a little table beside the chaise and pour herself a tiny cup of pleasantly scented tea, like a prostitute treating herself to a quintessentially bourgeois pleasure after her amorous labors.

"Let's get out of here. That awful little dog's going to sniff us out any minute now."

But the dog remained oblivious.

The aroma of the tea quickly filled the room, enveloping the furniture, making Fri-Fri sneeze and Madame Longstaffe sing. She sang an old song that went *mamba umbé yamamabé,* or something like that, with a mezzo-soprano voice well past its prime that rather grated on the ears of the two spies hiding in the shadows. *Omi mambambá, mamba umbé yamamabé,* she continued tunelessly. What with the song and the strong scent of the brew, for a moment Carlos thought he saw a glint of life in the eyes of a moth-eaten vixen in the glass case to his left. He gripped the witch's little bottle tighter—the last thing they needed was for him to drop it accidentally (or out of fright) and alert Madame Longstaffe, who was still sipping her tea from a cup so tiny she had already refilled it three times, as Carlos had noted. It was while she was pouring out the fourth cup that the fortune-teller began to speak. But at no point did she turn to face them, remaining supine on the chaise. All she

did was make her Venetian slipper bob a little more vigorously, so that it seemed to have a life of its own, or at least to be
speaking like a ventriloquist's doll: "He who believes he is
mortally ill shall die not by illness but by ice, and he who believes that words can kill should not keep them so close to his
heart."

Carlos looked at Nestor, who no longer seemed to be
amused.

And just then a laugh rang out and filled the room, coming
not from the talking slipper but from the ventriloquist herself.

"I knew you couldn't just walk away," she said. "Even those
who say they don't believe in omens, like you, Nestor, can't
resist the temptation to find out what destiny has in store
for them. Isn't that right? But destiny loves to play tricks on
us . . ."

Madame Longstaffe sat up on the chaise longue, folding her
legs beneath her so that her feet and the talkative slippers disappeared. In that position, she looked like a legless torso or a
speaking figurehead fixed to the prow of the chaise, with a cup
of tea in her hand.

"No, don't go yet," she said to Nestor, as if she could read his
thoughts. "I want to give you just one piece of advice, and if
you follow it, you'll be grateful to me, I assure you."

"Sometimes it's better not to know what the future holds,
madame. Especially when you know there's nothing you can
do about it."

But the old woman insisted. "Listen, all I will say is this:
Nestor shall not die—do as you please, enjoy yourself, my
friend, fall in love, write a scandalous novel, learn how to play

the bassoon, whatever you like. Don't worry about your future, because Madame Longstaffe has seen it clearly: Nestor has nothing to fear until four *T*s conspire against him."

The cook tried to protest, but the witch, sitting up even straighter, held her little cup out in front of her as if all the world's mysteries were floating in it.

"You're suffering from an incurable disease, but you need not worry about that, I promise you."

"All right, madame . . ."

". . . too many coincidences," she continued. "For your luck to turn, four *T*s would have to join forces, and that could never come to pass, could it? Although coincidences do occur. The gods are fond of practical jokes."

Madame Longstaffe laughed again, and her little dog seemed to be laughing with her. Then she added: "You shouldn't have hidden there behind the door." She wasn't laughing anymore. "You really shouldn't have done that, you know. If what you were after was a love potion for our young friend, you'd have been better off going somewhere else. Any old clairvoyant could have given you that, it's a piece of cake, but you wanted something else, didn't you? Yes, that's right, what you really wanted." (The Yoruba accent had come back in force, as if she were not a white fortune-teller but Mae Senhora herself, or Aspasia Guimarães do Pinto, the famous *yarolixá* from Bahia, minus the imposing Yoruba appearance.) "What you wanted was to discover your destiny, and now you have," she said, bidding her clients good night with an impatient wave of her hand. "Until that fourfold coincidence occurs, you have nothing to fear.

"Four *T*s," she repeated, with a hooligan's streetwise air. "Four *T*s." (Or was it teas?) "What an evil brew."

The voice might have belonged to Madame Longstaffe or Mae Senhora, or even Aspasia Guimarães do Pinto, but the face . . . it was definitely the face of Malcolm McDowell in *A Clockwork Orange,* no doubt about it this time. She even winked at them as she said, "Nothing to fear."

7

A TERRIBLE ACCIDENT

*L*YING, DECEITFUL, CRAFTY, and the worst thing is, sometimes she's actually half right, and that's what pulls you in; it makes you think all her predictions will come true. Despicable, cunning old witch, stealing people's hopes and dreams.

This is what Carlos was thinking as he knelt beside the body of his friend Nestor while the Teldis' kitchen filled up with people and noise. Poor Nestor. There they all were, staring at him. Little Chloe Trias, in her bare feet and possibly naked under a large T-shirt with PIERCE MY TONGUE, NOT MY HEART written on it. Behind her was Serafin Tous, a friend of the family, prudently keeping his distance, as if he were afraid the deceased might suddenly spring back to life like some kind of Lazarus. And there was Karel Pligh, too, trying to explain to the Teldis when and where he had found the chef. Beside him stood Adela (so beautiful, even at this hour of the morning, thought Carlos, with her freshly washed face and a knowing look in her bright eyes, as if none of this had come as a surprise to her), while Mr. Teldi listened impatiently to Karel's explanations, itching to take control of the situation—he was the boss, after all.

"All right, all right, let's calm down. There's been a terrible accident, that's all," he said. "In any case, we'll have to call the police. There's no way around that . . . May I borrow your pen? Where did you leave the telephone? Although, since it's a holiday, they probably won't answer or the line will be busy. You can never rely on the military—I mean the police. It's the same all over the world."

As he spoke, Teldi was holding the phone, ready to dial, and rubbing the cap of a pen on the kitchen table. The line turned out to be busy—what had he told them? As he redialed, his gaze wandered over the table, on which he noticed a perfectly clean egg whisk, a complete set of brand-new knives, and a copy of Brillat-Savarin with a folded tea towel lying on top of it, like a ceremonial cloth on a pagan altar. You had to admit the fellow was a first-class chef, he thought, and a bastard, an absolute bastard. Somehow this opinion had escaped from the world of his dreams, but he locked it away again promptly and dialed: 0 . . . 9 . . . 1, and then, more quickly, 091. Maybe this time . . .

"Police? Are you ready to take this down? Ernesto Teldi speaking, I'm calling from a house called the Lilies on Oleander Road, number 10B. There's been an accident, no . . . nothing dramatic, I mean, it could have been much worse, it could have been a member of the family."

While speaking on the telephone, Teldi removed the tea

towel with which Karel Pligh had so carefully covered the copy of Brillat-Savarin, and as the conversation dragged on and they put him on hold, then switched him through to another department, and another, he rubbed the cap of the pen up and down on the book's cover. For a cookbook, he noticed, it was remarkably clean: not a spot of grease or a pastry crumb; clean as a missal.

"You what? You want me to repeat the name of the house? All right, I see, the computer's taking its time. It's the Lilies, as in the flower."

Once again the cap of the pen began to wander over the book's cover, tracing around the gilded letters, pressing into the leather's smooth furrows, before going over the side and down the edges of the pages, where it ran into something that was sticking out: the sheet of paper Karel Pligh had hidden in the book after finding Nestor's body.

"No, number 10*B* on Oleander Road. There's an *a* and a *b* and this is 10*B*, got it? That's right, it's off Rockrose Road . . ."

Teldi toyed with the protruding sheet, plucking at it with his finger like a guitar string, but nobody was watching him. They had better things to do. Serafin Tous suggested that someone open a window, while Chloe Trias shrugged her shoulders (after a pointed look from her boyfriend, Karel) and decided to go upstairs and put on a pair of slacks. Meanwhile, Adela was using the opaque glass of a window (the kindest of mirrors) to adjust her hair before looking at Carlos, who was the only one thinking about the dead man. He had taken off his jacket to cover Nestor's face.

What a pity it isn't big enough to cover his whole body, thought Carlos. Nestor's body, spread-eagled on the floor, seemed larger now, as if his limbs in thawing out had uncurled like the petals of a funerary flower. Even his fingers had opened, although his blue-stained right thumb was still very stiff. Poor Nestor, Carlos repeated again (it was becoming a litany). Perhaps, before the accident, he had used that pen Teldi was playing with to make some notes. Perhaps in the quiet of the small hours he had taken the time to jot down a few lines in that moleskin notebook he always carried with him. Where could he have left it? It must be around somewhere, on the kitchen table or near the stove. I'll have a look for it when Teldi gets off the phone, thought Carlos. He would have liked to keep it as something to remember Nestor by.

"What?" fumed Ernesto Teldi. "You don't know Rockrose Road either? I don't believe this. The village *idiot* knows where it is, and you're telling me . . . Very well, young lady, it comes off the Coín-Ojén Road, near the twenty-four-kilometer post . . . That's right, now we seem to be getting somewhere. What other information do you need? So you didn't get that down either? Well, I'll just have to tell you again, won't I? My name is Ernesto Teldi. No, not Seldi, I said Teldi, T E L D I . . . yes, that's right, *t* for tortoise."

Carlos looked at him with a sad smile: his tone of voice, the way he was carrying on, that pathetic wisecrack. It was just the sort of thing that would have made Nestor laugh.

Poor Nestor. Carlos looked around the kitchen again, but he wasn't thinking about the notebook or Teldi and his telephone call. The others were right: there were more important things to do. Yet that voice filtered back into his thoughts, and it sounded almost as if Teldi the Spaniard had become Teldi the Argentine, improvising the lyrics to a weird sort of tango:

"Frozen to death, what a way to go. It's the luck of the draw, life's a bitch."

Part Two

SIX DAYS
IN MARCH

⚬─────────

Soothsayer: Beware the ides of March.

Caesar: He is a dreamer, let us leave him: pass.

SHAKESPEARE, *Julius Caesar*, Act 1, Scene 2

THE FIRST DAY

NESTOR'S NOTEBOOK

A FEW WEEKS before Nestor's body was found in the Teldis' house, before Madame Longstaffe proffered her highly oracular (some might say fraudulent) prediction of the events that were to take place, the characters in this story were leading their separate lives, and it might have seemed unlikely that their paths would cross. "Coincidences do occur," Madame Longstaffe had said that afternoon when Carlos and Nestor went to see her. "The gods are fond of practical jokes." But that was just part of her witch's patter. Both Nestor and Carlos soon forgot what she had said. Not all of it, though: they remembered the spell for finding the girl in the picture, or her double, and although Carlos didn't carry out the instructions with the recommended blind faith, he did take four drops of the prescribed love potion each full-moon night. You never know.

In any case, what with all the little tasks involved in the day-

to-day running of Mulberry & Mistletoe, the rest of what they
had heard that afternoon at Madame Longstaffe's house was
soon forgotten. And the management of that catering business
was an unpredictable affair, with months of frenetic activity,
especially in summer and spring, followed by months of dead
calm, like February and March. There were only three perma-
nent employees: Nestor, Carlos Garcia, and Karel Pligh, the
Czech bodybuilder, although Chloe Trias had recently joined
the team—a rather eccentric helper perhaps, but also very
cheap, since she hadn't asked for any pay at all.

Mulberry & Mistletoe somehow managed to survive from
peak season to peak season, through the months of hibernation
(as Nestor called them), mainly thanks to the owner's consum-
mate skill in making desserts and tarts, which famous Madrid
restaurants bought and passed off as their own. So when business was slow and the telephone wasn't ringing, when there
was really no point in them all just hanging around, Nestor
Chaffino would pull down the metal grille over the shop-front,
muttering, *"Porca miseria,"* give his employees the afternoon
off, and sit there looking at the white tiles on the wall.

Everything was dazzlingly white at Mulberry & Mistletoe: a
bright, well-located establishment consisting of two rooms.
The main room was the kitchen, at the back. It was spacious
and had the better exposure, with three windows onto the
street, so that all the passersby could see how spotless the food-
preparation area was. Looking in, you saw a large room completely lined with white tiles—even the walls and the little
benches—waiting to be transformed into a hive of creative activity. Copper pots and pans hung on one wall, and laid out on

the large stainless steel table in the middle was an array of the finest kitchen accessories, each patiently waiting its turn, accompanied by a little instruction card. Cleanliness, order, irreproachable hygiene: these were the fundamental principles of Nestor Chaffino's realm, which also extended to the smaller front room, used as a waiting room or reception area for clients. There, the ambience was more bohemian. Nestor, who had spared no expense in fitting out the premises, had decided to give the waiting room a certain *Ritorna a Sorrento* feel, or that, at least, is what he used to tell his clients. And although they didn't quite understand what he meant, they had the impression of having stepped into a scrupulously prepared theater set, part Sicilian villa, part trattoria (minus the tables but still with a gastronomic feel), and subliminally, the convivial atmosphere of the room set them dreaming of the delicious things that might emerge from the adjoining kitchen. While the kitchen at Mulberry & Mistletoe was spotless, the waiting room was charming. While the back room was scented with raspberry syrup and one of those upmarket cleaning products named after a fairy, the front room smelled of the most expensive wood and metal polishes, and the expense was justified, given the quality of the furniture. The waiting room was decorated with objects and souvenirs from trips to exotic lands: a model ship with SOLE MIO inscribed on the poop deck, a poncho draped artlessly—or so it seemed—over a sofa for the clients, a collection of Murano glass paperweights over to the left, and over to the right, a collection of seashells, little boxes, and pictures of saints. And watching over all these objects was a sizable collection of photo portraits autographed by more or less famous people, more or less forgotten now, more or less dead, all of whom had one thing in common: at least once in their lives they had enjoyed Nestor Chaffino's marvelous cooking.

⟍⟋

THE PHOTOS IN the waiting room at Mulberry & Mistletoe smiled down from the walls at the clients who came in to arrange a meal (when there were clients, that is; at the moment there were none). There was a photo of Aristotle Onassis inscribed with the words "*Epharistos*, dear Nestor, *epharistos.* Your Churchill sorbet is a splendid invention." And one of Ray Ventura: "*Ah, ton bavarois, mon cher, ça vaut bien mieux que d'attraper la scarlatine, dis donc.*" And María Callas: "Bravo, Nestor, bra-vo!" Now, *there* was someone who appreciated my chocolate fondant, thought Nestor as he sat there alone in the afternoon at Mulberry & Mistletoe, checking the accounts after his employees had gone home, faced with the fact that February had been an even slower month than January. He put the calculator back in its case and sighed. Hopefully, the good weather wouldn't be long in coming, and then the First Communions would begin, and the outdoor parties, and soon it would be Easter (Callas loved to be surprised with an Easter egg, and Nestor's eggs were quite exquisite), but Easter, alas, was still a good way off. *Porca miseria,* he muttered again.

⟍⟋

IT MUST HAVE been at such an idle moment in the off-season, while he was thinking nostalgically about his favorite clients, that the idea came to him: he would write down a little compendium of culinary secrets in his moleskin notebook. At that point no one even knew about the notebook except his employees. In a tiny, impeccably neat hand, he started writing—three secrets per page and diagrams where necessary—and this is how the text began:

LITTLE INDISCRETIONS
(A BOOK OF CULINARY SECRETS)
By Nestor Chaffino, Master Pastry Cook

PROLOGUE

All around the world, chefs will tell you that there's no point in giving out recipes, because it's not the recipe that makes an excellent dessert, it's the chef's talent. You have to have "a feel for it," and when the recipe says a pinch of ginger or vanilla, it might just as well say a dash or a smidgen. Let me be perfectly frank: pastry cooks, like chefs, always keep something to themselves, a tiny but crucial secret that makes all the difference to the result, and these little tricks of the trade are what I propose to reveal to the world.

PART ONE: COLD DESSERTS

Special tricks for the preparation of cold desserts and how to avoid the errors most commonly made by novice pastry cooks.

You must remember that to make a perfect *île flottante*, it is absolutely essential to use *fresh* eggs. You can beat them by hand or with an electric beater. To make the whites stiffen into peaks, some people use a

pinch of salt, but the truly infallible method is to use a coffee bean. This
is how to do it

Having got that far, however, Nestor interrupted the composi-
tion of this curious opus to write a letter to an old friend.

> *Don Antonio Reig*
> *Pensión de Los Tres Boquerones*
> *Sant Feliu de Guíxols*
>
> *Madrid, 1st of March . . .*
>
> *Dear Antonio,*
> *No doubt you will be surprised to receive this letter after so many*
> *years, and especially when I tell you that by the time you read it, I*
> *will be dead . . . or almost.*

Nestor bit the cap of his old fountain pen, a 1954 Parker made
of blue Bakelite with gold plating, which he had bought on a
whim at the San Telmo market in the company of Antonio
Reig, his friend and colleague, back in the days when they
were both living and working in Buenos Aires. It wasn't easy
for him to write this letter; he had been putting it off for weeks.
"By the time you read it, I will be dead . . . or almost." It
sounded like something out of a novel, especially the "almost,"
but there was nothing fictional about his lung cancer, and all
he could do was prepare himself and try to tidy things up a bit
before the time came. In a way, this eccentric cookbook he had
begun to compose was his last will and testament. No doubt it
would have been considered an act of high treason by the se-

cretive freemasonry of chefs—and pastry cooks in particular—
who never provide exact recipes for their creations. He had
thought of calling his compendium *Little Indiscretions*. The
title had a literary ring to it that appealed to him, and it suggested the treachery of his enterprise. The idea was to go public with the tricks of the trade: the little touch that makes the
difference between a proud, upstanding soufflé and a flop, the
closely guarded secrets that transform the pleasures of confec-
tionery into a veritable art.

*. . . Since I don't know how long I have left to live, given the state
of my health, I would like to send you this little culinary testament
in installments. At the moment I'm writing it in my spare time, in
a notebook, but I plan to send you ten to twelve tips in each letter.
I would be grateful if you could compile them for posthumous publication. Don't you think it's a delicious way of taking revenge on
those famous colleagues of ours who'll do anything to get their
fourth star in the Michelin guide, but won't give the public even a
glimpse of the simplest tricks that you and I use every day?* Little
Indiscretions *. . . it's a splendid title, don't you think? The other
day I was talking to my employees about it and they got completely
the wrong idea, poor lambs. "So you're going to reveal the shameful secrets of all those famous people you worked for before setting
up your own business?" That's what Chloe asked (she's the new girl
I've got working for me), and I let her think she'd guessed right.
Given the highly sensitive nature of my subject, it's not a bad idea,
as I'm sure you'll agree, to keep people in the dark about what I'm
really up to, which is something far more significant (and dare I say
it, yes I do: heroic) than gossiping about the foibles of Mr. X or*

Mrs. Y. Can you imagine what would happen if you and I started coming out with all the things we've seen and heard in our careers? Just think of the scandal that would create! For instance, you remember back in Buenos Aires . . . what was the name of that couple you used to work for? Seldi? Teldi? I wonder what's become of them. Funnily enough, I was thinking of them only yesterday, not because I was planning to write to you, but because I was trying to remember the recipe for that magnificent summer pudding I used to make for them. You must have a copy of it. Would you mind sending it to me in full? I've forgotten some of the ingredients. So there I was racking my brains when this Chloe girl I was telling you about came and interrupted me: "Go on, Nestor, tell us what you're writing, tell us one of those shameful secrets." Then I remembered that we happened to have a catering job to do that day for the Seldis or whatever they're called, and that gave me an idea. I said: "That's right, dear. My Little Indiscretions *is a book about people's shameful secrets, but not famous people, no, it's not like the gossip you get in the glossies. When you're a bit older, you'll learn that people who seem utterly normal on the surface often have something far worse to hide than those who are trying to shake off the paparazzi: poke around in their closets and you may get a nasty surprise."*

You're probably wondering why I lied to her like that, saying I was writing a book full of scandal and gossip when the thought had never crossed my mind. Well, I only did it to conceal my secret plan. Young people can't help blabbing . . . But the thing is, once I started lying, I just went on, making my story more and more elaborate. I couldn't help myself. Maybe it's because I'm a pastry cook: you start something, even if it's just telling a fib, and next thing you know, you're decorating it as artistically as you can, as if it were a big wedding cake: a few flakes of caramel here, a raspberry coulis there. Meanwhile, Chloe's hanging on my every word, so I look her gravely in the eye and add, "You're still very young, but someday soon you'll find out that there are many people in the world who have done something shameful in their lives. I don't mean anything heinous: a little affair on the side, say . . . a betrayal of trust . . . a minor theft . . . maybe even a one-off homosexual experience. In other words, an act they're ashamed of but which is really perfectly forgivable . . . The problem is that often, later on, sometimes many years later, in order to keep their shameful secret hidden, they have to do something far worse. They have to commit a real crime, do you see what I mean, my dear? Oh, you'd be surprised how often it happens: I've come across several cases myself." You should have seen the look on her face. She was absolutely convinced that this little notebook of mine was full of juicy secrets instead of dessert recipes. So much the better. That way she won't suspect what I'm really up to, and I can string her along, promising to tell her about some old scandal that no one cares about anymore and no one will remember after I'm dead.

But how to make a perfect chocolate fondant—now, there's a secret I'm duty-bound to hand on to posterity, don't you think, Antonio? So will you accept my offer? If you agree, I'll start sending you recipes in the next letter.

Anyway, you might be amused to hear what happened with this Chloe girl: she just went on and on at me, so in the end I had to tell her a little secret, and since I was already thinking about you and the time when we were both in Buenos Aires, the first shameful secret that occurred to me was one that you know all too well: that *business with Mrs. Teldi. I tell you, Antonio, I felt like that character in* Tintin, *Oliveira da Figueira, whose storytelling creates a diversion, keeping a crowd of listeners spellbound with a juicy morsel of old gossip. There I was, yours truly, telling the tale of Mrs. Teldi or Seldi or whatever the hell she's called. My audience consisted of the wide-eyed Chloe, Carlos Garcia, my trusty sidekick, and Karel Pligh, the Czech boy who's been helping out with the deliveries. There's been hardly any work the last few days, unfortunately, so I could take my time, and I have to admit I was rather proud of the realistic way I described that accident, shall we call it, that happened at the Teldis' house back in '82 or thereabouts, when Mrs. Teldi's younger sister came to visit with her husband. Of course I didn't mention any names—as you know, I've always preferred to err on the side of discretion—but I did tell them in some detail about the visit of your employer's sister-in-law and her husband from Spain, beginning with a little description of the visitors themselves: she was beautiful, I said, but with a melancholic air about her, yes, that was the word that sprang to mind, almost mournful . . . and her husband seemed to be one of those rare specimens: a man who is handsome but doesn't know it.*

Then I went on to tell them how we all noticed Mrs. Teldi flirting with her brother-in-law. But adultery was no big deal back then in Argentina. It was almost par for the course, and nobody made much of a fuss about it: we certainly didn't, and neither did her husband or anyone really . . . except, of course, the betrayed sister. "Because one fateful day, my dears," *I told my rapt audience,* "she found them together in one of the upstairs rooms, where nobody went as a rule, since those rooms were no longer in use . . ."

You should have seen them gape and stare as I told them all this.

Isn't it funny, Antonio, how people go on being fascinated by stories of adultery, even the young ones today, with their busy sex lives and all sorts of affairs: straight, gay, even incestuous sometimes. And yet there is something irresistible about love stories from another era and another world, the kind that reek of mothballs and secrets. I should say too that I was particularly inspired that afternoon, for instance in the way I explained in evocative detail how, a few hours later, we found Mrs. Teldi's younger sister dead, "lying crushed on the paving stones of the back patio, as if the poor thing had quietly, ever so quietly, let herself drop from that upstairs room, the scene of her defeat." Then I added: "Her face was destroyed by the impact, and yet, as we stood there looking at her, we could still see clearly the pain in those eyes, which had witnessed something intolerable. Relationships between siblings are always complicated—I don't know if you have brothers or sisters, but it's not like any other relationship. There's so much unfinished business: 'It's mine . . . you always try to take it from me . . . no, it never belonged to you . . .' The strong sibling versus the weak one, the same thing over and over, until one comes out on top . . . Anyway, in this story the strong sister obviously ends up with a guilty secret on her conscience. That brief affair, one silly fling among so many others, would never have mattered in the least if her sister hadn't opened the door of the upstairs room. But death can blow even a little indiscretion like that right out of proportion. And ever since that day, the brother-in-law and the surviving sister had to live with the image of those accusing eyes looking up at them from the patio below, her skull broken on the paving stones and her skirt riding up obscenely, exposing a pair of innocent white legs that never should have climbed the stairs to the top floor."

But what am I doing rambling on? This isn't what I meant to tell you. You know the story from start to finish, Antonio, so it isn't going to have any effect on you, but you should have seen those kids when I came to the end. They were impressed, I tell you. Carlos kept staring at me, Karel was speechless, while Chloe was hungry for more details: "And what was the name of the sister who died? Maybe she suspected they'd been shagging for ages, since before she married him, eh, Nestor? And what about the other husband? Sounds like he didn't give a shit. All this going on under his nose— maybe they both had their bits on the side, like my own dear olds."

"That'll do, Miss Trias," I had to tell her. "Enough chattering for today." She pulled a face. On anyone else you'd hardly even have noticed a frown like that, but you see Chloe has these two metal rings, one in her lower lip and one in her tongue, which you can see when she smiles (they say it's the fashion, I think it's disgusting), so the result was really quite frightening. "It's just an old story that doesn't matter to anyone anymore," I said. "I was only telling it to fill in time." She didn't answer, and just stared at my little notebook, as if it concealed a wonderful treasure. She's an odd one, that girl, and if I actually were writing a book about people's shameful secrets, I'd have to put her in it. Not that I think she's done something truly shameful, she's too young, but over the years I've developed a sense of what destiny has in store for certain people . . . Anyway, I'd better not drone on and on, this letter's becoming an epic. If I had time and could be bothered, I'd tell you what I know about Chloe Trias, but it's hardly worth it. She's a typical poor-little-rich-girl-turned-rebel, I'm sure you know the type. This one's a punk with an apathetic attitude and a Czech bodybuilder for a boyfriend, nothing very original really, and besides, what do we

care about other people's private lives? We've had enough of that over the years . . . So let's get back to business, shall we? Here's something I know you'll love, my little trick number 3, for making chocolate mousse. Something just occurred to me, though: don't you think some people are rather like desserts? I admit it's incongruous, but if someone asked me to describe Chloe, I'd say she's the human equivalent of a mint-flavored chocolate mousse, made with very bitter chocolate and slightly too much tangy mint. There's an observation for my little notebook—spot on, if I say so myself.

THE SECOND DAY

KAREL AND CHLOE

"IT'S GOTTA BE straight on the edges. Look, I'll show you. Give me the razor. Hey, watch it! Don't move, I could slash your jugular. And don't even think about looking in the mirror, okay? I feel like I'm shearing a sheep here. You're gonna look *so* cool. Gimme a break, will you?"

Karel Pligh leaned his head back against the chair and tried to concentrate on counting the number of times Chloe said *cool* in the course of the conversation, to keep his mind off the supersharp razor blade scraping at the skin under his lower lip. He had already learned something that day: the transformation of a common or garden beard such as he had been sporting since his arrival from Prague into a minimalist goatee is a delicate and time-consuming operation. In the twenty-five minutes it had taken so far, he had counted seventy-three *cool*s, thirty *wicked*s, not to mention a good deal of *fucking*-this and *fucking*-that. It's a good thing the vocabulary is so limited here, thought Karel Pligh before replying with a "cool" to one or another of Chloe's questions. At this rate, he thought with a certain self-satisfaction, I'll be speaking like a native in two or three months.

And so he was. Thanks to his girlfriend, Chloe Trias, and his undying passion for Latin music, a few months after his arrival in Spain, Karel could express himself fluently in a curious modern Spanish that blended the coolest hip talk with quaint turns of phrase from old boleros and congas.

He had more difficulty, however, mastering the secret code of Western love. Chloe was not the first Spanish girl to have burst into his life like a meteorite, catching him off guard. The situation wasn't totally unfamiliar (this had happened with Czech girls too): before he could ask what was going on, there she was, making herself at home. And the preliminaries were pretty much the same as back home: you go to a disco, you go up to a girl, ask her to dance, she offers to buy you a drink, you let her, and before you know it, you're in a strange bed full of soft toys or little pink pillows with YOU HAVE TO KISS A LOT OF FROGS BEFORE YOU FIND A PRINCE CHARMING written on them, while Brad Pitt or some other capitalist movie star watches your every move from a poster on the wall, to make sure you're acquitting yourself like a man. That much was familiar, but there were other things about Western love, other points of etiquette, that were harder for a recent immigrant to understand. For instance, the kind of kiss that signals the difference between a bit of fun and true love.

"Now, don't even think about moving, K, 'cause this little

Michael Douglas dimple you have here is very sexy and all, but it's a bitch to shave, so hold still for a bit, will you?"

Chloe had started calling him K the first time she had given him a true-love kiss, and Karel had been touched by this apparent homage to one of his most famous compatriots. Quite a few weeks went by before he discovered that Chloe didn't associate K with Kafka but with a brand of shoe polish that bore a vague resemblance to his first name. By that stage, however, they were in love. They had met a few months before, and rushed through the early stages, the exquisite exploration of each other's bodies, without their lips meeting once, for, as Karel had been rather stupefied to discover, in the West, you can touch countless bodies, lick and kiss them from top to bottom and penetrate various orifices in between without even imagining a kiss on the lips.

"No, man, no. It's not that things are really all that different here," a drunk apprentice philosopher told him one day in a bar, confessing his intimate secrets as men do only in the company of complete strangers. "The thing is, the chicks these days, the young ones, they've gone weird. Sex: not a problem. Whatever you like. But try and get them to give you a tongue kiss and you've practically got to pull out an engagement ring. Completely fucking crazy, I'm telling you. My theory is they all went off the rails after seeing that stupid scene in *Pretty Woman*. So now a bit of spit swapping is supposed to mean 'I will love you forever and ever, amen.' Fuck that!"

And perhaps that explains why it was only after working their way right through the *Kama Sutra* that Chloe said to Karel, "Kiss me, K."

⟨⟩

"JESUS, CAREFUL! THIS razor's really sharp, you know . . . what if my hand slipped?"

Chloe's hand was steady enough, but one night she literally lost control of her tongue. Karel often thought about that night. Since they'd met one morning in a supermarket—Nestor had sent him out in an emergency for nutmeg, and she was buying a bag of cheese-flavored chips and two bottles of Coke for breakfast—she had told him many things about her life, all of which had turned out to be true: that she and two Moroccan friends had been subletting an attic room without electricity for two weeks, that she liked Led Zeppelin and Pearl Jam, and AC/DC sort of (pity she had such eclectic tastes), that she hated her parents, didn't care about money, and had never been on a motorcycle. But one unforgettable night, when Karel had already befriended Chloe's roommates, Anwar and Hassem, who were observing Ramadan, he would make some disconcerting discoveries about his new girlfriend. All because of Ramadan and a kiss.

"Let's get out of here," Chloe said to him that afternoon in her attic. "The guys are really boring when they're on this fasting-and-praying trip."

And that's how Karel found out about the other side of Chloe's life. She insisted that they take a taxi, even though he had his motorcycle parked outside. It was getting dark when they pulled up in front of the sort of house Karel had seen only in old Hollywood movies. Before they could knock on the door, a servant appeared and took care of the taxi fare while Chloe asked him, over her shoulder, if the olds were in.

The olds must be her aged parents, thought Karel. And that's what he went on thinking until the day he actually met the olds: she was forty-something and looked like Kim Basinger, while he could have been the Marlboro Man. So there's something else I've learned about the ways of the West, thought Karel: rich, rebellious girls have walking ads for parents.

Why Chloe, who had a house bigger than the Sportovni Skola in Prague, chose to live in a dirty attic with a floating population of cockroaches, newspapers for carpet, and *lebdas* of dubious cleanliness laid out several times a day in the direction of Mecca, why she lived on chips and Coke: these were no doubt to be numbered among the inscrutable mysteries of the capitalist world. But that first night he spent with Chloe at the olds' house, a far more troubling ordeal awaited him: the first, long-delayed, this-is-serious kiss. Months later, forced to sit still by his girlfriend, who was determined to make him look presentable ("Gotta get rid of this prehistoric growth. Just sit down there and I'll fix you up. You're gonna look *so* cool, I promise"), Karel looked in the mirror, but instead of scrutinizing the tailored remnant of his beard or the very long, thin sideburns Chloe was beginning to shape on his jaws, he remembered that momentous kiss.

First the moist, yielding feel of her mouth, and then a metallic taste, a mixture of copper and tin perhaps. Am I up to this? he wondered. And then: Here goes, pushing his tongue so far in he thought for a moment it would tickle her tonsils. But he stopped himself just in time and opted instead to explore Chloe's perfect teeth with the tip of his tongue: molars, canines, incisors. Excessively clinical, he thought: meticulous and unromantically precise. But how the hell are you supposed to kiss a girl with one ring in her tongue and another in her lower lip?

Unsurprisingly, Chloe's bed was full of teddy bears. No pillow with instructions for kissing frogs, though, and instead of Brad Pitt, all three members of Nirvana on the wall, casting a critical eye on Karel's performance at this crucial moment.

The door shut behind them. They had sneaked into Chloe's parents' house and, for the first time, Chloe had given him a true-love kiss. "I love you, K," she said to him. "I want us to be together forever and ever. I don't ever want to come back to this awful house, not even to visit. You're all I have in the world. Can I come and live with you? Could I get a job where you work? I can cook. I can wait on tables, too. I'd do it for free. I don't care about money. I just want to be with you. Your boss at Mulberry and Mistletoe, do you think he'd take me on? Please say yes. Listen, to prove I really love you, I'm going to show you something. This is a secret; I've never told anyone," she continued breathlessly, diving into her backpack to find that small, red, rather battered case. But she must have had a sudden change of heart, because all she pulled out was a pair of Pearl Jam CDs.

"What's the fucking point," she said.

Karel was curious to know what she had almost shown him. Perhaps a photo of a former lover; girls always keep pictures of what they love most, even when it's dead and gone. But in the end, he didn't dare ask. Nor, while she was still wielding the razor, did he dare ask her if she really thought it looked *so cool,* what was left of his poor beard: a little doormat of fur under his lower lip and sideburns like ants marching single file. Had Karel known the old proverb about what to do when in Rome, this would have been a good time to remember it. Instead, what he thought was: I've still got a long way to go before I understand how things work in the West. But in the meantime, he was determined to help Chloe however he could. If she was prepared to work at Mulberry & Mistletoe without pay, it wouldn't be hard to persuade his boss to take her on. He could say he needed help with the deliveries, and there'd be no cost to the business. Nestor wouldn't mind, he was a good sort.

"Do you know how to ride a motorcycle, Chloe?"

"You know what you can do with your fucking motorcycle," Chloe shot back. But then, switching abruptly, as she often did, from anger to tenderness, she added: "Kiss me, K. Kiss me again."

And he did, not just because her words reminded him of a bolero, but also because by then he had grown accustomed to the sweet taste of her mouth.

THE THIRD DAY

LITTLE INDISCRETIONS
PART TWO: DESSERTS MADE WITH EGGS

You can't make an omelette without breaking eggs.

(Popular saying)

(A note for my dear friend Antonio Reig, to be sent with the recipes.)

I'm very tired tonight, Antonio. I haven't made much progress. It's late and I don't feel like writing. What happened was I went to see a fortune-teller—God knows what got into me—and though I don't believe in that nonsense, I have to admit she's got me spooked. Do you think it's possible to read a man's destiny and see how he'll die just by looking at his face? I know it sounds crazy, but . . . Anyway, to get my mind off all that superstitious stuff, I'm going to send you a recipe, just one this time. It's an idea that came to me while I was observing Madame Longstaffe's clients, or rather one in particular. (Madame Longstaffe, as you will have guessed, is the name of the fortune-teller I went to see.) It's a delicacy I thought I'd call Oeufs Intacts. *What do you think? Rather paradoxical, of course, but then it's meant to be. There's a lot of it about, you see: people dying for an omelette but too scared to break an egg. But enough private jokes; here's the recipe:*

Oeufs Intacts

Take two very fresh eggs and . . .

OEUFS INTACTS, OR SERAFIN TOUS BUYS A PIANO

THAT DAY, AFTER leaving Madame Longstaffe's house, Serafin Tous decided to walk home. It was six in the evening, still early. He could have called a friend to see if they had plans for dinner, a close friend, so he wouldn't have to be good company, or even polite, someone who wouldn't mind if he dispensed with the customary questions about their health: he didn't feel like making an effort. He knew that Ernesto and Adela Teldi were in town. He didn't like Ernesto, but he'd known Adela for ages, and over the years they had shared a good many secrets. He could have been alone with her—that would have been the perfect balm for his agitated state of mind. He could have called her; there was no danger. She wouldn't have probed him about anything he didn't want to reveal. His cell phone was in his pocket; all he had to do was choose a number from the memory, the third one, to be precise, and . . . "Just wondering if you were free tonight to put up with one of my silent moods." But instead of calling Adela or anyone else, Serafin switched his phone off as if making a resolution: Put up with it yourself, like a man, he thought, and kept walking down the street.

At the first corner he came to, he turned, leaving the Plaza Celenque, where Madame Longstaffe lived, and took the Calle del Arenal, heading west toward the Palacio Real, all this without any idea where his steps and his thoughts might be leading him. Recently, steps and thoughts alike seemed to have a mind of their own: disquieting, to say the least. A few weeks ago, they had led him to the door of Freshman's, and now, in the same unconscious way, they had taken him to Madame Longstaffe's house, although this time he did not regret it.

"We have come," he had said to the witch, as if speaking on behalf of himself, his steps, and his thoughts, "to ask you for help, madame." And he went on to tell her about his unsettling visit to the club, ending with a plea: "There must be a way. There *has* to be some way of turning me back into the sensible person I was before my wife died. It doesn't make sense, does it? Why should I suddenly start feeling those, um . . . inclinations again? It must be an illusion, mustn't it? It probably happens all the time, no? You come across a photograph of a boy, say, who looks just like someone you remember from years ago and it stirs up all these . . . inappropriate emotions. But that's all in the past, I swear to God, madame. All that is gone and forgotten. I mean, it's nothing, is it? This feverish feeling I've had

since the day I visited that horrible club, it won't last, will it?
Tell me it won't. You must have something that will turn me
back into the sort of man Nora wanted me to be. Nora was my
wife, did I tell you? She died just a few months ago, a terrible
loss . . ."

The Calle del Arenal was noisy and full of traffic. The
jostling crowd swept even the most pensive pedestrians along,
like corks bobbing in a stream. Tourists in sandals consulting maps, would-be artists hurrying off to cafés, pickpockets,
strollers, con men, and beggars, all moving together, a fluid
mass of humanity channeled between the road and the walls of
the buildings, sometimes diverted toward the window of a wig
shop or a 7-Eleven.

"And why do you want to forget this boy?" Madame Longstaffe had asked him, without waiting for him to finish his
plea. "Hmm? I notice that monsieur takes good care of his
lovely long fingers, pianist's fingers . . . Monsieur is a very respectable man, a gentleman."

It seemed that Brazilian fortune-tellers (a curse on the lot
of them!) sometimes addressed their clients in the third person, with the deference generally reserved for VIPs. Not that it
made Serafin Tous feel important, or even respectable. Had he
really been respectable, he wouldn't have felt that pang whenever he remembered the boy from Freshman's. It was as if
he'd come face-to-face with his past: Look at yourself, Serafin,
you're just the same, he thought, you haven't really changed at
all. This is exactly how you felt when you first met Pedrito
Martinez. You were barely eighteen at the time, and you spent
a whole year playing sonatas with him (among other things)

behind closed doors in a mezzanine on the Calle de Apodaca. Martinez, that was his name, your young piano student: Pedrito Martinez, such an ordinary name, but what a beautiful body . . . The agony of guilt but, oh, the ecstasy too . . . Admit it, Serafin, the ecstasy, the passion and . . . no! You didn't want to live like that, a sordid, fearful existence, always scared of being found out. Martinez, he was still a child, really. What would your dear parents have said if they had found out? And your friends? You know only too well: queer, faggot, shirtlifter, turd-burglar, poof, poof, poof.

IN THE CALLE del Arenal there is a bridal shop with shiny satin gowns and myriads of little artificial flowers for the headdresses. Nora would never have chosen one of those gowns for her wedding. She wore a wonderful simple raw silk dress that made her look taller, almost beautiful, even. And she was graced with the serenity of a woman who knows how to make her husband happy. So few women are capable of that. How lucky he had been to find her just in time. Intelligent, companionable Nora. Love gave her unfailing intuition: she never had to ask; she always knew, God bless her. You don't seem to understand, Madame Longstaffe, she was perfect, perfect for me, don't you see?

But Serafin Tous had left Madame Longstaffe's house behind him, and it was not the fortune-teller now but the human torrent carrying him along the Calle del Arenal that replied: Let yourself go, boy . . . don't hold back. Accept what you are for once in your life.

But what sort of nonsense was that? He wasn't a boy any-more, and he didn't want to let himself go. That was precisely why he had gone to see Madame Longstaffe. As she sat there looking at him with her head tilted to one side and her blond hair falling over her left shoulder, he had thought, My God, what's going on? For, viewed from that angle, she looked very much like a man. In fact, she was the spitting image of an actor whose name Serafin couldn't recall. Don't look at me like that, madame! Help me! You must have some way of warding off ghosts. It's the ghost of a man I chose not to be, coming back to haunt me after all these years. Imagine it, at my age: turning into an old queen, maybe even a pedophile, who knows . . . Luckily, just at that moment, the shopwindows of the Calle del Arenal came to Serafin's rescue. He saw a sign that read RELIGIOUS ITEMS. Immediately he felt calmer: it was like a life-line thrown to a drowning man. There were little plaster fig-ures of various saints: Anthony of Padua, that great miracle worker, and Saint Jude the apostle, champion of lost causes and intercessor for those in desperate straits. Desperate indeed.

"The gentleman's problem is very interesting," Madame Longstaffe had said, at which point Serafin thought he saw a glimmer of hope. But then the old woman added: "I'm sure you'll understand if I don't prescribe anything today. An un-usual case like this will require careful consideration. Don't worry, I'll call you shortly to arrange another appointment."

"But, madame, I really would prefer not to have to come back. I have to be careful. I'm a judge, you know. The public image of the profession is at stake. I wouldn't want to be asso-ciated with your . . . divinatory arts (which are, I'm sure, quite outstanding). You have to understand that somebody could recognize me and think . . . You must realize I'm risking a great deal by coming here."

"Oh be quiet, *meu branco*. Just wait for my call," said Madame Longstaffe, interrupting him and shifting from the respectful third person to a completely inappropriate Brazilian familiarity. Then, even more disrespectfully, she added: "Stop being such an old woman, will you? Off you go, shoo!"

⌒

AS PEDESTRIANS MAKE their way along the Calle del Arenal toward the Plaza de la Opera, they sometimes find themselves falling into step with the rhythm of a bossa nova or a samba, a tango or a waltz. There's a dance school with a window that opens onto the street, dispensing music, accompanied by the crisp one-two-three of the instructor.

"You can't just send me away like that, madame, without helping me. Surely it wouldn't be so hard to prescribe a potion, one of your famous little bottles. After all, I only want to forget, madame. I only want to forget a pair of young hands on a piano, a boy's fingers dancing on the keys." Serafin's words came back to him as the rhythm of the bossa sped up. Fortunately, the sonatas he used to teach Pedro Martinez in the Calle de Apodaca were nothing like the Vincius de Moraes song blaring from the dance school, so Serafin continued on his way, following his thoughts and steps, leaving all his musical memories behind. Farther down the street there was a pajama shop, then a Pans & Company fast-food place; beyond that, the elegant old Café del Real and a bar from which an electronic jingle emerged, indicating that someone had hit the jackpot on a poker machine. I'm all right, Serafin told himself, I'll be fine. The flow of the crowd is carrying me away from the music at last, helping me forget. I'll be able to hold out, at least until my next appointment with Madame Longstaffe. Stay calm, Serafin. In a few seconds all this agitation will subside into the unthinking, unfeeling, unspeaking numbness that has blanketed your life for years. It's all right now. Soon the memory of Freshman's will fade away, like the memory of that boy with his crew cut, his melancholy eyes and nervous fingers, like the memory of Pedro Martinez in that sad refuge on the Calle de Apodaca from which your beloved Nora came to save you, bringing years of love and peace. The flow of the crowd quickened his pace as the Calle del Arenal suddenly narrowed before opening into a new pedestrian zone. And there, waiting mutely in a shopwindow, was a piano.

When, two days later, a pair of very handsome young men delivered the piano, maneuvering it into position in the sitting room near the fireplace, Serafin found himself looking at a photo of Nora that one of them—the irony of it!—had set on the lid, as if that were its habitual place.

Don't jump to conclusions, Nora, it's not what you're thinking, he said to the image of his wife. I didn't mean to go to that music shop. Somehow my steps and my thoughts led me there . . . Anyway, it's only on loan, my dear. These days they let you try out even grand pianos. It will only be in the house for two or three days. Think of it as a kind of exorcism. That's all it is, I swear. Believe me.

"I just need a signature here, sir."

The young fellow was wearing blue sleeveless overalls. He didn't have the arms or the hands of a pianist, but Serafin couldn't help staring as he held out the clipboard: muscles tensing under young skin, smooth forearms covered with blond, boyish down.

"Here, a thousand pesetas for your trouble," said Serafin. And, having slipped the note into the chest pocket of the young fellow's overalls, he gave it two delicate pats, as if it were a little bird that might escape at any moment. "You've been ever so kind . . ."

THE FOURTH DAY

I. OF LOVE AND BLACKMAIL

Don Antonio Reig
Pensión de Los Tres Boquerones
Sant Feliu de Guíxols

Madrid, 14th of March . . .

My dear friend Antonio,
I can't tell you how sad I was to read your letter. A chef of your
stature ruined, banished from the kitchen, condemned to cook what
he can on a Primus stove in the bathroom of a run-down boarding-
house. It's just awful. You told me about your arthritis—sadly, it's
not uncommon among the practitioners of our art. Destiny has seen
fit to spare me that curse, which is something to be thankful for, I
suppose.

I'm afraid I can't offer you any work, Antonio. My little busi-
ness barely covers its costs, especially at this time of year. But don't

*worry, we'll find something for you soon. You also asked me to help
you get hold of the Teldis' address, that couple I was telling you
about the other day. [Poor Antonio, the arthritis shows in your
handwriting: there's so much pain in those wobbly letters, despite
your elegant green ink.] What do you want their address for? To see
if they will help you out, I suppose. At the moment I don't know
how to get in touch with them, but how about this for a coincidence: a couple of days ago I saw a photo of them in one of those
glossy foreign magazines. Remember how he looked back in the
seventies, when he was beginning to build up his fortune? Teldi the
Spaniard, they called him. Well he hasn't changed much, physically
at least; he still looks distinguished but slightly dodgy, as they say
over here. Why are you so curious about him? You kept mentioning him in your letter, but I don't know what else I can tell you. He
did always strike me as an odd character, Ernesto Teldi. The Argentine upper crust held him in high regard, even back then, but
you always said there had to be something suspicious behind that
smooth, refined exterior. If you ever found a skeleton in his closet,
you never told me, and besides, by now it would be a very old skeleton, hardly worth getting worked up about. The sins of the rich are
easily forgotten, aren't they? Peccata minuta, Antonio. For what
it's worth, here's what I read in the magazine—maybe it'll be
of some use to you: he's a well-known art dealer these days and a
generous patron of the arts, dividing his time between Argentina,
Spain, and France (his main base). In fact, in the photo I mentioned, he's wearing the little ribbon of the Legion of Honor on his
lapel. Just like him, isn't it? He's obviously done well with his
paintings. He was just getting into the art business when you were
working for him in Argentina. I used to come around now and*

then and we'd brew up a pot of mate *and chat, remember? But I*
mustn't keep going on about the old days. What I meant to do in
this letter was cheer you up and tell you what I found out about
Teldi, since you seem to be so keen to locate him. Right now I have
no idea where he could be, but that's exactly why I'm sure we'll find
him. This may sound crazy, but for a while now I've had this feel-
ing that my life is running on a track, like a train, and there's no
getting off it. Not just my life, the people around me too. The things
that are happening are like pieces of a puzzle, and though the pieces
are all different shapes, one by one they're falling into place. I don't
know how else to put it. I think it has something to do with going
to see Madame Longstaffe, the clairvoyant I was telling you about
in my last letter. Did I say what I was doing there in the first place?
I really just went along with one of my employees, Carlos Garcia,
to give him moral support. What he wanted from the witch was a
magic potion to help him find the woman of his dreams, in the flesh.
I know, I know, I think all that stuff's bogus too, but the thing is,
honestly, since that day, I keep feeling that destiny—or my destiny,
at least—is playing tricks on me, setting up coincidences. For ex-
ample: I happen to see a complete stranger in a compromising
situation. A few days later I run into him again in equally odd cir-
cumstances, and putting one and two together, I discover his dark
secret. You see what I mean? It's very strange. And then there's
Madame Longstaffe's prediction about my health, which she vol-
unteered without asking my permission. I know it's hard to believe,
but it's coming true, too. She said I had no reason to fear the cancer
that's eating away at me, and much to the surprise of my doctors,
since that day I've been feeling a lot better. So much better, in fact,
that if I weren't a natural skeptic I might think I was actually re-

covering. Now all we need is for Carlos to find his dream woman and for me to run into Ernesto Teldi in the street . . . But really it's no more than a bizarre series of coincidences. You're a rational person, so tell me: do you really think destiny likes playing Chinese boxes, taking odd bits of people's lives and fitting them together to make some crazy kind of puzzle? No, I don't either. It's just my imagination, I know, and that's why, despite what I just said, I'm still assuming I don't have long to live. Cancer is no joke, so I have to keep working on my secret project. But I've prattled on again, so I won't be sending you a recipe this time, Antonio. Next time, I promise. My book of little indiscretions is getting thicker every day, and now you'll have to excuse me. The phone is ringing.

"Mulberry and Mistletoe, who's speaking? . . . Yes, who's speaking? . . . Allô? . . . Pronto? . . . What do you mean, the number I've dialed doesn't exist? I didn't dial any number, *porca miseria.* Somebody was calling me. *Porca miseria,*" Nestor repeated impatiently. "Bloody telephone! Bloody government! It was probably an important client."

II. CARLOS AND ADELA,
OR LOVE IN ITS PUREST STATE

ADELA HUNG UP the phone. It was the third time she had called and the third time a robotic female voice had informed her that the number she had called was not in service. But she knew she hadn't made a mistake. The friend who'd recommended Mulberry & Mistletoe ("The very best, my dear. I wouldn't even think about a do without consulting my old friend Nestor—he's a genius when it comes to organizing parties; he takes care of *everything*") had repeated the number so that she could check it. But the robotic voice was implacable: the number you have called is not in service.

For a moment Adela considered going there in person. After all, the address on the card, at the corner of Ayala and Serrano, wasn't far from where she was now, on the Calle Miguel Angel. She looked at the card again, not that she really needed to: yes, yes, she could walk or take a taxi and sort it all out in a matter of minutes. That would be best, really—she told herself—it's always a good idea to talk to people face-to-face with this sort of business. Just then, a taxi pulled up a few meters away to drop someone off, as if the driver had read her mind. It was starting to rain. That decided her. As soon as the taxi's free, I'll hop in, she thought. First she would stop at Mulberry & Mistletoe. She'd ask the driver to wait while she went over the details of the party she was planning to have at her country house, and she'd still have time to get back to the Palace Hotel and meet her husband before three. Madrid is not a pleasant city in rainy weather. Now she just had to wait for that person to get out of the taxi.

A great mass of blond hair emerged from the depths of the car, followed by a foot encased in a silk slipper. Strange footwear for this time of year, thought Adela, but she said nothing. Over the years she had learned to remain indifferent to all kinds of extravagance.

"Excuse me," said the voice of the passenger, and for a moment they paused and exchanged glances. "Excuse me, but could you tell me if this is the Calle de Almagro?"

What a stupid question, thought Adela. They were on the Calle Miguel Angel, nowhere near Almagro, and anyway, no one gets out of a taxi without knowing where they are. So instead of answering the question, she put on a polite smile and murmured: "May I?"

She was determined to get into that taxi as soon as she could.

"Don't go today, madame," said the slipper. "Go another day. Tomorrow maybe. Yes, that would be better. What you had planned for today, leave it for tomorrow afternoon. It's starting to rain, haven't you noticed?"

It *is* raining, you mad old bat, thought Adela, but before she could say anything, the exotic slipper added: "Anyway, do you really know where you're going? Do you know the route you'll have to take to get to the Calle de Ayala?"

"Easy," interrupted the taxi driver, who had been quiet up to this point but was no doubt exasperated by his clients' chatter. "The quickest way from here is to go across the Plaza de Rubén Darío, down the Calle de Almagro, and then—"

"It's going to rain. Come back another day and take another route," insisted the slippered woman. "You wouldn't want your fur coat to be ruined, would you? . . . It's so pretty," she said. Only it came out "Ish so pretty," with a Brazilian accent. "Ish going to rain . . . anosser day." But in the end, she did get out of the taxi and allow Adela to take her place. The whole thing was absurd, and yet . . .

~

ONCE SHE WAS in the taxi, Adela did not turn around. She would never know what that woman looked like from a distance or how that voluminous head of blond hair stood up to the rain or whether, to step over the spreading puddles, she had to hitch up her green tunic and reveal her silk slippers. By the time Adela finally settled into the taxi, she had reconsidered her destination.

Before heading off, the driver asked her: "So you want to go to the Calle de Ayala?"

She shook her head. "No," she said without looking back, not even a glance. "Take me to the Palace Hotel." And then she added: "You don't have to go along Almagro to get there, do you?"

To which the taxi driver, who was talkative and a stickler for precision, replied: "No, it's easy" (apparently everything was easy for him). "From here, if you prefer, we can go down to Castellana, across Colón, and then straight ahead until we get to the hotel."

"Great—because my husband is waiting for me, you know," said Adela, as if the driver needed to know.

She didn't look out the window again until they reached the fountain of Neptune. That mad old bat was right. She could go to Mulberry & Mistletoe tomorrow. That way she'd be setting out from a completely different part of Madrid. It was raining, after all.

⁓

EVEN THOUGH Adela Teldi always liked coming back to Madrid, the city of her birth, there were certain streets she carefully avoided. Like the Calle de Almagro, for example, with its plane trees, whose downy leaves made you sneeze, and its footpaths, which had hardly changed since her childhood. So little had they changed, in fact, that if for some unimaginable reason she had found herself walking down that street, it would have been hard for her not to fall back into the silly games of her childhood: avoiding the cracks in the pavement or playing a kind of mental hopscotch. But there was no reason for Adela to go to that part of Madrid. Her Madrid had shifted, and the shops, the hairdressers, and the restaurants she frequented, even the houses of her friends, were all a long way from that block, once so familiar. Luckily. So the following day, around four in the afternoon, Adela set out from the Palace Hotel and had no trouble getting to the Calle de Ayala, where the catering company had its premises. And when she arrived, a young fellow showed her into a pleasant waiting room.

"I'll be with you in a moment, madame," he said to her. "My boss isn't in. He's almost always here, but something came up and he had to go out. It's a bit of bad luck, but don't worry, I'll be able to help you. I'll just go and get something to write with, Mrs. . . . ?"

And, as in an old film, Carlos left the sentence hanging for Adela to complete.

"Mrs. Teldi, with a *T* for Teresa," she replied. "And what is your name?"

"Carlos Garcia at your service, madame. I'm sure we'll be able to meet your needs. I'll be right back."

While he was in the other room looking for the list of menus, pulling out the albums with photographs of buffets and impeccably laid tables adorned with flowers and still-life

arrangements, he could see Mrs. Teldi through the gap between the curtains: she was walking around the waiting room,
surveying the portraits hanging on the walls. He saw her smile
at some of the personalities in the photos as if she knew them,
tilting her head occasionally to read a dedication. There's not
much variety in the things people do while they're waiting.
Some light a cigarette, others walk up and down as if taking
possession of the space by measuring it. And some settle in,
taking off their coats, undoing a button or two.

One more album, thought Carlos, mustn't forget to show
her the fruit arrangements, and he glanced guiltily at Adela: it
isn't good to keep the clients waiting. But she had made herself
comfortable on the sofa, having shifted a South American poncho that must have been bothering her. Now her coat seemed
to be bothering her too, though it wasn't all that hot in the
waiting room. Suddenly, impatiently, she removed first her
coat and then the scarf that was covering her throat. Mrs.
Teldi's movements were so hasty that for a fraction of a second,
the slight hollow at the base of her very white and fragile neck
was exposed.

What a pity, thought Carlos, spying on this stranger. That
neck must have been quite unforgettable once. Then he went
back into the waiting room with the papers and the albums.

⸺

TWO OR THREE days later, when the door of room 505 at the
Phoenix Hotel shut behind them, the rest of the world ceased
to exist for Carlos and Adela. The piped music could have
been "Love Me Tender" or a flamenco song: it wouldn't have

made any difference. When they paused in their lovemaking, they could have drunk Fanta or Bailey's without ice, it could have been light outside or not, cold or oppressively hot. None of that mattered: the only thing they sensed was love. It was the typical chance meeting between a mature woman and a young man: they began by talking business, how the party would be organized and so on, then they had sandwiches at the Embassy, got drunk together in the bar of the Phoenix, and ended up in bed. A casual encounter, predictable enough. But the next day they saw each other again, and the day after, and the one after that, and when the door of the hotel room shut behind them, off came the shirt with the Mulberry & Mistletoe logo, the Armani skirt, the red bow tie and the sky blue blouse, all in perfect silence, kisses guiding the way to nakedness. And, still without a word, they set about exploring that naked flesh inch by inch, with a passionate attention to detail. The piped music brought them the voice of Wilfrido Vargas singing, "There's nowhere left I haven't kissed," but neither was interested in what their ears might register. Carlos and Adela heard, saw, smelled, and felt through the skin—"every inch a source of bliss"—and bliss it was for Adela to run her smelling, seeing, hearing hands over that young skin, so young that, kiss after kiss, what it inspired was not so much desire as tenderness. How lucky, how lucky you are, Adela, she said to herself. Kiss him while you can, no questions asked, no past, no future. Make love the way castaways do, or the terminally ill, the way only old women like you can make love. Stroke his thighs, tangle yourself in his hair, don't let a morsel of that beautiful body go to waste. You're a lucky woman. And what about him?

What is he thinking? . . . It's just as well nature hasn't given us the power to read other people's thoughts. So kiss him, taste him, love him, Adela, she told herself. And afterward, forget. Don't forget to forget, for heaven's sake. Forgetting is essential, because the world is still there waiting outside the door of room 505.

⌒

THIS ADVENTURE HAD taken Carlos by surprise and swept him away, but not once did he look back. Falling in love is like the flight from Sodom and Gomorrah: if you stop to look back you may find yourself turning into a pillar of salt, a sterile, impotent statue, sensibly (all too sensibly) wondering: What the hell are you getting yourself into here, spending three afternoons in a row with a woman who could be your mother? Have you taken a good look at her?

No. Carlos hadn't taken a good look at her, because in the microcosm of room 505 the laws of perspective had been suspended, so it was impossible to view anything more extensive than the curve of a neck or the lobe of an ear. When you're under the sway of an all-consuming passion, love in its purest state, all you can see are millimeters of skin electrified by desire and ever-new paths opening before you. Carlos set off to explore without a compass. "I want to take the long way from your hips down to your feet . . ." He was not a big reader of poetry and had no special interest in Neruda, but in love, poets and waiters follow the same paths. Sooner or later, both have to overcome all the same obstacles on their amorous voyages: peninsular fingers, hill-like knees, the deep dale between the thighs. The route is long, and it may take the explorer some time to reach the Mount of Venus. There, for the first time in his life, Carlos lost control of his tongue, as if it had developed a mind of its own.

The role of explorer was not unfamiliar to him, but it had always been just that: a role. "This is what women like, or this . . ." The exploration was perhaps more clinical than passionate, but it always seemed to work. He considered himself an accomplished actor, yet until he stepped into room 505, his amorous experiences (as well as being a search for the woman in the picture) had always felt rather like taking an entrance exam. Was he worthy of admission to the club of surefire lovers? Or the club of tender lovers, who hug the girl afterward when all they really want is to get out of there—all right, all right, I'll cuddle her a bit, a little kiss here, an I-love-you there, but don't overdo it, stick to the script. They freak out if you start ad-libbing.

In room 505, however, there was no script, no map, no compass. And there was no need to work himself up by imagining that the line of an unfamiliar neck might fit the perfect curve he had discovered in an armoire all those years ago. With other women it had always been deceptively easy: all he had to do was shut his eyes and Lola, Laura, Marta, Mirtha, Nilda, Norma . . . and so on, through to the end of his neat and not so little black book, they all had the neck of the woman in the painting.

But that skin . . . Adela's skin (he hardly dared to say her name: it was superstitious, like the fear of looking back and turning into a pillar of salt), Adela's skin did not extend beyond the minute path marked out by his kisses. Love has eyes so weak they cannot pick out wrinkles or imperfections, so shortsighted they can admire a freckle simply because it's *hers*.

⸻

ADELA WAS NOT shortsighted. And she had long since quit the club of obliging lovers, which has different statutes for its male and female members. Women have to know how to sigh convincingly and how to turn up the heat by talking dirty at the appropriate moment: those are the golden rules. The language of passion is a delicate balancing act: you might, just might, get away with *cunt* in certain circumstances, but *fanny,* well, no, and *cock* is okay, but *knob* . . . excuse me! There are strict rules about these things, and sometimes acting is more convincing than sincerity, but you have to know how to pull it off, when to say what, how to soften or raise your voice, because obscenities are like exotic food: there are aphrodisiacs and purgatives.

Adela knew all this, of course, but none of it mattered to her anymore. She had given up employing those skills in her affairs years ago, and she certainly wasn't going to start again with this boy. Yet although she felt that her long years of acting had earned her the right to concentrate on actual pleasures without bothering to pretend, somehow the paths her kisses traced on Carlos's skin didn't seem entirely new. It was as if once, many years ago, her hands had explored this territory. It was a silly, absurd idea, but for the first time in ages, she felt she had lost control of what was happening to her. She of all people, after so many lovers, so many affairs, so many attempts to cauterize her solitude.

Her sister's name—Soledad, solitude—had slipped unexpectedly into her thoughts, giving her a start.

"What's wrong? Are you all right?"

"Fine. Don't stop kissing me."

But it was too late for kisses to blot out that name, linked to a story she would have preferred to forget. So, holding Carlos tightly, Adela resorted to a method that had served her well over the years. She had applied it successfully since the day her sister died: the best way to forget guilty caresses is to smother them with thousands more, because nothing diminishes guilt like the tireless repetition of the sin, which empties it of meaning. And that is what Adela had been doing all those years, trying to forget one particular body by loving so many others.

For a moment the trick seemed to be working. Adela smiled: the danger had been averted once again, and she was feeling rather pleased with herself, until she noticed that strange but familiar sensation in her thumbs.

By the pricking of my thumbs, something wicked this way comes. I've done all this before, she thought. I'm sure I've loved this body, this skin . . . But then she tried to shake herself out of it: Come on, Adela. The only wicked thing going on here is that you're falling in love with a twenty-one-year-old boy. Don't let yourself. Just keep quiet and enjoy it. You'll be able to love him again tomorrow, and Friday too, and maybe a fourth or a fifth time after that, but don't think any further ahead. As you know only too well, my dear, dreams do exist, oh yes, but only so long as you don't try to make them come true. Room 505 is paradise for as long as it lasts: two, three, four days, maybe even quite a bit longer. Think of that: you might be able to enjoy *months* of love just so long as . . .

Just so long as you're sensible about it, she told herself sternly. As soon as he walks out that door, ring up Mulberry & Mistletoe and cancel all the arrangements for the party; promise you'll do that.

As soon as he's gone, you're going to pick up that telephone and change your plans. The idea of spending a weekend with a houseful of guests plus *him* is just crazy. Out of the question. This is where your passion belongs, between these four walls, and only a hopeless dreamer would attempt to live it out in public. *Carpe diem;* kiss, don't think. Love and forget, Adela. Dreams melt away at the touch of reality. Enjoy yourself now and pay later by giving up on seeing him outside this room. Make sure you call that chef.

⁓

TWO HOURS LATER, when Carlos had left the room at the Phoenix Hotel and love had given way to practicalities, Adela sat down on the unmade bed to call the number, just as she had promised.

"Hello, is that Mulberry and Mistletoe? Could I please speak to Mr. Chaffino? It's Mrs. Teldi here . . . Aha, pleased to meet you, so to speak . . . Yes, that's right, exactly, Teldi, with a *T* for Teresa. I dropped in the other day to arrange some catering, and since you were out, I talked with your assistant. Did he tell you what we needed? Well, I'm calling now because I've changed my mind . . ." (Adela stroked the sheets and closed her eyes tight, although what she was really trying to do was shut off other, more obstinate senses, for the scent of Carlos's skin was still clinging to the treacherous sheets and was even more delicious than when he had been there in person— and more dangerous, too. Oh God, the scent of absence!)

Adela wanted to light a cigarette so as not to smell that perfume, but something stopped her.

"Pardon? Yes, sorry, I'm still here, Mr. Chaffino. I wanted to tell you that . . ." (Her hand ventured farther afield now and discovered forgotten patches of warmth. Careful, Adela. Many stupid things have been done on account of an empty hollow in a warm bed . . . but only by naïve, romantic women, who didn't know the rules of the game.)

"Can you hear me, Mr. Chaffino? I'm so sorry, I was thinking . . . You see, I called you because . . ." (Don't do it, Adela, don't do it.) "Actually, I called to confirm the arrangements," she said, crumpling, because the sheets still held the shape of Carlos's body. He hadn't been gone ten minutes, and she could still feel the kiss he had left on her lips, saying, "Till tomorrow, my love" . . . She could also feel that inexplicable tingling in her thumbs, warning her that something wicked was on the way.

"Yes, yes, that's right, it's all going ahead . . . except that instead of a whole weekend, we'll just do the dinner on Saturday night." (What a coward you are! As if that were any kind of solution. What difference does it make whether he comes for one night or a weekend?) "Is that all right then? I'll call tomorrow and we'll go over the details, what do you think?" (Game over: you lose. You're making the same stupid mistake as all those women you're always laughing at.)

"That's right, all settled then. Tell me, Mr. Chaffino, you and your assistants, how will you be getting there? . . . Excellent, I'll send you a check. So it'll be just the one day then, but a very special day."

~

THE FIFTH DAY

LITTLE INDISCRETIONS

PART THREE: SORBETS AND OTHER FROZEN DESSERTS

Madrid, 25th of March . . .

Dear Antonio,

I told you, I told you! The Teldis have turned up, just as I predicted.
You won't believe this, but the very same day I wrote my last letter
to you, Adela Teldi paid us a visit here in person at Mulberry &
Mistletoe. She wants me to cater for a party at this house they've got
in the south, called the Lilies. At first it was going to be a weekend,
with lots of guests staying over, breakfast, lunch, and dinner and so
on, the whole deal, but in the end it'll just be one big dinner on
Saturday night. It doesn't matter. It'll be less money, but the amaz-
ing thing is that my hunch was right.

So what does it all mean? Well, for a start it means I can help
you get in touch with them, like you asked me to. The Madrid ad-

dress is easy: they're staying at the Palace, and I'll give you their address at the Lilies too, in case you'd prefer to write to them there. And now let's get down to business—we mustn't let all these strange coincidences distract us from serious culinary matters.

Have I got a treat in store for you this time! My secret tips for making sorbets, the aristocracy of cold desserts. But before I launch into my little indiscretions, a request.

It makes sense for me to keep writing, since I'm sending you these recipes, but from now on I think it would be simpler for you to call me. Reverse charges, of course, it goes without saying. I hope you won't be offended, but I can barely read your writing. And what with the green ink you always use, it's like . . . well, like a row of tatty parrots perched on a wire. There are whole sections I can't make out for the life of me, like the paragraph where you're telling me about Teldi, something about the disappearance of political prisoners in Argentina, if I've understood it properly, and God knows what else. In any case, that part of the letter is practically illegible, though I'll try and decipher it properly tomorrow on the way down. But whatever it is you want to say to Teldi, I would strongly advise you to make an effort with your handwriting: no one's got the patience to read three or four pages of green scribble. He'll give up right away. It's the curse of our times, Antonio: no one has any patience anymore, everyone gets bored so easily.

Except for me, of course. Here are my plans, then: I'm off to Málaga to do this big dinner the Teldis are throwing for a group of collectors, God knows why. I'll keep you posted. I'm sure it'll be interesting. I love big parties with lots of houseguests; something unexpected always happens. I'm taking Chloe along to help (the girl I told you about in my first letter: she's not a bad waitress), along with Karel Pligh and Carlos Garcia. They've both done the country-house thing before, so I'll be able to concentrate on the food and my beloved desserts. I'm even planning to invent one specially for the occasion, a sorbet surprise worthy of the Teldis: cold, expensive, and very showy. What do you think?

Speaking of desserts: here are this week's secret tips. This time they're for making sorbets and gelati. But do remember what I said, Antonio: make an effort with your handwriting . . . You wouldn't be planning to blackmail Teldi, would you now? You have to be very careful with that sort of thing. Pardon my indiscretion, but I'm curious to know what you've got in mind. We are old friends, after all.

All right. Here they are then, finally: this week's two little indiscretions.

A trick used by le maître Paul Bocuse
to improve the consistency of a mango sorbet

To maintain the consistency of a fruit sorbet, especially if it's made with mango, you need to keep a sprig of marigolds handy, or, better still, two sprigs. What you do is . . .

THE SIXTH DAY

ERNESTO TELDI AND MISS RAMOS

THE ROTUNDA OF the Palace Hotel has featured in innumerable photographs as the calm and discreet backdrop for interviews with all manner of famous people. Its carpet, woven on the Royal Looms, has muffled the catlike tread of Julian Barnes making his way toward the ideal armchair in which to pose and display a pair of expensive French moccasins. The kentias in the lobby inspired La Toya Jackson to try something different: peering through the branches to reveal the oval of her pallid face, like a Versace medusa. Famous athletes and legendary actors, left-wing intellectuals and right-wing politicians (moderately right wing, of course): at some point they have all chosen this cozy yet well-illuminated space, unique in all Madrid, not just because the photos turn out well but also because it is one of those places that have their own significance. It adds the following message to a profile piece: I, ladies and gentlemen, am someone who appreciates quality but disdains ostentation, who is not averse to comfort so long as it is accompanied by a hint of cleverly simulated decadence. I honor the life of the mind, of course, but artistic sensibility is incomplete without that—how shall I put it?—that deft, almost imperceptible touch of sophistication.

The unique ambience of the rotunda at the Palace says all that, or at least that is what Ernesto Teldi imagined it to say, which is why he had chosen it as the setting for his appointment with the photographer and the journalist from *Patron of the Arts,* a trade magazine with around 350,000 subscribers throughout Europe (individuals, mostly, plus a very select group of institutions). This prestigious publication had been trying for months to set up an interview with Teldi—"A professional piece, of course, very classy, but with a human slant: the home life of the highflier, in the style of *Fortune* magazine. You know the sort of thing."

Teldi had been waiting for Miss Ramos and her photographer for some time. On the table in front of him, the remains of a frugal breakfast were arranged as if for effect: grapefruit juice, a cup of tea, crumbs (presumably from a slice of toast), while the lord of this little domain flipped through the pages of *The Financial Times* (the arts pages, naturally).

"GOOD MORNING, Miss Ramos. Agustina Ramos, isn't it?" A kiss for her, a firm handshake and a slap on the back for the photographer. "Allow me to introduce myself: Ernesto Teldi," he added, his manner poised between familiarity and reserve.

He had discovered that this worked well on the better sort of journalist, and especially on the likes of Miss Ramos: usually extremely well educated, sometimes left-handed, and occasionally cross-eyed (a trait that may add a touch of originality to an otherwise nondescript appearance). Often, remarkably often in fact, these journalists were also the daughters, nieces, or close relatives of some unknown or unjustly forgotten painter, a painter of enormous talent (what a barbaric world we live in), and for these reasons Miss Ramos and her ilk considered themselves hard done by. They were acutely aware that working for a glossy but pseudo-intellectual magazine like *Patron of the Arts* was a miserable waste of their intelligence, but what really peeved them was having to endure the company of Chema or someone like him.

Chema was the photographer. He was much younger than Miss Ramos, and was in the unforgivable habit of chewing gum and dressing with an absolute disregard for aesthetics: a dire combination of stripey Nikes and checked trousers, say, proof positive of his bad taste, which didn't stop him taking good photographs, so good, in fact, that they tended to overshadow the impeccable prose of Miss Ramos. This time, however, she was determined not to be overshadowed, which was why she had prepared a battery of penetrating questions for Ernesto Teldi. Some were hard-hitting, even impertinent, all were backed up by careful research: intellect and gossip, blended fifty-fifty, a foolproof recipe, mused Miss Ramos. She was going to show her stupid bosses at *Patron of the Arts* what a top-class interview should be.

"Good morning, Mr. Teldi."

Miss Agustina Ramos had almost vanished into an enormous sofa with claret upholstery, no doubt very comfortable, but far too voluminous for someone of her modest dimensions. Nevertheless, she got her tape recorder going.

"One, two, three, testing," she said, adding, by way of a label: "Interview with Ernesto Teldi, Spanish-Argentine art dealer and collector."

"Plain Spanish, I would say," interjected Teldi with a marked South American accent. "Many people think I'm an Argentine because I lived for a long time in Buenos Aires and my surname sounds vaguely Italian, but I assure you I'm Spanish through and through."

Miss Ramos didn't like to be interrupted. What a drag. Now she would have to stop and rewind the tape. And besides, there was absolutely no need for him to butt in. She had prepared the interview thoroughly; she knew perfectly well that Teldi had started out as a young man in Madrid with ambition to spare but not much money and that, at the end of the sixties, ignoring everyone's advice, he had decided to give up a steady job and try his luck in Argentina. It was hardly an ideal time to make the move—the country's glory days were well and truly over, and yet against all the odds Teldi had managed to make a fortune, especially in the seventies and eighties, buying up paintings in bulk at absurdly low prices (compared with what they'd fetch in Europe): Sorolla, Gutiérrez Solana, Ruisiñol, Zuloaga, even occasionally minor works by Monet, Bonnard, and Renoir, gems that had come to Buenos Aires at the beginning of the century. Thanks to these good deals, Teldi was now a successful businessman, a highly respected professional, and he had recently become a generous patron of the arts. All this made him an ideal subject for the magazine Miss Ramos had the misfortune to work for, which was interested in the rich and in artists who were famous only because of the price a bunch of philistines were willing to pay for their work. Nevertheless, there are dark corners in the life of every eminent man, and Teldi was no exception. Miss Ramos was determined to seek them out, even if it meant opposing the directives of her insufferably ignorant bosses. She would show them what a real arts journalist can do. But before going for the jugular . . .

"Tell me, Mr. Teldi, for you, is art business or pleasure?" she asked, because this highly original question was an obligatory part of any interview with *Patron of the Arts*.

Same old drivel, thought Teldi, silently cursing Mr. Janeiro, the developer who owned the lavish magazine as well as a chain of shoe stores, which allowed him to devote his time to humiliating serious people like Miss Ramos, forcing them to ask hackneyed questions like "Business or pleasure?"

Teldi leaned back in his armchair. Privately, he agreed with Miss Ramos about the stupidity of the question: everyone knows that art these days is a business first and foremost. Nevertheless, he trotted out an appropriate reply.

"Well, of course, it's neither one nor the other. Art is a source of aesthetic experiences, part of the common heritage of humanity. It is what distinguishes us from the animals and brings us closer to the gods."

Right, thought Miss Ramos. Now that she had discharged her obligation, she could get down to business. She pulled out a little notebook in which she had patiently summarized the key facts and dates from Teldi's CV. Are you ready, Mr. Teldi? she said to herself. Brace yourself; here comes the first cruise missile. And she launched into her first penetrating question, cleverly laced with vitriol; but before she could get to the end of it, two sounds distracted her. The first was emanating from the jaws of the photographer, who was chewing gum in time with the second sound: *click, click, click, CLICK,* went the shutter as Chema dodged around Teldi, taking photo after photo. This always drove Miss Ramos up the wall, but there was no point complaining: the editor of *Patron of the Arts* believed in having the photos taken during the interview. "They've got more life and authenticity that way, Ramos. You don't get it, do you? You still haven't realized we're living in a visual culture. A gesture's worth a thousand words. Do us a favor and stop whining."

So Agustina Ramos didn't whine, not even when Chema thrust himself between her and Teldi to immortalize the way the dealer stroked his chin as he replied to the tough question that the young lady had left dangling.

"No, no. I'm afraid you're mistaken, my dear. It was easy to buy paintings back then, but I can assure you it had nothing whatever to do with Argentina's political problems or the repression and the horrendous crimes committed by the military. The art boom had begun before all that. You realize, of course, that I've been a member of the UN IC for years" (IC for Investigating Committee, of course). "As I said, I'm a member of a body set up precisely to investigate human rights violations; so I'm hardly likely to have taken advantage of those unfortunate circumstances to—"

"To get rich by ripping off families that, as well as being torn apart, also had their property devalued during the dictatorship."

"Quite, my dear," broke in Teldi, who knew that the best way to handle this sort of virago was to confront her directly and get the upper hand as soon as possible. "That's precisely why we set up the PFVST, the Philanthropic Fund for the Victims of State Terrorism, and it's well known that I was one of the founders of the fund, at considerable personal risk, believe me. Remember, we're talking about the period from 'seventy-six to 'eighty-three—not the best time to go playing the hero, I can assure you."

He was looking at her. His suave philanthropist's gaze seemed to settle tenderly on Miss Ramos's ankles, which were the most attractive part of her anatomy. "Nice ankles," he seemed to be saying with his eyes, and Miss Ramos almost smiled, because she wasn't completely immune to the masculine gaze, especially the gaze of a connoisseur. Nevertheless, like a true professional, she managed to continue in the same aggressive style as before:

"Yes, yes, perhaps it wasn't a good time for heroics, but curiously, with everything that was going on, it seems to have been a good time for making a great deal of money. As you mentioned yourself, those were the years of state terrorism. So what's your secret?"

"There is no secret," Teldi replied (his gaze sliding down from Miss Ramos's ankles to her shoes, which she suddenly wanted to hide, lest those gallant eyes discover that her seemingly expensive looking footwear was fake). "You see, Agustina" (such a pretty name, the way he said it), "in the period we're talking about, there was only one way to succeed: a good deal of hard work and contempt for the military. But we're here to talk about art, not politics, aren't we, my dear? So perhaps we should sharpen the focus of our conversation."

At this point, Chema took advantage of Teldi's emphatic pause on the word *focus* to capture an image of him making his point with an expression of such royal grandeur that a lady having breakfast two tables away let out a stifled "Oh" and elbowed her husband in the ribs.

"Look, Alfredo, it's someone famous!" she said. "Look, over there, on the left. Isn't it Agnelli, the owner of Maserati? He looks just like a Florentine cardinal!"

And the husband, apparently up on such things, informed her that Agnelli had nothing to do with Maserati; he was the owner of Olivetti, the multinational, didn't she know anything? Meanwhile, Chema went on firing off his flashes and Miss Ramos made a valiant effort to back Teldi into a corner with her tough questions.

"All right, it's true that no one has ever been able to link you with the military, and that's to your credit, because if a link were to be discovered, well, the stain would be indelible. So let's leave all that aside and talk about art, but even where art is concerned, there have, I'm afraid, been a number of rumors about your highly profitable dealing. Is it true, for example, that you once bought a magnificent Monet for a ridiculously small sum, then sold it for twenty times its value while the former owner of the painting, unable to pay his debts, ended up committing suicide?"

"Well, it's true about the transactions," said Teldi with a charming smile, "but the rest of the story is a little fanciful. The former owner of the Monet is not only alive and well, he's also a good friend of mine and now one of the richest men in South America. I like to help people out and expect them to do the same for me. Is there something reprehensible about that, Agustina?"

Mr. Teldi was coming to seem less and less reprehensible to Miss Ramos. Especially when their eyes met, which didn't happen very often, just often enough to make her want more. In fact, Miss Ramos, who prided herself on being an infallible judge of character, had to admire the way he was handling her aggressive questions: smiling calmly, even once (just once alas!) stretching out his right hand toward the sofa where she was sitting, although he didn't actually go so far as to touch her. The perfect gentleman, naturally. His gaze settled on her again. Miss Ramos felt as if she were melting and would soon be no more than a puddle on the claret-colored sofa. My God, his aura! No camera could ever capture it, the aura of this exquisite philanthropist and patron of the arts. Besides, she thought, however hard I try to do my duty as an aggressive interviewer, the facts speak for themselves: as he says, hard work and a passion for art, that's how he earned his money; and you have to consider what he's done with it, too.

"Setting up two schools for abandoned children, my dear" (two little words that were music to her ears) "and scholarships to foster talent, not just for painters but for musicians and writers too. We can never do enough for the arts. Life has given me so much, I feel I should give something back, you see."

Of course she does: Miss Ramos can see clearly now. This man is so sensitive, so wonderfully straightforward, and what he says is so true.

"I've got it," said the wife of the man named Alfredo, sitting two tables away. "It's not Agnelli. He's an actor, that guy. What's his name . . . ? Sean Connery? No, I don't know, that mustache and the gray hair . . . But I'm sure I've seen him in a film. They never stop acting, even in real life, but it always seems so natural, doesn't it, Alfredo?"

Alfredo had no opinion on the matter. He couldn't have cared less. Distinguished-looking men with gray hair fascinate a good many wives, but husbands are, on the whole, far less susceptible to their charm, especially husbands who happen to be bald. Besides which, Alfredo couldn't hear what they were saying, although he knew two things for sure: it wasn't Sean Connery, and that poor girl, the journalist, was falling into the same hypnotic trance as his wife. If you ask me, he's a small-time con man, thought Alfredo. But all he said was: "Forget it, Matilde."

Meanwhile, Teldi was saying to Miss Ramos: "Yes, yes, but let's not restrict ourselves to Art with a capital *A*. It's all very well to talk about Monet and congratulate oneself on being the lucky owner of so many wonderful works, but there are other things in life that give me much more pleasure, things I feel I can talk about with someone like you. I'll let you into a secret, my dear. But perhaps if you switch off the tape recorder first . . . You see, it's not the sort of thing that would interest a magazine like *Patron of the Arts,* with its three hundred and fifty thousand subscribers among the . . . they really should call it *Art Shark,* don't you think?"

Miss Ramos couldn't have agreed more. She switched off her tape recorder. Then she looked at Chema to see if he was going to butt in and spoil everything as usual. But Chema, who had finished taking photos, was chewing gum about ten meters away, inspecting his exposure meter.

"Perhaps it's rather frivolous, but it's the sort of thing I really enjoy, and I know you'll find it amusing. The philanthropists you interview are probably always telling you how they hobnob with other famous patrons of the arts, getting together to talk about the pieces they're planning to buy or throwing parties just to show off their latest acquisitions to friends and rivals—a Byzantine virgin, say, bought from some dealer who specializes in extracting such objects from Eastern Europe. You know the type, swindlers the lot of them. Not that I don't occasionally participate in that sort of pantomime myself. I do—I go along to their cocktail parties and do business with them, but the people I really like are the ones who are passionate about Art with a capital *A,* my dear, and by that I don't mean things that cost a fortune but things that are truly unique. Just to give you an idea, let me tell you what I'm organizing for next week . . ."

You can tell me anything, Ernesto Teldi, thought Miss Ramos. What do I care about my art-shark bosses and penetrating interviews and all the stupid, unscrupulous people who try to fling mud at you? There are always slanderous rumors about anyone who really stands out. If only I could . . . if only I knew . . . While all these thoughts were running through Miss Ramos's mind, she maintained the outward appearance of a dispassionate journalist, thanks to her professional reflexes. Resist, Agustina, she said to herself, as if her scruples were the walls of a besieged city. Keep on resisting. But Agustina's gunpowder was damp.

"Look, I'm organizing a little get-together in a few days' time. You really must come," said Teldi, as if the idea had just occurred to him and it wasn't a devious way to sidetrack Miss Motormouth, with her artistic pretensions and her dangerous questions about his past in Argentina. "I come from a humble background, and I like to mix with simple people. I should explain: I've invited some collectors to my country house. Not big collectors, mind you, the kind with more money than sense, who hoard Picassos or collect Folio editions of Shakespeare and never read past the first page of *Hamlet,* though they're always quoting 'To be or not to be' without knowing the rest of the speech, which is better still, don't you think?—'Who would fardels bear, / To grunt and sweat under a weary life . . .' and so on. You know what I mean: the kind of people who love possessions rather than art. No, the guests I've invited are not like that at all."

Ernesto Teldi then proceeded to seduce Miss Ramos (and, incidentally, the magazine's 350,000 subscribers, including all the major players in the international art game) with one of his original ideas.

"Naturally, I wouldn't want you to mention this in *Patron of the Arts.* You can keep the sharks happy with the politically correct side of my activities, if you see what I mean. You can tell them about the artists I sponsor, my efforts to bring art to a wider public, my scholarships to foster young talent—that'll do for them. They haven't got the sensitivity to appreciate this sort of thing. So it's just between you and me, all right?"

And as if to drive his point home, he went on to explain that he would be delighted if she could join them the following weekend. It would be an opportunity to meet some truly eccentric collectors: tin-soldier fanatics, seekers after exotic daggers and *stiletti,* not to mention beer-mug and stuffed-animal fanciers or connoisseurs of saucepans, porcelain dolls, and books of ghost stories. "People who really appreciate the objects themselves, above all. The way they love those sublime odds and ends, it's so pure, and that, for me, is how all art should be appreciated."

Ernesto Teldi prudently avoided mentioning that by gathering eccentrics such as these (and plying them with the contents of his cellar), he was often able to pick up very rare pieces for a song before they came onto the market. Miss Ramos didn't need to know insignificant details like that. What someone of her aesthetic sensibility couldn't help but recognize, however, was the generous spirit of his initiative: bringing together a varied group of real experts, in the most tasteful and refined of settings, free of snobbery and greed.

"And you're more than welcome to come if you'd like," he insisted.

Life is so unfair, thought Miss Agustina Ramos. She was still half buried in the claret-colored sofa, and for a second the enveloping warmth of the cushions helped her imagine what the gathering might be like, with all those interesting people. No famous, insufferable painters, no filthy-rich philistines incapable of telling a Monet from a Manet, none of the usual *Patron of the Arts* pond life. Just genuine aesthetic sensibility, she thought, looking at Ernesto Teldi's handsome hands, which had once again advanced toward the armrest of the sofa. He was watching her, waiting for an answer.

"Well, Agustina? Hmm, my dear?"

It was so unfair. Agustina my dear would have given anything to be able to say yes, but, just her luck, that weekend she had to be on the other side of the world, interviewing a Japanese collector who owned a van Gogh suspected by many of being a fake. Now, *there* was an art shark who had better watch out. She'd be cooking up her nastiest questions for him. A boring assignment in Japan instead of a party at Teldi's house. Typical, she thought. I never have any luck, never.

"That's such a pity, such a pity," said Teldi, who had chosen this psychological moment to bring the interview to a close. "I do wish you could come. But don't forget, my dear, not a word about our little secret. People are so narrow-minded," he added. "It's really quite sad: all they want to know is how much money I give to young artists and how much I spend on sponsorships. Money, money, money, it's all they can think about. But we may as well give them what they're after, don't you think, my dear?"

Agustina said good-bye. He kissed her hand, the hand that wrote for *Patron of the Arts* and would compose an extremely boring and conventional but glowingly positive profile of Ernesto Teldi, a man who, in the space of a few short years, had risen to become a philanthropist of international standing.

"You're a truly remarkable person, Mr. Teldi," she said to him as he bid her farewell with a wink of complicity almost as intimate as a kiss.

"Good-bye, Agustina. We'll be seeing each other."

And as Miss Ramos walked toward the door with a voice in her head crying, When? When?, and Ernesto Teldi sat down again with a sigh of relief, like someone catching his breath after an obstacle race, two things happened almost simultaneously.

"Now I remember who that man is. It's the actor who played the cannibal in *The Silence of the Lambs,*" exclaimed the woman two tables away. "Alfredo, do you think he'd mind if I asked for an autograph?"

"Mr. Teldi," said a bellboy who had appeared from nowhere, as bellboys should. "A letter has come for you. It was just delivered."

Alfredo's wife was approaching Teldi. Soon she would be able to hear his voice. So would her husband.

"Shit!" he exclaimed, standing up abruptly when he saw the envelope in the bellboy's hand: it was the second such letter he had received in twenty-four hours. Both had been written in a crabbed hand using green ink; the letters looked like a row of parrots on a wire.

"Did you hear that, Matilde?" said the gentleman named Alfredo to his wife. "You see? I told you he wasn't some foreign actor."

ERNESTO TELDI COULDN'T decipher the signature at the bottom of the page, but part of the text, written in capital letters, was clear enough for him to make out five words that had figured in the previous letter: "Lieutenant Minelli . . . Don Torcuato Airport," and then, in a tangled scribble that almost seemed to be a burst of laughter: "Remember, Teldi?"

Part Three

THE NIGHT BEFORE
THE DEPARTURE

Others apart sat on a hill retired

In thoughts more elevate, and reasoned high

Of providence, foreknowledge, will, and fate,

Fixed fate, free will, foreknowledge absolute,

And found no end, in wand'ring mazes lost.

MILTON, *Paradise Lost*, Book II

EDITOR'S NOTE: The recipe that follows is the last one Nestor Chaffino sent to his friend Antonio Reig. He had supposed that after his trip to the Teldis' country house, their correspondence would continue. As we know, this was not to be. Destiny had decided that Nestor's fascinating work should remain unfinished and unfinishable. The chapter devoted to petits fours is dated the twenty-seventh of March. It must, therefore, have been written the day before his departure. As usual, Nestor occasionally interrupts his culinary notes to pass on news.

LITTLE INDISCRETIONS
PART FOUR: PETITS FOURS AND OTHER
AFTER-DINNER DELICACIES

One of the high points of a good meal is the arrival of the little after-dinner treats that are usually served with coffee. Chocolate truffles, caramelized cherries, biscotti with or without almonds, mille-feuilles with *glacé* oranges . . . there's no better way to round off a menu than with these delicious morsels, and as we shall see in a moment, they too have their little secrets, jealously guarded by the professionals. For example, Lucas Carton's tiny soufflés. The recipe is as follows:

[. . .] *but first, dear Antonio, let me digress for a moment, I promise it won't take long. Remember in my last letter I was telling you I had this strange feeling that the various parts of my life were com-*

ing together to form a peculiar puzzle of coincidences? (A discon-
certing feeling, to say the least, I'd even say creepy if I wasn't half-
Italian and worried about bringing bad luck on myself: gettatore,
gettatore.) *Anyway, it seems to have stopped. A wrench got into the*
works of fate, and at least one of Madame Longstaffe's supposedly
infallible predictions has turned out to be wrong. It had to do with
the love life of my assistant, Carlos Garcia, the one who's responsi-
ble for getting me mixed up with this fortune-teller in the first
place. You may remember we went to see her to get a love potion
that was meant to help Carlos find the living image of his ideal
woman. Well, to my great surprise and relief, not only has my
young friend lost interest in love potions (before finishing the bot-
tle), he's also lost interest in his ideal woman (the one in the
painting). He told me he's fallen in love with a real woman—a
flesh-and-blood, living, breathing woman—and has forgotten all
those fantasies he used to have. I don't know her, and although I've
tried to draw him out, so far he's refused to tell me her name. My
guess is she's a bit older. Maybe some thirty-year-old divorcée, who
knows? It wouldn't surprise me; they can be so attractive . . . Any-
way, if you're interested, I should be able to give you more details
in my next letter, because I may well meet her tonight. You see,
Carlos urgently needs to sell the apartment he inherited from his
grandmother, so he's asked me to help him. I put him in touch with
an acquaintance who works in real estate, and we're going over in
a bit to take a look at the place. So today I'll get to see the apart-
ment and the portrait and most likely the girlfriend, too. She'll
probably be there to give him moral support at such a crucial time,
don't you think?

Anyway, I'm nattering on like I always do in my letters. You don't need all these details. The important thing is that the spell has been broken and I don't feel like I'm being driven along a path anymore. It was like a sort of determinism. I think that's what it's called when your destiny is fixed in advance. But that's all over now. Madame Longstaffe's potion didn't work, and the boy has fallen in love with another woman, who has nothing to do with any predictions, so you see I feel free. It's such a relief to realize that no one can know or determine your destiny, not even some crafty old witch. That's why I'm feeling so good today, dear Antonio. In fact I feel so good that before I give you Lucas Carton's recipe, I'll slip in another one that's even better. This is my most precious indiscretion. Here goes:

In 1911, the chef at the Waldorf-Astoria in New York discovered an infallible secret method for making a cold soufflé that looks exactly like a hot one. These days one of the most interesting petits fours being made is a cold pistachio soufflé. Because it is so small, it is perfect for

1

NESTOR AND THE WOMAN
IN THE PAINTING

"Small but perfectly formed: ideal for the client I have in mind," said Juan Solis, the real estate agent, with an admiring little whistle. "What a *find,* Nestor!"

Nestor Chaffino and Carlos looked at each other and then at Solis, who was opening and closing drawers, inspecting the contents of biscuit tins, expertly pacing out the distances, walking around and weighing things up, as if making a complete inventory. He had broken a personal rule in coming to Number 38 Calle de Almagro with Nestor and Carlos. In twenty years as a real estate agent he had never agreed to see a property on a Saturday night—absolutely out of the question; he spent his Saturdays practicing Tai Chi. It was the only way he could maintain his emotional balance in such a stressful profession. But the sacrifice had turned out to be worthwhile. Solis felt he had discovered a pearl, and didn't mind saying so, over and over again. He was full of praise for Number 38: the height of the ceilings, the ideal orientation of the windows, the quality of the woodwork, and he kept emphatically repeating the bit about it being "small but perfectly formed," just right for his client.

Nestor was not particularly curious about this client, who apparently considered a 250-square-meter apartment "small" (and on the Calle de Almagro, no less). But as he walked away, leaving them to it, he heard Solis mention, in a discreet but intentionally sonorous whisper, somebody by the name of Baggerscheit.

"A kid who sings heavy metal," added the whisperer, by way of explanation. "He's huge, a real phenomenon."

No doubt he is, thought Nestor before slipping away through a door on his left. He was disappointed. Carlos had come on his own, without his new girlfriend, so he would have to wait to satisfy his curiosity. Now he had a choice: he could either follow Carlos and Solis from room to room, admiring the apartment and making the appropriate noises, or he could entertain himself. Off you go, Juan, he thought. Discover the unexploited potential of Number 38. In the meantime, I think I'll sit down and wait here in this little room . . . I can note down a few things I mustn't forget for tomorrow's trip.

Switching on the light, Nestor realized that there was nowhere to sit. Sheets covered all the furniture in the room, and underneath the dustiest of them all, the looming shape of what seemed to be a large armchair was hardly inviting; it had the air of a relic from a bygone age. He looked around and discovered that he had stepped into a semicircular room with walls that must once have been yellow. At the far end was a fireplace, and there, sitting in the hearth, like a woman looking out at the world through a window frame, was the portrait of a lady.

Nestor approached, examining her features curiously. This must have been the young woman he had heard so much about, the lady in the armoire . . . Because of Carlos's straitened circumstances, the room was lit with a single bulb, which dispensed such a feeble glow that the cook had to open the door wide so that the light from the hallway would illuminate the portrait at the far end of the room.

"Baggerscheit's going to love this purple foyer," said Solis's voice. "It is purple, isn't it, kid? You can't see a damn thing in here."

And it was true. Even with the door wide open, Nestor couldn't see a damn thing. He rifled through his pockets. Cooks, even if they don't smoke, often carry a lighter, or matches at least, and sure enough, in the pocket of his vest, Nestor found a small box of Mulberry & Mistletoe matches decorated with the company insignia, a motif at once floral and magical: the mulberry tree, favored food of silkworms, and mistletoe, a talisman for finding hidden treasures. Most appropriate. Anyone else would have seen the portent in those symbols, anyone but Nestor, who innocently lit a match.

"Listen, kid, my client will want to know how much of the furniture's coming with the apartment, and remember he's keen to buy the lot if he can. He's about your age, actually, but absolutely rolling in it. Have you heard his latest hit, 'Kill Me with the Lawnmower'? Great stuff."

Solis kept calling Carlos "kid," and his insistent voice worked its way into the little yellow sitting room. Nestor could hear every word of the agent's patter, which went on and on as if to provide an odd counterpoint to his own silent activity. He had lit a match and, with the uncertain precision of someone who doesn't yet know that he is on the point of making a strange discovery, he was moving the flame up and down in front of the picture. First the halo of light illuminated a woman's forehead, then her platinum blond hair, then it hovered a little too long in front of a pair of blue eyes, so that by the time it moved on, the flame was nearly spent. Nestor tried to use the fading glow to reveal another of the girl's features, her mouth at least, but the flame shrank and died, as if it were trying to preserve a secret. Too late: the secret was out. While Nestor was looking for another match, he could have sworn that under cover of darkness those mocking lips said, in a dimly familiar voice, "Ah so it's you, Nestor, back again?" or, more simply, "Good evening, Nestor."

The flame of the second match opened a breach in the darkness of the yellow sitting room and the voice fell silent immediately, dispelled by the light, like all enchantments. But when he examined the girl's lips up close, it seemed to Nestor that they remained slightly open, as if she had just been speaking.

"What's in that room there, kid, the one with the open door?"

It was the voice of Solis, the pioneer, discoverer of unknown lands. But Carlos diverted him with a request.

"Hang on, Mr. Solis. Let's leave that room till last. First I'd like to show you this one here on the right. It's a dressing room. Your client may want to use it as a gym. I think there might even be an old massage table in here."

"Excellent! You're in luck, because Baggerscheit wants to buy it all—everything. Let's have a look."

So Nestor had a little longer to make absolutely sure, not that he needed to: the blond girl in the painting was Adela Teldi, the woman he had met in Buenos Aires when she was thirty-something, the perpetrator of that little indiscretion he had told his staff about one afternoon to stop them from asking questions about his moleskin notebook full of culinary secrets. Nestor no longer needed confirmation, but the third match, like a meticulous clerk, verified the presence of Adela's features, one by one. Experience had yet to accentuate them, but they were all latent in that smooth young face: the somewhat absent expression, the blue eyes he had seen staring at Soledad's lifeless body. Even now, by the flickering light of the match flame, he could detect a hint of incredulity in those eyes, just as he had when the broken, lifeless body of her sister was found on the paving stones of the patio three floors below, three floors closer to hell. Nestor, Adela, and all the other witnesses could see Soledad's head, tiny and black like a period, while her twisted body lay in the shape of a stupid question mark. It's her sister, it's Mrs. Teldi's younger sister, all the eyes confirmed, while down below, a dark stain had begun to spread from the question mark. It was the beginning of Soledad's long revenge on two of the onlookers: her unfaithful husband and Adela. The bloodstains left by suicide are stubborn. They never wash away completely.

Piecing together the coincidences, Nestor turned his thoughts to Soledad: for Carlos, her son, she was faceless. And now, of course, it all made sense: the apartment at Number 38 Calle de Almagro, where Carlos's father was not welcome, the frosty grandmother, the silences . . . and the portrait, the one he was examining, relegated to the back of an armoire by Teresa, the grandmother, who no doubt wanted to forget both of her daughters: it was too painful to remember Soledad, and it was better to banish Adela from her mind than to hate her.

AGAIN, THE MATCH went out. Nestor lit a fourth, and this time his gaze slid down over the young woman's shoulders to her hands. What was that green spherical object she was holding in her fingers? It looked like a jewel or perhaps a cameo . . . But rather than lingering over it, he lifted the flame back up to her eyes, and as it flickered out, the last pieces of the puzzle fell into place. What surprised him most was Carlos's blindness. In the picture, Adela couldn't have been more than seventeen or eighteen years old. Nestor had recognized her instantly, but of course he had the advantage of having known her when she was still young. That day at Mulberry & Mistletoe, Carlos had attended to Adela, but amazingly, he hadn't made the connection. She was the one he had been searching for everywhere, endlessly seeing her eyes or her neck in those of other women, so how could he not have recognized her? Three days earlier, at Madame Longstaffe's house, he had said: "I never see whole people, Nestor, only parts. I only notice the little physical details that make them unique . . ." Like a man lighting his way in the dark with a match, thought Nestor, without realizing that this was exactly how he had discovered Adela.

He who sees reality in fragments will not take in the whole picture, as Madame Longstaffe might have put it.

"Of course, 'Kill Me with the Lawnmower' isn't my client's only hit. 'Shitless in Gaza' was huge too. What? You're kidding. You've got to get out more, kid. You're telling me you've never heard of it? It's only sold two million. And just think, he'll be writing his next hit right here," said Solis. "Your apartment and everything in it will be his."

Yes. Let's hope he does take the lot, that Baggerscheit. That would be the best, thought Nestor as he stroked the frame of the picture, which, unlike the rest of the objects in the room, didn't seem to have gathered any dust. Sell the house and everything in it, all in one go. It's creepy how some places seem to attract coincidences, like Number 38 Calle de Almagro. One day Soledad's body must have been taken from this apartment to a grave that Carlos had never visited, and one day Carlos's father must have been barred from entering. But now Number 38 had opened its doors to Nestor, revealing secrets within secrets: a story of adultery between brother- and sister-in-law, the sad fate of Soledad . . . You might have thought that would be enough bad luck to last a lifetime, but twenty years later, the gods had seen fit to add a few more twists: a boy who doesn't remember his mother's face falls in love with a portrait of the woman who was responsible for her death. Then he happens to meet this woman but doesn't recognize her. Honestly . . .

what next? he asked himself. Surely there had been enough coincidences.

Nestor's hand was still resting on the frame, as if on a window ledge, and it struck him that he and the woman in the picture were an odd couple: she on her side of the mirror, he on his, she looking out at him, seeing nothing, while he could see all too clearly and he didn't much like what he saw. Destiny likes to arrange coincidences, he thought. Life is full of them, when you think about it. It must happen all the time that two people who share a common history walk past each other in the street without realizing . . . or two brothers separated at birth sit next to each other one day on a bus . . . their paths might cross, or they might not, he thought . . . There are so many amazing coincidences, but most of them go unnoticed. And sometimes it's better that way. By the time Nestor joined Carlos and Solis, who were about to inspect a room at the end of the hallway, he had decided what he was going to do.

"This is one of my favorite rooms in the whole apartment, Mr. Solis," said Carlos. "I know it's not much to look at, but see that armoire? I used to play in it when I was a kid. It was full of junk—still is. When I inherited this place, the only thing I salvaged from in there was a painting I'm very fond of, the portrait of a lady."

And that armoire is where you belong, Adela Teldi, or at least where your story belongs, thought Nestor. It was clear to him now that chance occurrences, however uncanny, didn't become coincidences unless a witness was there to point them out. He had always considered that discretion was the wisest policy for someone in his position, with intimate knowledge of so many private lives. Most of the tricks that destiny plays on us pass unnoticed, he thought, and so will this one. Your story will stay in this apartment, Adela Teldi. You're staying right here, my dear, as if you were still locked up in that armoire, you and your little indiscretion with its unforeseen consequences, your homemade Greek tragedy and your soap opera scandal, because that's how I want it to be. We'll go to your house, we'll serve your guests, I'll prepare my finest desserts . . . and no one will ever know about the strange connection between a respected client of Mulberry & Mistletoe and one of the firm's employees.

"Carlos, are you there?"

"Hang on, Nestor, I'll be with you in a minute. I just have to see what Mr. Solis wants."

"I'm interested in this copper washbowl, kid, and that old lamp too, but what I'd really like to see is that portrait you found in the armoire."

NESTOR WASN'T LISTENING to any of this. No doubt Carlos and Juan Solis were making good progress in their negotiations, but all our chef could think about was his discovery, and how it wasn't all that hard to cheat destiny. If the gods can play tricks, so can I, he concluded with a certain self-satisfaction. And then, predictably employing a gastronomical simile, he vowed that this little indiscretion would never be divulged, because coincidences, he thought, are like soufflés: they come to nothing unless someone takes the trouble to beat, stir, or otherwise agitate the egg whites.

From where Nestor was standing, he could see Solis, who was still measuring and estimating the value of the place, like the shrewd real estate agent that he was. He even went over and measured the painting of the woman. It's not as if the secret's bound to come out, thought Nestor, seeing the agent so interested in the portrait. This house will be sold, and soon it will all be forgotten. Luckily, Carlos seems to have found himself another woman who's made him forget the one in the painting. And that's a blessing, because now he'll never know that since he was a child, he's been in love with . . .

"A very nice picture, son, but it's not worth much. I'd advise you to sell it with the apartment. You're in luck, because Baggerscheit loves blondes. I hope you don't want to hang on to any of the other furniture or fittings."

"Just the picture," said Carlos. "It has sentimental value. It's part of my childhood."

"Oh do grow up," said Nestor, butting into the conversation. "I thought we had agreed that you were through with fantasizing about ghosts."

"Oh, there you are, Nestor," said Carlos with a start. "Where have you been?"

But instead of answering the question, Nestor simply said: "I've seen her, Carlos, and she belongs in that yellow room. The picture shouldn't be moved. Leave it where it is."

Carlos didn't understand. He didn't understand at all. He even found his friend's reaction funny. "Hang on, what's happening? Don't tell me you've fallen in love with her too."

"Come on, she's not that gorgeous," said Solis. "How much do you want for her?"

"The thing is, I don't think I want to sell her. I've already told you, the picture is part of my childhood. You don't sell things like that, even if they don't mean as much as they used to . . ."

But both Solis and Nestor seemed determined to make an issue of it:

"Come on, kid, sell it while you can. Don't be silly. Where else are you going to find a buyer like this?"

"Think about it, *cazzo* Carlitos. You don't even know who the woman is, and you're being offered a nice sum of money. What difference does it make to you now? It was just some fantasy you had."

"He's right. If you're smart, you won't let a chance like this go by, because Baggerscheit," said the agent, stressing each syllable of his millionaire client's name, "he'll take the lot, childhood memories and all. At a fair price, of course."

2

CHLOE TRIAS AND THE GHOSTS

THE NIGHT BEFORE leaving for the Teldis' house, Chloe thought it wouldn't be a bad idea to pack some clothes. Maybe she wouldn't get a chance to wear her bikini, but she might as well take it, just in case. Everybody is hungry for sun in March, even apathetic girls like Chloe Trias. But then she suddenly realized that when she'd walked out of her parents' house and slammed the door behind her two or three months earlier, she'd left her bikini behind. She'd have to sneak back and get it. Just as long as she didn't run into her olds—what a fucking drag that'd be.

Chloe examined the house from outside. There were lights on in five of the downstairs windows, so there must have been something special going on. Upstairs, however, two dark balconies laden with dim, forgotten objects revealed that the Triases had become "a childless couple," as they liked to say wryly. Since Chloe's departure, they had rearranged the house in response to the new situation, so the large ground-floor rooms

were full of people, while the windows upstairs were shut-
tered. It was one way of enduring the absences.

Chloe knew this. She understood. The gravel near the front
door crunched under her feet, but luckily that sound, so evocative of childhood, no longer reminded her of the games she
used to play there as a girl with her brother, Eddie. All things
fade away in time. Any pain can be anesthetized by carefully
covering it up with layer after layer of insignificant memories.
Many years had passed since the day Eddie left, so Chloe felt
no nostalgia as she walked up the path and heard the gravel
crunch. There was only one part of the house that was dangerously charged with memories, and she had no intention of
going there. She looked up. The darkness of the windows was
reassuring.

The bedrooms of dead children are shrines to their absence
but also a refuge for the cowardice of the living. Few have the
courage to live with their memories and weave them into the
present. Only the strongest parents can keep a photograph of
the dead child in the sitting room, facing the questions of people who don't know, enduring the sight of that perpetually
fresh smile, indifferent to the passage of the years. The rest of
us grow old while they, by contrast, seem to grow younger, filling us with guilt for not having made the most of their brief
time among us, for not having guessed that they would disappear, leaving everything unfinished, not just their lives and
their dreams but also, more wrenchingly, the things that happened on the day of their death: a silly argument, say, that will
never be resolved, an argument about nothing, really. And all

we can remember are a few hurtful words that can never be taken back now: "If only" I hadn't said this or that . . . "If only, if only . . ." But nothing can bring the dead back to life or accomplish their destinies.

That is why most of those who remain prefer to forget those who have gone, without completely betraying them. They shift the departed out of their daily lives while keeping them present in some part of the house: a guilty but reassuring shrine, like Eddie's bedroom.

Just as deep wounds heal, leaving a layer of hard, insensitive scar tissue, when children die or run away, the loss heals eventually, absence fading into nothingness. While the photos of Eddie, his books and belongings, and Chloe's things too, had gradually disappeared from the rest of the house, their rooms had been preserved intact, beds made and clothes in the armoire, as if they were still children and might come home from school at any minute. They were at once absent and present. Not a bad way to deal with it, really. After all, you have to go on living.

Chloe crept past the door of the sitting room on tiptoe, so as not to have to say hello to anyone. She knew exactly what was going on beyond that inch of wood: the holy ritual of her parents' canasta night. There would be two card tables covered in green cloth, one on either side of the window. Her mother would be presiding over the noisier table while her father directed proceedings at the other—the perfect couple, an advertiser's dream, as Karel Pligh had described them one day. And he couldn't have put it better. They were the perfect imitation of a successful couple. She was good-looking and so was he. Both were moderately unfaithful, moderately unhappy, and moderately prone to insomnia.

As she crept up the staircase, Chloe couldn't help stopping for a few moments in front of one of the wooden banisters, the fifth to be precise, which was darker than the rest. This was an old ritual—as a child she had been convinced that she could see the face of a gnome in its grain and that by scrutinizing his expression she could tell how the day would turn out. He's laughing! Great: I'll pass my math test. He's frowning: better not tempt fate . . . As she came to the banister, Chloe realized she was now too grown-up to read the grain, yet, prompted by an old superstition, she stroked it fondly, like a talisman that had lost its power. One more step, and another, and another, and Chloe had reached the top of the staircase without the old wood creaking and betraying her presence. She crossed the landing and passed her parents' bedroom without stopping. Hers was farther along, and she was thinking about the clothes she wanted to take to the Teldis', just a bikini and a pair of T-shirts. It would only take a couple of minutes to grab what she needed and get out of there. Easy: everything would be in its place, clean and ironed, because her pretty plastic TV mother made sure it stayed that way: "This is Chloe's room, these are Chloe's teddy bears, those are Chloe's nice clothes—everything's just as it was, nothing has changed."

But before she reached the door of her bedroom, Chloe hesitated. The voices of the canasta players drifted up from the sitting room, amplified by the stairwell: an indistinct murmur from which a strident voice emerged now and then. There's always one especially raucous chicken in the coop.

"Bunch of assholes," she said. "Just as well I don't have to see their ugly faces."

At which point an ugly and all too familiar face appeared in a doorway downstairs. Spying between the banisters, Chloe could see Amalia Rossi, her mother's old Italian friend, coming out into the hall, and she must have had more to drink than usual, because she was saying: "Let me go, Teresa, I'm practically one of the family, after all. Why shouldn't I go upstairs? What's the problem? Is it my fault if your *caro sposo* has been in the smallest room for an hour? You don't want me to pee on the carpet, do you? Come on; don't be silly! I know the way. I'll just pop into Clo-Clo's room."

And up she came, the bitch. Chloe could hear her steps on the stairs. She passed the silent gnome and kept coming. There was no alternative: Chloe had to go back down the passage to the door at the end, a door she never opened (when it came to memories, she wasn't brave, either), and try to hide, pressed up against the jamb. Maybe she wouldn't be obvious, but there wasn't much space. Carosposo would have to be completely drunk not to see her shoulders protruding. So when the heavy breathing drew nearer, all she could do was open the door. Fucking hell, it's Eddie's old room. That stupid bitch! Now what? Well, what else could she do, now that she was inside, but shut the door and switch on the light . . . It had been a long time, fucking ages.

CAN SOMEONE'S SMELL survive for seven years after his death? It can. Shrines to dead children never smell of must or mothballs, however long they have stood empty. Even their most inaccessible corners remain free of mildew, and the air stays fresh, without a whiff of neglect. Or that was how it was in Eddie's room, at least. It is no simple feat to create the illusion that such a room is still inhabited. All the talents of a brilliant set designer had been deployed, and Chloe was drawn in, captivated by the lifelike effect created by the curtains and the bedspread with its ink stain, which seemed to say: "Come in and see for yourselves, ladies and gentlemen; nothing has changed—smell, touch, look." You could quite easily imagine that the occupant of this room had just slipped out for a beer with his friends. And yet on closer inspection, the fixity of death was subtly apparent in certain details, particularly the excessive tidiness. Everything was precisely in its place: Eddie's bookshelves, from which he would often choose a marvelous story to read to her. His collection of model cars, lined up with morbid precision on the shelves, and next to them his sporting trophies, encircled by a scarf. And there was something artificial about the objects laid out on what had once been Eddie's desk: the papers and folders neatly piled up, the pen and pencil strewn at romantic angles yet not quite offsetting the overall theatrical effect.

Yet what struck her most on entering her brother's bedroom was neither the deceptive smell of life nor this excessive neatness but the *size* of everything. The years had gone by outside, but Eddie's room had been frozen in time, with the curious effect that all the objects in it had shrunk, as Chloe discovered to her amazement: the bed, the bedside table, and the sofa, where Eddie used to lie with his legs up on the backrest—everything was so much smaller than she remembered. And like Alice bewildered in Wonderland, Chloe discovered that a bedroom remembered from childhood can produce the same amazing effect on a girl as a mysterious little cake that says EAT ME. She must have grown too big; that must be it. She must have become enormous, because it wasn't like this before. Before, her brother was big and she was small, but now the room as a whole seemed the right size for her, she thought, sitting down on the tiny chair where she always used to sit. Gathering her courage, she began to explore, opening an armoire to find Eddie's clothes: his little shirts and shoes, all so small by contrast with her oversize memories. The clothes were too neatly folded under their plastic wraps, but apart from that, it wasn't funereal. Small, yes, but not dead, because the smell of Eddie was still clinging to the fabric. It was so real that Chloe recoiled in wordless shock and bumped into her brother's old desk.

And as with the rest of his things, the desk at which she had so often seen him writing no longer seemed massive but just right for her. Feeling like Alice, she sat down on the chair, her feet resting comfortably on the ground, and she could reach out and touch Eddie's notebooks, which he never used to let her read. She opened one and, for the first time, started leafing though his drafts: twenty pages written in a tight, childlike hand, followed by a passage with so much crossing out it was illegible. The bit that was so hard to read must have been something secret; perhaps the pages he didn't want to show her the day he died. "Please, please, Eddie," she had implored

him so many times. "Tell me what you're writing. I bet it's
a story with adventures and romance and crime and stuff, isn't
it . . . ?" But her brother's reply was always the same: "No, Clo,
not yet. One day I'll let you read what I've written, I promise
you. This is nothing, nothing important." And now, trying to
read her brother's notebooks, all Chloe could make out was a
handful of disconnected ideas, sketches of plots, and lots of isolated, unfinished sentences that didn't make any sense. "Nah,
this is rubbish, Clo-Clo. I guess before I can make up a good
story, I'll have to have tons of experiences, get drunk, fuck
hundreds of girls, kill someone or something . . ." And hearing
her brother's voice in her memory, Chloe tried to smother it,
because she didn't want to remember the last things he had
said before leaving forever. That's right: I don't want to, I don't
fucking want to remember. Fuck you, Eddie. If you hadn't had
that stupid idea of going off on a motorbike at two hundred
kilometers an hour looking for stories, you'd be with me now.
I *hate* you. You had no right to go away like that . . . Chloe
reached out toward her brother's bookshelf and the pile of
folders. Like a spoiled child who was not getting her way, she
swiped at the papers and knocked them off the table, mixing
up all of Eddie's scribblings, his attempts to put together beautiful words, his incoherent notes full of clumsy sentences . . . all
those futile attempts that, as Chloe saw it, had cost him his life.

"Hey, Teresita," said an indiscreet voice, the kind that carries through doors, in this case the door of Eddie's shrine.
"I don't believe it. It's absolutely incredible. I almost died of
fright when I saw her . . ."

There was a murmur, then someone interrupted the voice

with a question that Chloe couldn't quite catch. And then: "Yes, dear, I mean the photo of your daughter Clo-Clo I just saw in her bedroom, the one on the table. A lovely photo, and it's recent, too, isn't it? I have to say, it gave me a start. It's amazing what's in the genes, don't you think, my dear? If I hadn't seen it with my own eyes, I wouldn't have believed it. Chloe has become the spitting image of her brother Eddie. She *has,* my dear. Don't look at me like that. The eyes are different, true—Eddie's eyes were very dark—but apart from that, I swear, even with that pasty look she has, like a half-starved Hare Krishna, if she took out all those rings she insists on putting through her lips, she'd look exactly like your son, *poveretto mio,* God rest his soul."

"God rest his soul," said Carosposo's grating voice once again, coming from somewhere near the bottom of the staircase. Despite the distance, Chloe could hear her distinctly through the closed door of the bedroom-shrine that seemed to have shrunk down to her size . . . And what if it turns out you don't like getting drunk, Eddie? What if you don't get to fuck hundreds of girls or you don't have the guts to be a killer? Now the memory of their last conversation distracted her from Carosposo's chatter. Chloe could hear the voice of the little girl she was back then, questioning her brother, and, as if the magic shrinking room had assumed Eddie's role and transcribed his reply, Chloe's gaze fell on one of the scribbled sheets, where, in the midst of a great mess of crossing out, she saw a legible sentence of fourteen words, written in her brother's unmistakable hand: "In that case, Clo-clo, I'll just have to kill someone, or steal a story."

"Just like her brother," someone said, but Chloe could no longer tell the voices of the guests downstairs from those that inhabited her brother's old room.

"Chloe's going to be twenty-two soon, isn't she? The same age as Eddie. I don't know about you, Teresa, but for me that girl, wherever she is now, however punk or grunge or whatever she tries to be with all that piercing everywhere, she's the reincarnation of her brother, may he rest in peace."

3

SERAFIN TOUS AND THE PIZZA

ON THE NIGHT before leaving for the Teldis' house, two of the characters in this story were feeling lonely. One was Karel Pligh, whom Chloe had left in a bar, promising she'd only be a few minutes, but she still hadn't returned.

The other was Serafin Tous.

It's just as well no one can see how people behave when they are alone, in private, because otherwise even the most sensible individuals would appear to be quite mad. If a window cleaner, for example, or an indiscreet neighbor, had looked through the windows of Serafin Tous's apartment, he would have seen a middle-aged gentleman with a three-day growth, attired in only a very dirty pajama top and unlaced shoes, sitting in front of a grand piano and staring at a telephone, as if he had spent months in this position. On closer inspection, the window cleaner or prying neighbor would have noticed that the man was not as naked as he appeared at first glance. Now and then he jiggled his leg in time with some inaudible tune, revealing (thankfully) a pair of striped shorts beneath his filthy pajama top. The sense of relief would have been short-lived, however, for the observer would also have discovered that, rather than sitting on a stool, the gentleman was balanced on an uncomfortable-looking pile of art books, his elbows resting on the lid of the piano, and he was clasping a box containing a half-eaten smoked-salmon pizza, details that added a rather greasy and sordid touch to the picture. And what with the character's glassy eyes, his sloping shoulders, and hair slicked down with sweat, the scene was a sad one indeed. In short, Serafin Tous, with his catatonic hands and his eyes glued to the telephone, looked like the archetypal victim of anxiety and unrelenting insomnia. And there was nothing deceptive about his appearance: it was nine o'clock at night, he hadn't slept for three nights, and it looked very much like this would be the fourth.

Observant people know that there are two ways of looking anxiously at a telephone. There's the edgy look of the person who's hoping it will ring, desperately hoping it will transmit the sound of a beloved voice, or perhaps the offer of a job that was promised long ago. Serafin Tous, however, was fixing the phone with the other sort of anxious look: as if it were a diabolical device, a malevolent magnet luring those who have no wish to use it: Get thee behind me, Satan, or, if you prefer: My Father, let this cup of damnation pass from me.

⁓

WHILE THE PIZZA was still warm in its box, it had been relatively easy for Serafin to stop himself from dialing a number that was firmly lodged in his memory. It was an absurd but effective method: he took a bite of pizza, got melted cheese all over his fingers, spilled a bit of tomato . . . then another slice, and another . . . and so he kept temptation at bay. It was as if he were poised between two contradictory impulses: he hated pizza, but there he was eating it; what he wanted most in the world was to dial that number, but he wasn't going to let himself.

How long had he been sitting there like that in front of a piano he was trying not to play, eating food he detested, and stopping himself from picking up the phone? A long time. This was the sordid culmination of night after night spent trying to be sensible, only to find his good intentions undermined by the image of a red door with a nameplate on which the word *Freshman's* was inscribed in Gothic lettering. He swallowed another mouthful of pizza. The taste of the fish was disgusting yet somehow pleasant, too. Now he knew how it could happen, the slide into squalor and degradation you see in certain American films, those characters who don't get dressed or go out for days on end, holed up in their evil-smelling apartments surrounded by overflowing ashtrays, empty bourbon bottles, and take-out food containers (chop suey or pizza, as a rule). Those apartments are the cinematic representation of the pit into which even the most respectable person can fall at any moment. Once you're on the slippery slope . . . And to judge by Serafin Tous's apartment, he was slipping dangerously. Luckily, he neither drank nor smoked, so at least he was spared those aspects of the squalor: the acrid reek of a thousand cigarettes, bottle after empty bottle feverishly drained without quenching the terrible thirst. But all the other signs were there: he was descending into hell.

When night fell, Serafin didn't switch on the lamp; he stayed put, in the same position, enveloped in darkness, illuminated only by the lights from the street. It was better that way; neither he nor anyone else could see his unsightly stubble or the glassy look in his eyes. What a ridiculous situation. The best thing for him to do at this point would surely have been to dial the damned number and be done with it. The only way to get the better of temptation is to yield to it, said someone who no doubt knew what he was talking about. So why not do it? It's really very easy: you pick up the receiver and with a finger you key in the number you've learned by heart. Then all you have to do is say, with a firm and impersonal voice, "Good afternoon. Is this Freshman's? Listen, it's . . ." But there Serafin hesitated: even making an imaginary phone call, he couldn't bring himself to give his own name. "It's . . . a client. I'd like to speak with one of your young men. His name is Julian. Is he there?"

Yes, it would have been easy, and he wanted to do it, but Serafin's hand did not reach for the phone. Instead, he gripped the pizza box like a shipwrecked man grasping at a raft. He opened the box and ripped off a piece of cold pizza. It stuck in his throat. The dough seemed to be swelling; the cheese was rubbery and the tomato had an acid aftertaste . . . his gorge was rising. He felt sick enough to throw it all up. If only I could, he thought, at least it'd get all that bloody filth out of my gut.

Shocked by the vulgarity of this expression, which was most

uncharacteristic, he sat up straight and, with the air of a guilty child, looked around for the portrait of his wife. It wasn't on the piano, as it had been a few days before, nor was it on the mantelpiece, where it had lived for so many years. Nora, my dear, where are you? And just at this point the telephone rang.

The sound was so unexpected that Serafin jumped, as if Nora herself were making a long-distance call from heaven. He wiped his hand on his pajama top and was about to answer when a crazy thought came into his head: what if it was *him*? Fat chance. Young Julian, the boy with the blond crew cut, was the last person who'd be calling him. Meanwhile, the phone went on ringing. He'd have to answer eventually, so he reached out and picked up the receiver.

"Hello."

At first he didn't recognize Adela Teldi's voice. And he couldn't make out what she was saying. Sorry, what was what? She was chattering on in the quick, flat voice people use when talking to old friends—a torrent of words from which Serafin gradually managed to extract some sense. Finally he grasped what was she was going on about: an escape plan; that is what she was proposing, in effect. She wanted him to come along to a little party her husband was organizing for a group of art dealers at their house down on the coast. "And I won't take no for an answer, my dear. It's exactly what you need. You can stay two or three days, soak up a bit of sun, take it easy. You really haven't been looking well recently. Life goes on, you know. It's about time you started forgetting your dear Nora."

It wasn't his wife whom Serafin couldn't forget, but the invitation was like a lifeline all the same. The piano, the pizza,

the tomato stains, the terrible state he was in, and the temptation of the telephone: all that could be over in an instant.

"Yes, of course. I'd love to," he said, amazed that he could
still muster the will to escape.

"We're planning to leave tomorrow morning. Would you
like me to come over and help you pack?"

Serafin trembled in fright at the mere thought of Adela or
anyone else entering that pigsty.

"Absolutely not, my dear, everything's perfectly in order.
You'd be amazed," he said, and after listening to a few more
details about the party, he hung up abruptly, as if he were
afraid that she might notice the foul smell over the telephone.

For a moment he sat clasping the receiver like a friend's con-
soling arm. Then he reflected that the invitation had come just
in time, miraculously. He had to get out. He had get away. It
didn't matter where. The only problem was that the plan involved Ernesto Teldi. He had never warmed to Adela's husband.

Sitting in the same position, still unable to detach himself
from the telephone and move away from the piano, Serafin
wondered why he felt that way about Ernesto Teldi. Everyone else seemed to admire him, but Serafin remembered several occasions on which Teldi's conduct had struck him as less
than wholly admirable. Perhaps I envy him, he thought—who
wouldn't? And really, should I be sitting in judgment when
just a moment ago, before destiny threw me a lifeline, I was all
at sea myself?

God bless Adela, he thought. May God bless her and keep
her safe from that awful husband of hers.

Spite and disdain are very effective antidotes to all kinds of passion. To his great surprise, Serafin realized that during the few minutes he had spent thinking about Teldi, he had actually started to feel better. He looked at the pizza box and thought: I have to tidy up. He caressed the piano, even opened the lid, and for once the sight of the keyboard did not make him think of his visit to Freshman's or remember that angelic boy who had turned his life upside down. Strange how uncharitable thoughts can suppress desire—and as if to test his new method, Serafin decided to go on being spiteful. He sat up straight on his makeshift seat, let his legs swing back and forth, and thought about what a stuck-up prig Adela's husband was. And once again, miraculously, he managed to forget what had been obsessing him until then, and forget it so completely that his hand could come to rest calmly on the piano keys without the usual shiver running down his spine. It was all right. The descent into hell had come to an end. And, as if to prove it, his fingers touched the keys, playing a few unrelated chords that were not reminders of a shameful past but delicious promises of a bright future. Maybe he would be bored out of his mind at the Teldis' house, but there are times when boredom is a godsend. Serafin was hardly aware of it, but his fingers had begun to gain confidence, improvising in a style as conventional and monotonous as the Teldis' party would probably turn out to be. There wouldn't be any boys, of course, just a group of dull art experts droning on endlessly about paintings and sculptures and so on. Perfect, perfect, he thought, although (and for a moment his fingers froze) from what he remembered of Adela's hasty explanation on the phone, if he had understood correctly, the guests might be slightly more interesting on this occasion. "Eccentric collectors" was the expression she had used, before adding that they were also potential clients for Teldi. Potential suckers, thought Serafin. He might be long in the tooth, but he's as sly as ever. And now Serafin's fingers played a few bars that harmonized with his opinion of Ernesto Teldi: the piano did a remarkable imitation of a horn trio. It was Prokofiev's *Peter and the Wolf,* the stealthy tread of the wolf in the snow. It had come to him quite unconsciously as he thought about Adela's husband.

⁓

THE RESPITE LASTED ten minutes. For ten long minutes the boy with the crew cut was absent from his thoughts. And that was by far the longest stretch of peace he had enjoyed since the day it had occurred to him to visit Freshman's. The pang returned, of course, but by then Serafin had discovered how spite can provide temporary but effective relief from an unhealthy passion. Who would have thought? In any case, it had been more effective than going to see that famous fortune-teller, Madame Longstaffe. She had promised to look into his case and help him, but he still hadn't heard from her. I wonder what the old charlatan is up to now, thought Serafin.

4

KAREL AND MADAME LONGSTAFFE SING *RANCHERAS*

At number 29 Calle Corderitos, on the edge of Malasaña, there's a little bar called Juanita Banana, a favorite with tropical-music fans. In the afternoon and evening the crowd is more enthusiastic than discriminating: they love anything Latin and are keen to practice the merengue and conga steps they've just learned at one of the many local dance schools. Until this crowd leaves, around three in the morning, there are soft red cushions on the seats to make them comfortable for cuddling. The waiters are Latin American girls and boys with nice bodies but not much experience in hospitality, and the music is pleasant enough but relentlessly commercial. The playlist features Juan Luis Guerra (an all-around favorite), Ana Gabriel's *rancheras, vallenatos* courtesy of Carlos Vives, and Gloria Estefan's Cuban-American *sones,* which get everyone singing along noisily. While they dance and chat with their friends, the clients put away a good number of *mojitos* with Bacardi or shots of tequila with salt, gulped down to cries of

"Dele nomás" ("Knock it back"), supposedly adding to the authenticity of the atmosphere, from which they emerge in high spirits: that Latin music is *fan*-tastic, and we had *such* a great time.

Yet, as the last neophyte Latinophiles wander off singing, *"vacilón, qué rico vacilón / cha-cha-chá, que rico cha-cha-chá,"* as their voices die away and the stragglers disappear, an altogether different club springs to life as if by magic on the premises of the Juanita Banana: a secret club, to which only the initiated have access. The Juanita Banana seems to withdraw into itself. The red cushions vanish from the seats, exposing bare wood, and in no time at all the place fills up with a sort of fog, as if someone behind the curtains were blowing out clouds of cigar smoke, while the young, good-looking waiters are replaced by a different crew. The first to arrive is René, a Cuban with a snub nose in the middle of his broad, dark face. René is the barman, a master of the daiquiri, and also the creator of a number of remarkable Congolese concoctions made with plants like *kolelé batama pimpí* (sesame, to the uninitiated), which, as everyone knows, has an aphrodisiac effect when mixed with coffee, as well as being an effective treatment for asthma.

Another key figure in the exclusive late set is Gladys, who waits on tables with as much agility as her ninety-seven kilos of ample Colombian flesh will allow (though she is as light on her feet as any young girl when she dances to a *son* by the maestro Escalona). The third staff member—or members, rather—are the identical and inseparable Gutiérrez twins, a pair of virtuoso musicians who between them can play any instrument from Cuban drums and bongos to the peasant accordion, including the guitar of course, Mexican trumpets, and even the reed flute, not that there's much call for Andean instruments at the Juanita Banana, where the music is predominantly Afro-Caribbean.

One night, as it happened, two individuals were making their separate ways toward this extraordinary establishment, both hoping to relax and forget the worries of the day with a little singing, accompanied by the Gutiérrez brothers. One was strolling on the left side of the street, hands in pockets, whistling a tune as if anticipating a special pleasure. The other was walking along the right side, protected from curious gazes by an enveloping overcoat. They reached the door at the same time . . . After you. No please, madame, after you, I insist. Madame Longstaffe stepped inside, followed by Karel Pligh, who was determined to make a night of it before heading off to the Teldis' country house. Their little exchange was marked by the cool and deferential politeness of complete strangers who have realized they belong to the same sect or secret society.

Having taken up positions at opposite ends of the bar and ordered drinks (caipirinha for Madame, a daiquiri for Karel), each settled in for a night of pleasure. There was no one else in the club, a situation that tends to break down the barrier between staff and clients. Three caipirinhas later, René had come out from behind the bar to sit with Madame Longstaffe, while Gladys and Karel were improvising a duet on the dance floor. They had chosen one of Bola de Nieve's songs, which, with the Gutiérrez brothers' instrumental accompaniment, had a lilting, Santiago-de-Cuba feel that delighted the clairvoyant. After this performance, Madame Longstaffe asked Karel his name, and he told her. She also invited him to try a drink from her Brazilian homeland.

"It's called *cachaça*. Try it. Does wonders for your musical intepretation."

So Karel gave it a try. Minutes later, all the staff were watching and listening as Karel cleared his throat, preparing to launch into heartfelt song, with Madame Longstaffe perched beside him on a bar stool.

If Nestor Chaffino had been able to observe this scene, he no doubt would have found further confirmation of his theory that chance encounters only become coincidences if a witness puts the pieces together. Karel and Madame Longstaffe spent a wonderful evening together singing "Aurora," "Yo tenía que perder," "En eso llegó Fidel," and even "The Girl from Ipanema" in Portuguese, but since they were complete strangers, it never crossed their minds that they might have friends or acquaintances in common. Despite her formidable paranormal powers, Madame Longstaffe failed to make the connection. It should have been simple for such a renowned clairvoyant to give some indication of the events that were to take place the following day at the Teldis'. Like her ancestors, the Weird Sisters, she could easily have foreshadowed Nestor's imminent death. She also could have warned Karel about the curious circumstances in which the death was to occur. At the very least, she could have repeated the prophecy she had already pronounced for Nestor and Carlos that afternoon when they had gone to see her: Nestor has nothing to fear until four *T*s conspire against him. She could have revealed all this to Karel

Pligh as well as explaining how the events would result from a combination of strange forces brewing in the ether and a series of little indiscretions. But Madame Longstaffe made no mention of these things, perhaps because she was too busy teaching young Karel a pretty song by Paquita la del Barrio, perfect for a duet.

AND YET PERHAPS, in her own crooked and darkly humorous way, she *was* trying to tell him something. The question still hangs in the air of the Juanita Banana, like the lyric of the song they sang together, propping each other up, their voices hoarse from the *cachaça,* accompanied by the Gutiérrez brothers, one on guitar, the other on piano, after Marlene Longstaffe had made Karel Pligh practice the chorus three times. It wasn't a Cuban or a Brazilian song but a famous Mexican *ranchera,* and it went like this:

> *I cheated on you once, I cheated on you twice,*
> *I cheated on you three times, and after those*
> *three times, I never want to see you again . . .*

5

ERNESTO AND ADELA
IN THE ELEVATOR

THE NIGHT BEFORE they set off for their country house, the Lilies, Ernesto and Adela Teldi went over their arrangements for the party.

"If we count Mr. and Mrs. Stephanopolous, that makes a total of thirty-three. I've never liked that number," said Ernesto Teldi.

"Why? Because that's how old Jesus was when he died? And Alexander the Great, and Evita Perón, too, no?" said Adela. "I really don't think you should worry about it. You're not usually superstitious, not about that sort of thing anyway."

They were talking on the phone. At the Palace Hotel, the couple occupied adjoining rooms with a communicating door, but neither had ever taken advantage of that discreet facility so thoughtfully provided by the management. So many secret lovers must have blessed that door, safeguarding their respectability, allowing them to make their separate exits without fear after an assignation. In this case, however, the door had precisely the opposite function: in appearance it joined the rooms, but in fact it was never opened, because the Teldis led parallel lives. Their lives were like two lines traveling through time, one beside the other, never to meet this side of infinity . . . or perhaps they wouldn't have to go quite that far: social conventions would no doubt bring them together in the same tomb, since that is the ineluctable destination for any well-matched couple, even if husband and wife couldn't care less about each other.

"Did I tell you about the problem with Mr. Algobranghini, Adela? He hates Stephanopolous. I think they had a fight once over a Persian scimitar. Very touchy, the pair of them. Just make sure they don't end up at the same table and spoil our evening."

Stephanopolous and Algobranghini figured alongside dozens of other exotic names on the list of guests Adela was consulting as she spoke with her husband. Next to each name, a note in Ernesto's businesslike hand indicated the collector's specialty: there were two knife collectors, three "Dickensiana fetishists" (so he had written), three individuals with a passion for Greek icons (so long as they featured Saint George), a "Rapanui statuette fan" (a what? wondered Adela for a moment), and the rest of the list consisted of collectors with less outlandish tastes: the letters of famous people, tin soldiers, books of ghost stories, or Fabergé eggs. Adela went through the list to see if she could recognize anyone, but none of the art world's big names were there. She smiled, wondering which of the guests was Ernesto's prey. Algobranghini, the knife and sword collector? The ghost-story specialist, Miss Liau Chi? Or perhaps the chosen one was the only guest whose name was not accompanied by a note, a certain Monsieur Pitou. Adela shrugged her shoulders. After many years of observing her husband exercise his dealer's flair—making a killing from the resale of treasures picked up for a song—she had begun to find the game amusing. Especially in the last few years. Teldi was rich enough now to forget about profit occasionally and set off in pursuit of a rarity. Acquiring unique pieces and curiosities was the culmination of a lifetime devoted to art. There could be only one reason for a party with such a guest list: the capture of a piece that was presently in the possession of an eccentric collector whose reluctance would soon be overcome by her husband's sweet-talking flattery.

"I don't want fixed seating arrangements, Adela. It should all seem casual, but I'm counting on you to make sure Stephanopolous and Monsieur Pitou sit with us: Pitou on my right and Stephanopolous on yours."

Monsieur Pitou. Adela found the name on the guest list. But what could his special interest be? Whatever it was, Adela was sure this mysterious gentleman was the prey, because Ernesto always made sure that the guest in whom he was particularly interested was seated on his right. But what was he hoping to acquire at a bargain price after the party? An especially rare Turkish dagger? A billet-doux, perhaps?

"Anyway, don't worry, we can talk about the details later. Leave it, Adela, there's no time now," said Teldi. "How long will it take you to finish getting dressed? Can we leave at nine? It takes over an hour to get to the Suarezes' place."

THAT NIGHT, ERNESTO and Adela Teldi had been invited to dinner by some friends who were not involved in the art world. It was a quarter past eight. Adela was sitting on the bed. She still hadn't put her face on, but she was an expert at quick makeup jobs.

"Let's meet in front of the elevator and go down together," she said to her husband.

And they met precisely at the appointed time: punctuality was the only virtue they had in common. As they stepped into the elevator, Adela took the opportunity to examine herself in the mirror. Three floors, she thought. She had three floors of delicious descent during which to ascertain that she was indeed looking beautiful—naturally, since she had dressed for *him*. Carlos Garcia had not, of course, been invited to the Suarezes' dinner, but a woman in love (no, not in love, Adela, don't even say that as a joke, a woman under the illusion of love) always dresses for her lover, even if he can't see her. Which is why, like a bride adorning herself for her groom, she had drenched herself with perfume and emerged from her room radiant and new, bright-eyed and glossy-lipped, giving off such a powerful aura that even her husband couldn't help noticing.

"You're looking very beautiful tonight, Adela. You have a very youthful glow," he said, and she received the compliment with a smile, because she knew it was true: whatever lies the cosmetics companies come up with, love (or the illusion of love) is the one and only fountain of eternal youth.

The elevator went down past another floor, the last before reaching the lobby: a few seconds left, thought Adela, in which to savor my happiness. Tomorrow, tomorrow, we will be together for a day, a few hours, my kingdom for a few hours. Then the elevator came to a sudden halt. The lights flickered, looked as if they would go out, but then stayed on dimly, bathing them in the sickly half-light of emergencies.

"Christ almighty," said Teldi, looking for the telephone. He soon found it and called reception to ask what was going on.

"A blackout sir, we're very sorry. It's not the hotel, it's the local supply. The whole block is blacked out. Is there something I can do for you?"

Crossly, Teldi asked her to call and inform the Suarez household that they might be delayed, before adding: "And do me a favor. Call the electricity company or city hall or whoever, but keep me informed. We're not in the third world here. They should be able to fix this right away in Madrid."

"Yes sir, of course. I'll let you know as soon as we have any information."

The Teldis looked at each other in the yellowish light. Ernesto shrugged helplessly while Adela studied the walls and the door. Would they have enough air to breathe? Would the temperature rise sharply and ruin her makeup? What a disaster! Even faces rejuvenated by happiness can crumple in absurd situations. And this situation was absurd. To say the least.

"If only there were a little seat, like in the old elevators," said Ernesto. "It's easier to be patient sitting down, isn't it? But the worst that can happen is that we'll be late to dinner. And that doesn't really matter; they're pretty boring people anyway."

Ernesto sighed and loosened the knot of his tie. It was a reflex more than a reaction to the heat. Trapped with her husband, Adela found herself thinking about him, while he was thinking about a love letter. Accustomed to dealing with unexpected situations, Ernesto remained unruffled and made use of this unforeseen holdup to go over every word of a beautiful love letter he was planning to buy the following day from one of his guests. "I want you, I trust you, I am coming to you": so began the document, in the hand of Oscar Wilde, no less. It wasn't an extract from the manuscript of *An Ideal Husband,* as one might be forgiven for thinking, but a plea written three years earlier in a letter addressed to a mysterious and unidentified Bertie. Who could the owner of that eminently Victorian name have been? Teldi had come up with a fascinating and scandalous hypothesis, but he wouldn't be able to verify it until the letter was in his possession. *I want you, I trust you, I am coming to you,* he repeated to himself, savoring the words with a collector's glee, entertaining the possibility of keeping this find for himself and declining all offers to sell it, although for such a document they would be very considerable. More and more, however, Teldi preferred possession to profit. A beautiful love letter, he thought, deeply moved, an exquisite love letter.

LOVE AND TENDERNESS were far from Adela's thoughts. She had become suddenly, intensely conscious of her husband's physical proximity. They had not been so close to each other for a long time. There had been no friction between them in the almost thirty years since they initiated their convenient matrimonial arrangement (I don't interfere with your life, and you don't interfere with mine: all very civilized, really). Parallel lives meet only at infinity or in the grave, and at that point nothing matters anymore. Adela pondered this idea for a moment: Together for all eternity. It sounded like a punishment. She had never been able to understand why people worried so much about where their mortal remains would end up and the company they would keep: lovers' ashes scattered over the sea or a field of daisies . . . all very romantic, even sublime, but ashes are just ashes, and dead bodies are dead for good. Adela was not so arrogant as to believe that her remains would go on loving or longing for anyone.

Life, however, would go on administering its doses of desire, pain, love, or agony; the life she was living in the here and now would put her through all that and more . . . Suddenly she was physically aware of the distance separating her from Carlos's body, while her husband's, which had never bothered her particularly until then, felt far too close. And for a moment Adela considered what happens when two strangers end up in an elevator together: they move to opposite corners so that their bodies don't touch and look at the roof so that their eyes don't meet. They fidget uncomfortably, pretend to whistle or consult their watches, willing the door to open, come *on,* open, because having your personal space invaded by a stranger is unbearable.

Teldi was leaning against the wall in one of the corners. He wasn't bothered by the proximity of Adela's body. Why should he have been? She was part of him, part of his identity, after all. Since they had made their implicit pact to lead parallel lives all those years ago, Adela had been as much a part of him as his hands, his legs, his skin, or the clothing covering his body. And he loved her, naturally, the way we love something we have always looked on as an extension of ourselves.

Adela had felt the same way about their marriage until now. She had taken lovers to make her feel alive, and sometimes she had even loved them and considered leaving her husband. But in the end she had stayed. Why leave when she could already do just as she liked, when their parallel lives were functioning perfectly and their shared territory was large enough for them not to get in each other's way: two beds in separate rooms, two bathrooms, two doors to come and go through as they pleased. One of the major and often overlooked advantages of having money is being able to dispose of a large amount of space.

In the elevator, however, unable to distance herself from her husband, who had just undone two buttons of his shirt and was now proceeding to remove his shoes, Adela was overcome by something like nausea. As she looked at Teldi's mustache, in which droplets of sweat were gathering, and the artificially abundant hair beginning to stick to his scalp with the heat, the memory of Carlos came back to her, and he seemed all the more handsome by contrast. She gasped as if she were running out of air, and all her muscles ached with the desire to get out of there, to flee into other arms, not Teldi's, arms that didn't smell of old flesh. Once again, Adela was scared: had she let herself go too far this time? Remember, dear, she said to herself (trying to remain aloof and detached despite her predicament), love is eternal, so long as it lasts. I will always love you until eight-thirty. That was the prudent strategy she had used with her other lovers. She had learned early on that the verb *to love* should be conjugated only in the present tense. Adela repeated these precepts to herself while trying not to look at Teldi, trying not to see how his shirt was sticking to his body. "The only way to make passion last is to ration it out in small doses and never to consume it all, so there's always something left to desire . . ." In the past she had always followed these sensible rules.

It had become unbearably hot and sticky. They were breathing each other's air. Ernesto called reception again, and in addition to his grating shouts and complaints, Adela had to put up with his physical presence: the rancid smell of his sweat and his slippery hand, which had fallen inadvertently onto her right arm. The contact sent an electric shock down her spine, precise and terrible as a revelation. She realized that she had been able to live with this old body, with a husband whose hair stuck to his scalp when he sweated, simply because she didn't usually notice all the details she was seeing now, in the forced proximity of the elevator. They had always been independent of each other, turning a blind eye, traveling a good deal, keeping out of each other's way, respecting each other's territory, and expecting the same in return. But that freedom will shrink with time, thought Adela suddenly. One day, inevitably, her role as a socialite, the only thing that made her life bearable, would come to an end and she would be reduced to sharing her solitude with *him*. No more friends, no more travel, just more of *him,* more aches and pains, more illness. God, that's what old age is: losing all of your personal space.

Fifteen minutes. Adela would never have imagined that being confined in an elevator with her future for just fifteen minutes could spin her world around and overturn the convictions of a lifetime. When the elevator lurched into action, the movement made her feel so dizzy it was as if she were dropping down through the lobby into hell itself. And during the brief descent, with the lucidity of those who are about to die, Adela saw her entire love life flash before her in the mirror. She saw the young Adela Teldi, beautiful and remote, whose only desire was to collect lovers who would make her feel still more beautiful and more remote.

Then a twinge she had been trying to ignore for years made her linger over the image of a faceless man, melting into her sister Soledad's blood, spilled on the patio of her house in Buenos Aires. Fortunately, the film didn't stop there but rushed on to show other trivial affairs intended to blot out the memory of that blood. A long string of inconsequential adventures culminating with the appearance of Carlos's beautiful body in the mirror, as if he were physically there.

Then the elevator reached the ground floor and the door opened.

"At last, about time," said Teldi, gathering his things. He looked for his tie, which had ended up in a corner, then his shoes. "Where's the left one? How can I possibly have lost it in such a tiny space? We just about melted in here."

Adela bent down. She was about to pick up the shoe and

give it back to him without further ado when a perverse impulse stopped her and she froze in that servile posture. She looked at Teldi and, as if needing to confirm with an act what she had discovered in the last fifteen minutes, she said to him:

"Let me help you, Ernesto."

Kneeling before him, she made herself put his shoe on.

"What are you doing, Adela? Have you gone crazy?"

But Adela hadn't gone crazy. She wanted to smell that old flesh again; she wanted to plunge to the very pit of all miseries to be sure that when she got out of the elevator, the daily routine wouldn't make her forget what she had felt in the last fifteen minutes, that foretaste of what the future held for her. Old age is losing all your personal space, she repeated, and by the time it comes, I won't have the strength to flee or any reason to change my life, because my life will have shrunk so much there will be nowhere to go, and no one to go with. The heat had made Ernesto Teldi's foot swell; she had to force his heel into the shoe, and the stiffener broke.

"Leave it, will you. What the hell are you doing? Come on, get up," said Teldi, and when he saw her face, he added: "You look terrible, Adela. You should get changed, and me too."

"Yes," she said. "But this time I think I'll take the stairs."

Adela didn't look back. She didn't know if her husband had stayed in the elevator to go back up to the room or what he had done. All she knew was that she had three flights of stairs to climb while thinking about Carlos and trying to sort out her feelings. It's too late to cancel the dinner now, she told herself.

I'll go ahead with life as planned for the next few days, but then it's good-bye, Ernesto. Adela was not tired. She felt as light as a child climbing those three flights of stairs, because she had just sworn that for once in her life she was *not* going to do the sensible thing. She was going to give love a chance.

Part Four

THE MIRROR GAME

"There has been in this incident," he said, "a twisted, ugly, complex quality that does not belong to the straight bolts either of heaven or hell. As one knows the crooked track of a snail, I know the crooked track of a man."

G. K. CHESTERTON

The Innocence of Father Brown

"This trick is done with mirrors, isn't it?"

AGATHA CHRISTIE

1

ARRIVAL AT THE LILIES

HOUSES IN WHICH a sudden death is about to occur do not differ noticeably from more innocent dwellings. Their wooden stairs do not groan like crows cawing, nor do their walls stand guard like melancholy sentinels waiting for something evil to happen. And Westinghouse cool rooms whose doors are destined to click definitively shut behind someone in a few hours' time do not purr invitingly, tempting the reckless to step inside. All that is sheer fantasy, and yet there on the doormat of the Lilies was an enormous cockroach, plain for all to see. Cockroaches are unpleasant creatures, with an obstinate team spirit. Often, as soon as you dispose of one, another will appear as if from nowhere to replace it, a second offender just as fat and shiny as the first, imitating its behavior with a sort of stoic exactitude, like the several cockroaches that the characters in this story kept finding on the doormat as they arrived at the Lilies.

If this renewed presence was some kind of portent or sign, it was a sign that everyone could see, sitting there, bold as you please, wiggling its antennae. And each guest, noticing this insect on arrival, did what people normally do when they see a cockroach: step on it.

⌒

ERNESTO AND ADELA TELDI were the first to arrive at the house and set eyes on that ugly insect. It gave them something to say to each other. They hadn't spoken in the plane from Madrid and had exchanged a bare minimum of words during the trip from the airport to their house, which was near Coín. It was an old house largely covered with wisteria, which ignorant people often mistook for the lilies that gave the place its name.

"I told you those caretakers you took on were hopeless," said Ernesto Teldi. "You don't often see a cockroach in the garden. I hate to think what it's like inside."

As he pushed the key into the lock, he glanced around. The rest of the garden seemed to be in reasonable shape: there were blue hydrangeas on either side of the front door, and the flower beds were looking good. A few leaves could be seen swirling in a corner of the otherwise carefully raked lawn, which stretched away to a little fountain with lilies and, beyond that, a box hedge.

"At least the gardener seems to be doing his job," said Teldi. "But the caretakers are a lazy pair, not even here to let us in. I wonder where they can have gone," he added as he turned the door handle.

Stepping in, Ernesto Teldi squashed the cockroach, which

went *crunch* under the sole of his shoe. "Shit," he said, wiping the remains of its carcass onto the doormat. Inside the Lilies, Ernesto and Adela were to be confronted with another domestic setback. They found the caretakers in a state of high anxiety: a very serious family problem had come up and they had to leave urgently for Conil de la Frontera. "It's terribly serious, madame," they said. "We're awful sorry, such a bad time."

"Well, go then, right now, and don't bother to come back," said Teldi, looking not at his employees but at Adela, as if she were the one who should have been awful sorry.

But Adela poured oil on troubled waters and persuaded them to stay until the team from Mulberry & Mistletoe arrived, so that they could explain all the ins and outs of the house. Teldi then deigned to address the caretakers directly with the tone of offended authority generally reserved for deserters: "One last thing: do me a favor and remove that dead cockroach. Then I never want to see the pair of you again."

❧

"GROSS! A COCKROACH!" said Chloe two hours later when she found an identical creature on the doormat, but very much alive, waving its antennae to welcome her. "It's dis*gus*ting; someone's got to kill it. It's against my beliefs to harm animals and all, but this is *too* gross."

Nestor and Carlos stooped to examine the insect. Like all chefs, Nestor found cockroaches deeply repugnant, as he told the caretakers when they came to open the door.

"I don't know where it can have come from," said the woman. "We just got rid of another one like it. Mr. Teldi must have brought it in on the sole of his shoe, because there are no vermin in this house. The kitchen is clean as a whistle, I swear. Come in, come in and have a look."

Nestor went in with the caretakers.

"And what about this bloody cockroach?" asked Chloe. "You kill it, Carlos."

So Carlos, who had no problems with that sort of thing, squashed the insect just as Ernesto Teldi had done.

"Done," he said. "Come on, Chloe, take that stuff to the kitchen while Karel parks the van. I'll go help unload the rest of the gear."

OH YUCK, A disgusting *šváb*! thought Karel Pligh, seeing a third cockroach on the doormat, as glossy and slimy-looking as its cousins. Now, how the hell do you say *šváb* in Spanish? He hesitated for a moment without realizing that, thanks to his comprehensive knowledge of Latin music, he had on many occasions sung a famous Mexican song named after the insect in question. But right then Karel didn't have time for further entomological or musical reflections—he was carrying a basketful of pots, pans, and other kitchen utensils that Nestor needed to prepare the meal at the Lilies that night—so he squashed the *šváb* with all the force of his Nike and continued on his way to the kitchen: there was a lot to do before the guests arrived.

THE TELDIS AND the staff of Mulberry & Mistletoe spent the whole of the morning and a good part of the afternoon getting

ready, each in his or her own particular domain. Ernesto shut
himself in the library to make a series of phone calls. He wanted
to be sure that none of his guests would be prevented from at-
tending by a last-minute hitch. As for Adela, she had a lengthy
discussion with Nestor about the details of the menu. (How
odd; she was certain she had seen his face somewhere before,
but where? Where had she seen that mustache? It would
probably come back to her in a minute, but in the meantime it
was best to pretend she hadn't recognized him, always the wisest strategy in such a situation.) Then Adela told him she
would prefer not to have to deal with his staff directly.

"If you could look after everything, Mr. Chaffino, including
the flower arrangements—you can take what you need from
the garden. I have a few things to sort out with my husband
upstairs, and as soon as I'm free, I'll come down and we can
discuss any changes of plan."

Nestor put her mind at ease: that was what he was paid for,
after all, to take care of everything so that the hosts could relax.
She needn't worry about the food or getting the house ready (in
spite of the caretakers' desertion). "We're a small but efficient
team," he said, "and we get on well together. That's the main
thing. It's almost like a family business. The young ones are like
children to me, as you'll see, my dear, especially Carlos."

After this declaration, culminating with that surprisingly
familiar "my dear" (he must say that to everyone, thought
Adela; it doesn't necessarily mean anything), she watched Nestor slip away discreetly like a true hospitality professional.

FROM THAT MOMENT on, Mulberry & Mistletoe took possession of the Lilies.

The Teldis handed the reins over to Karel, Chloe, Carlos, and Nestor, who proceeded to organize everything, setting tables, arranging flowers, moving furniture. "Do whatever you think is best," Mrs. Teldi had said, and having catered for many similar parties, they knew just what needed to be done. Soon they were coming and going as if they'd known the place for years. Each employee worked without supervision, at his or her own rhythm, and so each came to discover a different facet of the Lilies. Some say the personality of a house is completely subjective: the same house can be charming or menacing, beautiful or ugly, inviting or hostile, depending on the eye and state of mind of the observer. Some say that no two visitors will see the place in the same way, and it may well be true, because the Lilies certainly made a different impression on each member of the Mulberry & Mistletoe team. Nestor, for one, got a fright when he entered the sitting room intending to give it a quick dust. An uncomfortable little chill ran down his spine, but it wasn't so much the style of the décor that disagreed with him as one object in particular: the mail tray.

"What are you looking at?" asked Ernesto Teldi, who had come in to get the paper.

Nestor started flicking the feather duster with a dexterous wrist action and moved away, intently scrutinizing the walls and sundry insignificant objects while raising a protective cloud of dust.

"Lovely room, beautifully decorated," he said. "With a bit of dusting and some flowers from the garden, it'll look splendid," he added, turning his back so Teldi couldn't see what had caught his attention.

Ernesto then picked up the only thing on the mail tray: a thick envelope addressed unsteadily in green ink.

Shit, he thought, before disappearing with the envelope.

Shit, thought Nestor, too, flicking the feather duster even more vigorously, as if the house were suddenly full of invisible cobwebs.

FOR CARLOS GARCIA, however, the Lilies was a calm, light-filled house that reminded him strongly of his childhood. While trying to keep his mind on the job, he found pretexts for visiting one room after another, haunted by the impression that he was at Number 38 Calle de Almagro—not the run-down, neglected property that he was about to sell but the mysterious apartment full of nooks and crannies that he had known as a child, the domain of his grandmother Teresa. For Carlos, the Lilies and Number 38 were like mother and daughter. He noticed that even the choice of colors was identical. The entrance hall was painted red, the sitting room yellow, and what colors would the bedrooms be? For a moment Carlos forgot that this house belonged not only to his lover from the Palace Hotel but also to her husband, and like a curious child, he decided to investigate each of the bedrooms, hoping perhaps to find a lavender-hued dressing room or a secret chamber with an armoire in it.

"Might I inquire what you're doing up here?" said a voice that, luckily, did not belong to the owner of the house but to

Nestor Chaffino, who was standing in the doorway. "What the hell are you doing opening armoires?"

"Nothing, Nelly. Nothing, I swear," said Carlos.

Nestor looked at him quizzically. His expression was quite different from Nelly's when she scolded him for looking in the armoire, but the situation was the same.

"Aren't you going to say anything?" asked Carlos. He would have preferred a reprimand to the inscrutable silence of his friend. "Aren't you going to tell me to stop ferreting around in other people's armoires and get back to work? Aren't you going to ask me why, Nestor?"

But Nestor, who was already leaving the room, turned back and said: "*Cazzo* Carlitos, one day you'll learn that in life there are times when it's best not to ask questions. Especially when you suspect you'd be better off not knowing the answers." And then he added, in a different tone of voice: "Come on, let's go down to the kitchen. I need you and Chloe to help me prepare the dinner."

FOR KAREL PLIGH, the Lilies wasn't warm or yellow or full of nooks and crannies. Nor did it revive childhood memories. To him it seemed like the sort of place you only read about in novels, an unreal mansion full of bathrooms, more than one per person, he calculated, and all that wasted space; at least fifteen families could have lived in it. He was walking up and down the dining room positioning the chairs around the five tables, on each of which he had placed a candelabra and a floral arrangement. He was amusing himself, setting the scene with a meticulous attention to detail. In the West, he thought, you feel like you're living on a film set. It was a feeling Karel enjoyed. In the course of the evening he would no doubt learn a good deal about sophisticated gatherings of this sort, and if he was observant and did his job well, who knows, maybe one day he would be a guest at a dinner like this or even have a house like the Lilies. It was just a question of hard work and good luck.

Chloe would be proud of me then, he thought. Or maybe not. Karel wasn't so sure. Who knows what goes on in the mind of an adorable, capricious girl like Chloe, with her pierced lips and her hair shaved up the back? And, stumped again, all he could do was to count it among the mysteries of the inscrutable West.

CHLOE WAS IN the kitchen with Nestor and Carlos, peeling tomatoes. Hundreds of tomatoes, mountains of them, which left her no time to think about the house. She would no doubt have found it every bit as awful as her parents' place, a show-piece rather than a home. Its welcoming appearance was fake, the inviting warmth of the entrance hall a lie, the homeliness of the open fire a sham. No genuine feeling anywhere in this shit heap, Chloe would have concluded if she hadn't been so busy peeling tomatoes.

But she soon tired of this repetitive task and said to Nestor: "This is a drag. When me and my brother were kids, we used to hang around in the kitchen and they'd always come up with a story to tell us. Have you got your book of little indiscretions there, Nestor? Why don't you read us something to pass the time? Come on, read us something."

"Fifty-four, fifty-five. Just concentrate on the tomatoes for now and forget about stories. We need exactly sixty-six skins to make the decorative flowers, two per dish. I'll be watching to see how yours turn out, Miss Trias," said Nestor firmly.

For a few minutes the conversation lapsed into silence as they went on working methodically. The Lilies was abuzz with the noise of different activities. From where he was standing, Nestor could hear sounds emanating from various places: Carlos breaking ice in the kitchen sink, Karel setting the table in the dining room next door . . . And Ernesto and Adela, what were they up to? Nestor imagined them far away, up in their rooms, although Adela would have to come down to the kitchen soon. It was getting late.

"Come on, Nestor, this is a real pain in the ass . . . Why don't you tell Carlos and me another one of those stories you've got hidden away in your notebook? I love stories," she insisted, "but not for the gossip value, seriously. People are always getting the wrong idea about me. I know you think all I want to do is have a good time, but I'm interested in other things, too, like literature for example. I bet you wouldn't have guessed that. It's 'cause of my brother, Eddie, who wanted to be a writer, like you, Nestor."

Chloe chattering on in her usual silly way, thought Nestor. A cook with a meal to prepare for a large group of important guests has no time to lose, so he didn't pay much attention to what she was saying. He missed the bit about her dead brother and the bit about how he wanted to be a writer, but he did catch the "like you, Nestor" at the end.

Like me? he wondered, then burst out laughing. "So I'm a writer now, am I?" But then he had to attend to a pan of béchamel sauce that was boiling over.

It was always the same: when Nestor was busy at his work, he forgot about everything else. All he could think about were his saucepans, or in this case the tomato flowers that would be used to decorate the plates for the warm lobster salad. Had he not been such a conscientious and meticulous cook, he might have been alarmed by what happened next.

Chloe went on talking louder and louder in a vain attempt to provoke some reaction from Nestor or Carlos. "Come on, Nestor, lighten up," she said. "Just one story. It doesn't matter if you've already told it. Tell us that one about the woman whose sister topped herself in Buenos Aires. You know, the girl who threw herself out the window. That was a cool story."

Nestor was completely focused on his béchamel sauce and didn't notice the door opening. Chloe didn't notice anything either. Only Carlos realized that Adela had her hand on the door and was about to step into the room, but when she heard what Chloe was saying, she froze.

"Yeah, it was like a horror movie," Chloe went on. "Tell us that one again."

The door closed again just as it had opened, and Carlos went on breaking ice while Chloe chattered away as if nothing had happened. Just as well, thought Carlos. When she saw me, Adela decided to come back later, and that was the right thing to do. It's better if no one's around when we meet for the first time here. If she'd come in just then, unprepared, Nestor would have been able to tell from our faces.

"Fucking hell, Nestor. And you too, Carlos," said Chloe. "You could at least *say* something to me. I don't see why work has to be incompatible with a bit of communication between human beings."

But neither Nestor nor Carlos was listening. One was thinking about sauces, the other about love, and Chloe got bored and let her gaze wander until it came to rest on the door of a large cool room on the other side of the kitchen. WESTINGHOUSE 401 EXTRA-COLD, she read distractedly before noticing her reflection in the stainless steel door. Her face was distorted and enlarged, as in a trick mirror. Chloe amused herself readjusting her hair and checking how cool all her studs and rings looked, especially the one in her lip. This mutating fairground mirror-image made her laugh, and she stopped thinking about Carlos and shameful secrets and Nestor's little moleskin notebook.

Twenty tomatoes later, when all the flowers had been carefully placed on the plates, Chloe asked Nestor what else he wanted her to do. After consulting his watch, Nestor said he didn't need any more help in the kitchen, so she could go upstairs and get changed. "It's still early, but you need to make sure your uniform isn't crushed and the apron is spotless. Off you go. Carlos and I will finish this. You go and give your uniform a good iron, all right? And after that, you know what you have to do, don't you, dear? All those rings and studs and other bits of metal you're wearing are coming out, aren't they? You can pack them away in that enormous backpack of yours. I can't imagine what you've got in there. Anyone would think you were heading off for two weeks in the desert.

"Ah . . . women," Nestor added with a smile. He was in very high spirits: everything was going exactly according to plan.

⁓

A PEARL JAM CD was playing in the room that Chloe Trias and Karel Pligh had been given to share. Chloe had already taken a shower and, with her wet hair wrapped in a towel, she was rummaging through her backpack in search of her maid's uniform: a severe gray smock with a white collar and cuffs, an organza apron, and one of those little lacy caps that prestigious catering companies like Mulberry & Mistletoe have rescued from oblivion to give their services that extra touch of class.

"Where the fuck is that maid's getup?" she said, pulling the clothes out of her backpack, all the clothes she had picked up at her parents' house the day before. There were far too many things: shirts, a bikini, a pair of Bermuda shorts made in China (just the thing for strolling around the garden at the Lilies), everything except the uniform. As she continued rummaging, Chloe started to get worried. Jesus, don't tell me I left the fucking thing at the olds' place—what a fuckup! I was in such a rush I don't know what I took anymore, and it's not here, so what do I do? Nestor's a good sort, but when he finds out I haven't got my stuff, he's not going to be happy, that's for sure.

It was seven-thirty. Early still, but not early enough to solve the major problem of having left her uniform in Madrid. Shit, shit, shit! Chloe paced up and down in her room. Suddenly she had a lifesaving idea. It was her only chance.

She looked in the armoire. Karel had brought two waiter's uniforms. Yes! Such an organized young man! You could count on Karel to bring a spare set of work clothes. In the hospitality business you have to be prepared for all eventualities, and luckily, Karel was. So now Chloe knew what she had to do.

"It'll be fun dressing as a guy," she said.

AN HOUR LATER the front doorbell rang. It was still too early for the guests to be arriving, so rather than opening the door, Karel Pligh put his head out the window. He saw an affable-looking gentleman with a crew cut standing in front of the main door holding a small suitcase.

"Good evening. I am Serafin Tous," said the man.

"And you're here for the party?" asked Karel from the window, unsure as to what the protocol was in such cases.

Serafin smiled. He was in good spirits, all the more so when he realized that Karel's handsome face, like a portrait in the window frame, had not provoked any of those distressing urges that had been plaguing him recently.

"I have been invited for the party, and to spend the night. Ask Mrs. Teldi if you like. Go and ask."

Serafin waited a few seconds while Karel came around to the door.

"Good evening, sir," he said.

And behind Karel, Serafin could see the serene interior of

the Lilies. Such a peaceful house, he thought. Perfect, perfect. As I always say to Adela, it reminds me of a spa, a place where all anxieties are cured.

"May I take your suitcase, sir?"

As Karel Pligh picked up the case and headed off ("Follow me, sir, I'll show you the way"), Serafin Tous noticed a large, shiny, wet-looking cockroach waiting on the doormat to greet him. But he was shortsighted and in good spirits, so he mis-identified the insect. Oh, a sweet little dung beetle, he thought, giving it a nudge with his shoe. Ah, nature! The country life! It was just what he needed: a haven safe from people who might know about his secret.

"Off you go, off you go," he said, very gently, to what he thought was a beetle. "Off you go and roll some balls."

NOT LONG AFTERWARD, Serafin Tous had completely changed his mind about the Lilies. If the incident with the cockroach had occurred two hours later, he would certainly not have mistaken it for a beetle. The Lilies, so blessedly peace-ful when he arrived, now struck him as an old pile full of junk, the house of a collector with far more money than taste. Yes, that's what Serafin thought, sitting on the terrace with a news-paper in one trembling hand and a glass of sherry in the other, thoroughly shaken by what had just happened. As he settled down to read the paper and sip his sherry, Nestor's unmistak-able pointy mustache had appeared at one of the windows giv-ing onto the terrace—the mustache he had encountered at Freshman's and again at Madame Longstaffe's.

"Good evening," said the mustache. "I'll just leave these here if you don't mind. They're for decorating the terrace."

As Nestor put the candles on the table, he smiled, and that smile was so disturbing that Serafin couldn't help himself: he spilled the sherry on his trousers. A suspicious-looking stain began to spread across his crotch.

Dear God, he thought. Nora darling, isn't there something you can do to save me from this terrible coincidence?

2

EVERYONE WANTS
TO KILL NESTOR

$\mathcal{I}$F MADAME LONGSTAFFE, the famous fortune-teller from Bahia (and keen collector of taxidermic specimens), had been invited to this party for collectors of rare objects, no doubt she would have sensed the shadow of a crime hovering over the Lilies. Or perhaps not, since even if she had been among the guests, none of them were present when that sinister, negative energy took possession of the house.

The collectors had not yet arrived and would still be a while coming; the only people in the house were the characters who have already figured in this story, each of whom was getting dressed for dinner. As they performed this routine task, their thoughts wandered freely, unconsciously, and it so happened that four of them were thinking the same thought simultaneously: they all wanted to kill Nestor. Or at least they were all wishing, fervently and hopelessly, like souls in torment, that they had never set eyes on the chef who knew too much.

Why did he have to turn up tonight of all nights? It's completely stupid, stupid and unfair, thought Ernesto Teldi as he took a pair of cuff links from a little box. A curious pair they were, in the form of gaucho spurs: a rather unfortunate choice, for the sight of them spurred his memory back to a region of the past he had tried to leave behind. A long time had passed since his return from Argentina, and for more than twenty years now his respectable and impressive CV had gone unchallenged. The only thing he had left out was starting off as a smuggler, but was that really so terrible? Hadn't other respectable fortunes begun in a similar way?

And now, years later, this character has the nerve to turn up in my house thinking I'm not going to recognize him. I come to my country house, I open the door, and there he is, flicking at my furniture and my artworks with a feather duster, pretending to be one of the caterers. It's outrageous! But I never forget a face or a name, though I was very careful not to let on when we ran into each other. "No doubt about it: he's Antonio Reig, our old cook from Buenos Aires," muttered Teldi, immediately disproving what he had just affirmed.

Sitting brazenly on his bedside table were three letters written in green ink. He had received the first just over a week ago. The signature was no doubt deliberately illegible and the writing was difficult to decipher, but the content was only too familiar: the roaring motors and the screams that filled his nightmares. The one name he had been able to make out was clearly linked to an episode that he thought everyone had forgotten. That name was Minelli. Other scribbly paragraphs reminded him of the young men's shouts, the dark sheen of the Río de la Plata, a one-way trip, and his little smuggler's plane, which had been used to commit a crime. And what was the purpose of these wavering lines accusing him anonymously from the bedside table? What were they asking for?

Why, money, of course.

Completely unfair, said Teldi to himself, looking at his little silver spurs, the symbol of everything he had achieved in life through hard work: money, success, respect. He had earned it all, and it was rightly his, because the only shameful thing in his past was that one night when Minelli had asked to borrow his light plane and Teldi had lent it to him, no questions asked. "Not something to be proud of," said the green lines. All right, it wasn't something to be proud of, but it wasn't really that terrible, either, and he had paid dearly for it already. Ever since then, his nights had been inhabited by nightmares and screams, repeated over and over, hour after hour. People think that men like me don't feel anything or suffer at all, but what do they know? What does anyone know, really? Teldi looked back over the years and convinced himself that he had spent half his life getting rich and the other half apologizing for being so successful. All that work: his generous patronage of the arts, the vast sums of money he had donated to worthy causes, setting up charitable organizations . . . for what? In the end, none of those good works had redeemed him in the eyes of others. People think that men like me give money away to buy forgiveness for a sin or out of vanity, when really it's the winner's pathetic tribute to the loser. Look at me, we seem to be begging, I need you too. I need you to accept me, to admire me, to love me.

And now, thought Teldi as he fastened his right cuff link

(which is always harder to do), now all that hard work is at risk. "You and I know what happened in 1976," said the last of those knotty lines in green ink, which looked like a row of parrots on a wire. Teldi was convinced that if the author of those lines were to tell the plain truth, no one would believe him. Who would believe that the only thing Ernesto Teldi had done wrong was to lend his light plane to Lieutenant Minelli? Lending a plane to an army officer, just once, without asking what for, is hardly a serious offense, so the truth would have to be embroidered a little. It would be so easy to cross the fine line between telling it the way it was and claiming that he had collaborated in the Dirty War. A blackmailer can twist the truth however he likes—all he needs is a single detail, a subtle nuance. "Be careful, Teldi. Remember how easy it would be for me to go to the papers with your story," said the letter. "You think about it. I'm not going to write to you anymore. I'll get in touch with you directly so we can sort out this little misunderstanding . . . perhaps by telephone or perhaps . . ." Here the green writing became completely illegible, but Teldi could tell where the blackmailer was heading. So he decides to turn up at my house, bold as brass, he thought. And here he is, under my roof. What a nerve! How dare he!

I suppose he thinks he's invulnerable, thought Ernesto, having finally secured his cuff links and putting on his jacket now. He doesn't know that I've recognized him, and he's waiting for the moment to catch me off guard and screw the money out of me. And the worst thing is, I'll end up paying what he asks, however much it is, just to be rid of the filthy leech.

Ernesto Teldi was about to leave his room. I'll work it out

later, he thought, after the party, how much I'm prepared to pay him. Life goes on and I've got other things to worry about. At least I've got money. It does have its uses, like fixing this sort of problem and disposing of leeches like Reig.

As he reached for the door handle, the silver spurs knocked against it with a little *ting*. The sound was almost imperceptible, but it rang like an alarm in his head. He realized his mistake: money wasn't the solution; it would only make the leech fatter and greedier. You spend your whole life achieving respectability, then someone comes along and destroys your reputation just like that. The only good leech is a dead leech, he thought, surprising himself. He had always been a firm and efficient man, but he preferred to avoid conflict. Sometimes, however . . .

Was it better to fatten a leech with money (since he did have enough to tolerate a bit of bleeding), or should he find another way to get rid of it? The question would keep needling him all through the evening.

⌒

MEANWHILE, SERAFIN TOUS was in the grip of a similar anxiety, and wondering what magic he could call on to eliminate Nestor. Not a magic spell, the sort Madame Longstaffe might have pronounced, or her ancestors the Weird Sisters. No, while Ernesto was pondering leech control, Serafin was toying with the sort of homemade magic remedies we have all fantasized about at some stage. If only I could press a button and make him disappear, I'd do it without a second thought, mused the inoffensive Mr. Tous. Oh God, if only there were some secret device I could activate to make him vanish, with a simple click. I can't let him wander around. If I could just seal him away hermetically, like bacteria in cold storage or patients in a plague hospital, isolated for the public good.

Serafin Tous was sitting on the lid of the toilet. In outward appearance, he was a respectable judge, with his close-cropped gray hair, his legs crossed tightly, and his clasped hands resting on his thighs as if in prayer. The party would be starting soon. How on earth was he going to get through it, maintaining the serene composure expected of a judge? Three, four, maybe even *five* hours of social interaction awaited him: participating in banal conversations, smiling, admiring the works of art Ernesto Teldi would undoubtedly show them, while being manifestly delighted by the comments of the eccentric guests. Would he, in short, be able to perform the familiar routine of social gymnastics given his fragile state of mind? With a mechanical gesture, Serafin tore off a piece of toilet paper as long as the night ahead and used it to wipe his brow.

But the party was just the beginning, he thought, and it wouldn't be the hardest part, far from it. Nestor would be so busy with the catering, he wouldn't really have time to indulge in malicious gossip; he probably wouldn't get a chance to tell anyone where and in whose company he had encountered the venerable judge. Thanks to the party, his secret would be safe tonight, at least. But it would only be a momentary respite. Now the fellow knew his name and his profession. He also knew who his friends were, and it would be simple for him to ensure they found out about Freshman's. The real danger would begin in the morning. It was impossible to predict just when he would strike: tomorrow, the next day, the following week . . . Such was the exquisite torture that he would be forced to endure: the waiting and the uncertainty, until one day a caustic smile or the attitude of a friend would confirm that everything was lost and that his one little slip had become public knowledge. Serafín pressed his knees together, keeping his legs crossed in a desperate X as he reflected on how malicious rumors spread. Often, ironically, it's frivolity rather than malice that sets it off, he thought. He had seen it happen so many times. It's terrible to think that the most shameful secrets are often revealed simply for the pleasure of sharing a little indiscreet gossip among friends: You'll never guess where I met Serafín Tous the other day . . . you know, that judge, a pillar of the community. Did you know he was a queer, a poof, a pedophile? Didn't you know? A few remarks like that and everyone pricks up their ears. Really? Do tell . . .

I've seen it happen, thought Serafín, still sitting on the lid of the toilet. Careers cut short, lives ruined. And the most extraordinary thing is that people don't do it because they're evil or unthinking, or even because they're jealous. It's vanity. All they want is to be the center of attention for a few minutes. Honestly!

From where he was sitting, Serafín could not see his face in the bathroom mirror, just his hairline and his wrinkled forehead. A whole life spent trying to flee, trying to forget that delicate boy with whom he had played the piano all those years ago, only to end up giving himself away like this. He winced, and the wrinkles on his forehead deepened. Behind them was a crowd of jostling thoughts, but the most insistent was that silly, childish wish: if only I could push a button; if only it were that easy to get rid of a pest, I'd do it without a second thought. And Serafin Tous, who normally wouldn't have dared to hurt a fly, swiveled around to examine the flusher, wishing he could use it to free himself of Nestor and flush away all his fears and anxieties. He pushed the button, and a thundering roar made the little room tremble as if the plumbing were about to burst. Good Lord, thought Serafin, you can tell they don't come here often: nothing works properly. But vacation houses are always like that. So many things can go wrong: flooding, cracks in the walls, even dangerous short circuits. Serafin stood up, and, as if a household spirit had been waiting to confirm his theory about the dangers of vacation houses, when he tried to switch on the light over the mirror, there was a flash. The bulb had blown. Just as well he had good reflexes and was able to jump out of the way, otherwise he might have gotten a shock. This place really is dangerous, he thought. I'll have to tell Adela. Someone could have a nasty accident here. Or maybe, thought Serafin, falling back into his childish wishful thinking, maybe it would be better to say nothing. After all, sometimes you do happen to be at the right place at the right time. You might witness an accident, for instance, and do nothing to help the victim. You hear him shouting and know that you should reach out and give him a hand, but instead you stand there unmoved and do nothing—or, worse, you decide to give destiny a little nudge. Serafin examined the lightbulb, which was giving off a delicious burned smell. Accidents can happen so easily, he thought. You don't actually have to do anything, just be ready to give bad luck a helping hand, and that can be as simple and easy as pressing a button. Yes, thought Serafin, emerging from the bathroom with a more positive outlook and a few new ideas. All sorts of unexpected things can happen in the course of an evening. You never know, do you?

⌒

WHILE ENJOYING THE delicious meal organized by Adela and talking with the guests at his table, Serafin Tous would toy with the idea of provoking an accident. It would give him something interesting to think about for the next couple of hours.

⌒

THERE WAS A third person who also would have liked Nestor to disappear, and that was Adela Teldi. But she was not yet making plans. Instead, she was thinking: Careful, remember what he said. Carlos is like a son to him. Don't forget that.

As she was getting dressed for the party that evening, Adela tried not to look at herself in the mirror. She was scared of what she might find in her eyes: the anxiety caused by two discoveries she had made quite by chance that afternoon. First, she had recognized Nestor and remembered that he was a friend of Antonio Reig, who used to be their cook back in Buenos Aires. Then she had discovered something even more disturbing. Like a doubting Thomas, she wouldn't have believed it possible unless she had seen it with her own eyes and heard it with her own astonished ears; there were simply too many coincidences, and none of them fortunate. Not only did the caterer happen to be someone who knew about her past, but as she was entering the kitchen unannounced, she had been lucky (or unlucky?) enough to overhear him talking with his employees, and from what she heard, she was sure he had told them everything that had happened in Argentina, including the death of her sister.

Trying to repress that memory, as she had done so often in the past, Adela inspected her body, searching for the paths traced by Carlos's hands, hoping they would help her forget. But this time, instead of giving her pleasure, the inspection was painful, so painful that she almost expected to see wounds on her arms and shoulders. There were no wounds, but the pain persisted and Adela expressed it as a kind of sum, the arithmetic of her anxiety. One, this man has recognized me. Two, he has already told his employees what he knows about my life. And three, he said that Carlos was like a son to him. You don't have to be very smart to put these three things together and realize that, given how fond he is of Carlos, he's bound to warn him not to get mixed up with the likes of me. But of course he wouldn't even think of doing that unless he knew about our relationship, and he doesn't, not yet, I'm sure of that at least.

This gave her some relief. The pain ebbed, but only for a moment, because she soon realized that it was just a matter of time before Nestor found out about her and Carlos. Love, she thought sadly, flaunts itself, as you well know, my dear. Love can't help giving itself away: a beatific smile, a slight trembling, a special tone of voice, a glance . . . at some point Nestor would surely discern one of these symptoms in her or Carlos. And then the game would be up.

She was afraid her eyes in the mirror would betray all this—
the fear, the danger, the impending end of her love affair—so
she turned away. But it isn't easy to get dressed without looking at yourself. Adela had chosen a dependable plain black
gown. In a woman's wardrobe there are always some things
that require the use of a mirror and others that don't. There
are temperamental dresses, which call for a considerable
amount of testing, tweaking, and adjusting in front of the mirror, while others are less capricious and can be relied upon to
do the job, like the one Adela had taken from the armoire. She
put it on quickly, without thinking, but then she faced the
problem of how to fix her makeup and hair without looking in
the mirror. She would have to take a glance at herself, but just
a quick one, so as not to let the other, left-handed Adela, who
lived on the dark side of the moon, tell her something she
didn't want to hear, something along the lines of: You see? I
told you. It had to happen. You should have listened to your
thumbs; they've always warned you when something unpleasant was in the offing. And omens and portents aside, what did
you expect, you silly old thing? Did you think you'd be able to
get Love with a capital *L* for free? It was only to be expected;
something was bound to go wrong. Face it, twenty-five years
of marriage and a long string of lovers take their toll, to say
nothing of that painful secret you've been trying to hide even
from yourself. You were so brave yesterday when you decided
to make a clean break, promising that when the party was
over, you would risk it all and give love a chance. Perhaps you
thought you were paying a high price. Well, that was nothing.
Yes, you'll have to endure uncertainty and the fear of losing

him, but that's not all. The past always comes to collect its debts, Adela: your dead sister, the affair that led to her death, the guilt . . . It's true those memories are only ghosts, but ghosts have a nasty habit of coming back to haunt the living. They come back when you least expect them, in the most unlikely forms, and the ghost of what happened in Buenos Aires is here now in the form of a cook with a pointy mustache.

The mirror could not tell Adela any of this, because she would not look at it. As she had done so often in her life, she simply stopped herself from thinking. If you prevent ideas from forming, they don't exist, or at least they can't hurt you. But that was just a trick. Whether she looked at the mirror or not, whether she thought about it or not, Adela knew that she would have to do something to prevent Nestor from putting an end to her newfound happiness. The best thing would be to get in first, talk to Carlos, and tell him the truth, because in the end, thought Adela, why would he care about an old story, something that happened years ago, in another country, to people who meant nothing to him? A youthful error, a silly fling that ended badly, true, but who hasn't committed a little indiscretion at some point in their life?

By the pricking of my thumbs, something wicked this way comes. As she tried to zip up her dress, Adela's fingers brushed against her bare skin, and she could feel her thumbs pricking. A strange presentiment made her fingers retract as she was struck by the similarity between the feel of two bodies and the form of two names, one fresh in her mind, the other buried deep in her memory: Carlos Garcia and Ricardo Garcia. She imagined them side by side, like father and son. The strange sensation persisted in her thumbs, prompting the realization: the same skin, that same feel, the same surname. But where do you get these crazy ideas from, Adela? That's ridiculous! As if two men with the same last name had to be related! Garcia, for God's sake, it's one of the most common names in Spain. You really are losing the plot, my dear. Why don't you stop being silly and have a proper look in the mirror? It's no good trying to do it like this, you'll go out looking a fright, like a witch on a bad hair day.

But Adela didn't dare. She was too scared of what she might glimpse in the background: another coincidence, too awful even to imagine. What if Carlos Garcia *was* the son of Soledad and Ricardo? What then? A one-in-a-thousand chance, and the odds against that gossipmonger of a cook putting it together must be a million to one, but what if . . .

What if it were true and he knew, thought Adela, looking into the mirror now for the first time, unafraid. I'd just have to silence him for good. But fortunately that won't be necessary. There couldn't be that many coincidences. Stop worrying and finish getting dressed; you're going to be late.

Then Adela did something she hadn't done for years: from her jewelry box she took the green cameo that her mother, Teresa, had given her for her fifteenth birthday. She couldn't remember ever having used it as a brooch, but that old jade disk with its gold setting went well with the austere black dress she had decided to wear. And now stop being silly, she told herself as she headed for the door. She opened it, and shut it behind her. She looked around at the landing, at all the things she would soon abandon forever, and she smiled. A small price to pay, really, for what the future holds, as long as nothing goes wrong. And nothing will go wrong. I'll make quite sure of that.

Adela went down the stairs. She was going to play the role of Mrs. Teldi the model hostess one last time, and tomorrow . . . whatever happened, tomorrow would be the first day of the rest of her life.

⁓

AS ADELA WENT downstairs, Chloe was in the room over the garage at the Lilies, which she was sharing with Karel Pligh, thinking, Nestor! I could strangle him. Only he could have come up with a waiter's uniform like this. It's like a Mao suit or biker's leathers or something. It's so tight I'm going to fry like a chicken.

Nestor had not been amused to discover that Chloe had left her waitress uniform at her parents' house. It always gave Mulberry & Mistletoe's catering a nice touch of class, he felt, to have a girl waiting in a dark smock, a little cap, and a white organza apron. "But I guess if you've left it all in Madrid, there's nothing else we can do. All right, Chloe, go and put on Karel's spare suit. But if you're going to dress as a man," he warned her, "do us all a favor and play the part convincingly. Walk like a man, lower your voice so as not to give the guests a fright, comb your hair back, and above all, for God's sake, remove those rings and studs and things, will you?"

Chloe had already put on the trousers and the severe-looking jacket, which buttoned right up to the neck like a biker's leathers, and she was standing in front of the mirror, removing her rings and studs, gently, so as not to hurt herself, reciting the origin of each metallic object: this is the one my pal Hassem gave me for Christmas; I bought this one in a one-pound shop; and Karel gave me this one . . . he's so sweet, and gorgeous too. As she removed them, one by one, she realized it had been ages since she had seen her face unembellished, and faces change, it's fucking amazing how they change. She decided to comb her hair before removing the ring in her bottom lip, because she knew it was going to hurt. She looked in Karel's kit and found a comb and a tube of gel, then turned on the tap. She was starting to get into this cross-dressing thing. She began to imitate the way she'd seen any number of men, from Karel Pligh to her brother, Eddie, comb their hair. The Travolta method: the right hand wields the comb while the left follows, stroking. Hey, this is fucking cool. It looks good. I look like . . . and her hands acquired a life of their own, combing away, stroke after stroke, slicking all her hair back until she looked like a boy, a young man of twenty-two. That was how old she would be next month.

"What the hell are you doing in there, Chloe? Hurry up, for God's sake. Nestor will be furious."

Off in her own world, Chloe vaguely heard Karel Pligh's words through the bathroom door and her hand froze.

"What? What is it? Who's that?"

"Karel, who else could it be? We're really late. Open the door or I'm going down without you."

Instead of acceding to this demand, Chloe kept looking for

the eyes she thought she had seen in the mirror. Without turning around, she said: "You do that, K. Go down and stop giving me the shits."

And as she spoke, she realized that the eyes looking back from the mirror were not blue like hers but black and stern, and they seemed to be saying: Don't talk like that, Clo-Clo. You never used to talk like that.

"Is that you, Eddie?"

The face in the mirror looked like Eddie's, but it wasn't. It was hers: the ugly and possibly unhygienic ring in her lower lip was a giveaway. Not Eddie's style at all.

"Hang on Eddie. Just a minute, I'll take it out for you. I promise I'll never wear it again." And, very carefully, she removed the last ring from her lip so that her brother's reflection could smile back unimpeded from the mirror. There, that's better. Now, let me touch you.

The whole scene lasted no more than a minute. Chloe was back in the world of her dreams, playing with her brother, but then she reached toward the reflection to caress his eyes, so different from hers, and as her fingers touched the glass, she realized that the spell had been broken and the face looking out from the cold surface of the mirror was a girl's face, her own.

"I'm not going to warn you again, Chloe. Nestor has called us three times."

All the mirror showed now was a girl dressed as a boy. She looked like Eddie, true. She had the same hairstyle, and the suit she had put on was even reminiscent of the leathers he had worn that last afternoon, but the eyes were different. Once again those dark eyes had abandoned her.

THAT NIGHT, AS she waited on the tables and attended to the guests, Choe would keep trying to find her brother's eyes again in all the mirrors of the Lilies.

"Are you playing hide-and-seek with me, Eddie?"

3

THE DINNER AT THE LILIES

Ernesto Teldi raised his glass and said: "It's a great privilege for Adela and myself to have been able to gather thirty-three of the world's most original and important art collectors and to welcome you all to the Lilies tonight."

From their appearance, there was no way of telling that the thirty-three people seated around the dining room at the Lilies, their gazes converging on Ernesto Teldi, were all specialist collectors, each expert in a particular kind of art or antiquities. Most trades and professions have some kind of distinguishing characteristic, a way of dressing or talking, a particular form of pedantry or snobbery, but collectors of rare objects have nothing in common except their idiosyncrasy; each is a unique specimen, in the most literal sense. Take Mr. Stephanopolous and Mr. Algobranghini, for instance. Both knew all there was to know about knives and swords, but apart from that, the only thing they had in common was an immoderate fondness for tawny port. When the Teldis were charging their guests' glasses for a toast, both Algobranghini and Stephanopolous had rejected the Cava, opting instead for a slim red glass of '59 vintage Royal Port. In all other respects, their personalities could not have been more different. Despite his Greek name, Stephanopolous was a pure product of the British ruling class: Eton, Oxford, a life in the country, surrounded by dogs, cats, and horses. Algobranghini on the other hand looked like an old-style tango singer. Karel Pligh was captivated by his pin-striped suit, the carnation in his buttonhole, and his slicked-back hair. Every inch the Buenos Aires spiv, he thought as he refilled the collector's tiny glass for the tenth time. The reincarnation of Carlos Gardel, I swear.

A curious observer would have been struck by the bewildering diversity of styles on display that evening. It was an odd assembly to say the least. Despite her name, Miss Liau Chi, the famous collector of ghost stories, seemed to have stepped out of a novel by Wilkie Collins (rather than off a plane from Hong Kong). The three "Dickensiana fetishists" looked, respectively, like an overweight boxer, a severe Breton matron (in the mold of Becassine, from the old French comic books), and, more appropriately, the living image of Mr. Squeers, the stingy teacher in *Nicholas Nickelby*.

Also present were the icon collectors (a young woman who looked like a model, an Orthodox priest, and a young man with a smooth, angelic face, who appeared to be much younger than his passport said he was). On seeing this youth, Serafin Tous couldn't help thinking, What an exquisite creature, but immediately his gaze slid from the cherub to the kitchen door, behind which Nestor was no doubt lurking among his pots and pans. I hope he burns his hand and has to be taken to the hospital, thought the judge. Was it really so terrible to wish a little household accident on someone, a little time off work . . . or maybe a serious accident that would dispose of him for good and leave Serafin and his friends in peace.

But leaving these bad wishes aside (the air at the Lilies was thick with them that night, and all were meant for Nestor), let us resume the description of the guests. The rest of the lineup was composed of conventional-looking ladies and gentlemen, with two exceptions: the "Rapanui statuette fan," who looked like the reincarnation of Humboldt the naturalist, and Monsieur Pitou, the guest of honor, an eminent expert on the love letters of the famous. All through the evening Monsieur Pitou had been the object of Ernesto Teldi's subtly seductive attentions. He was a tiny man, barely more than four and a half feet tall. He had exquisite hands, and his limbs and trunk were perfectly proportioned, but his face . . . The owner of the world's most beautiful love letters was spectacularly ugly, and his body was shrunken, as if a love spell in reverse had turned him from a prince into a frog.

Having sat down again after his conventional words of welcome, Teldi said: "Now, dear Emile, before we go into the library, I'd like to thank you for having given me one of the most moving experiences of my life."

With a conspiratorial gesture, he opened his jacket to reveal the white corner of a love letter that Pitou had sold him before dinner. The sale had gone smoothly. There had been no need to bring out the heavy artillery of his bargaining skills. An odd fellow, Monsieur Pitou. There was something alarming about the way his froggy mouth was smiling back at him now, displaying a magnificent set of teeth. It had been a bit too easy to buy that curious love letter signed *Oscar Wilde*. And the price was very low. Could his guest have tricked him? "I want you, I trust you, I am coming to you . . ." The handwriting was indubitably Wilde's, and the date proved that it had been written three years before the author had used the same sentence in one of his most famous plays. It was really quite a find, as long as it wasn't a fake, of course. But I'm being paranoid. No one's going to try to cheat a dealer of my reputation . . . my *current* reputation, that is, he thought uneasily, remembering the letter scribbled in green ink sitting on his bedside table. Then he thought about how in the hard world of art dealers a little scandal, a little indiscretion, was enough to label you as one more shady businessman. Imagining the worst, Ernesto Teldi saw himself transformed overnight into one of those pathetic individuals, those ridiculous has-beens stripped of all respect, fair game for any scam. Perhaps it was happening already. Pitou was an intuitive dealer with a gift for anticipating the market. Had he guessed somehow that Ernesto Teldi's reputation was not so unimpeachable after all?

Monsieur Pitou was sitting there in front of him with his toadlike eyes, smiling. What Teldi saw as he looked at him, however, was not an amphibian but a more insidious and harmful creature. Filthy leech! If my reputation is ruined, it will be your fault, he said to himself, thinking of Nestor, not for the first time that evening. Again and again as he chatted with his guests and played the charming host, a question kept nagging at him: What the hell am I going to do about this leech? The toad poked out a very long tongue, as if he were trying to catch a fly, then pulled it back in with a smile.

"Are you feeling all right, Teldi? You're looking thoughtful."

And Teldi, having slipped the unexpectedly cheap love letter back into his breast pocket, where it would be safe and warm, close to his heart, told himself there was no way he could allow that blackmailer, that leech in the kitchen, to ruin his career or in any way diminish his hostly charms. I should just squash him and be done with it, stop him from interfering with my life. But how? *How?* Maybe there's a way . . . yes, I think I can see a way . . . but he can wait.

"This way, this way please, Monsieur Pitou," said Teldi to the collector of love letters, taking him by the arm. "Let's go to the library and have a glass of cognac. I want to introduce you to Mr. Stephanopolous."

ERNESTO TELDI'S LIBRARY is so renowned that it hardly needs to be described. Anyone who reads *House & Garden, Architectural Digest,* or other such magazines is bound to have seen a photograph of it: a room that testifies to its owner's exquisite taste and passion for unique pieces. The whole is perfectly harmonious, not dominated by one or two features clamoring for the visitor's attention. Often, in collectors' houses, objects are piled up as in a Turkish bazaar. Not so in the library at the Lilies. The visitor is not overwhelmed by abundance. There is a certain artlessness to the arrangement, as if, over many years, the objects made themselves at home, each in its place. On the right, for example, a little Manet hangs on the wall, watching over the entrance: a bust of the model whose naked presence in *Le déjeuner sur l'herbe* caused such a scandal. Here, however, elegantly blending in with the other paintings, she could easily be overlooked by all but the finest of connoisseurs. Across the room, an Art Deco statuette of a faun keeps watch over Manet's model, by happy chance it might seem, yet the symmetry is deliberate. And so it is with the other magnificent pieces, none of which are ostentatiously displayed, while comfortable seats of various kinds—chesterfields, chairs, little poufs—invite the lucky guests to sit back, make themselves at home, and let their five senses be delighted. The discreet harmony of the whole is in no way disturbed by the glass case containing a small but intriguing collection of tin soldiers or by the panoply of knives, daggers, and *stiletti*.

"I sold that dagger with the red handle to your husband last year, Mrs. Teldi," said Gerassimos Stephanopolous to Adela. "Since then, its value has tripled. And do you know why, my dear? Because last month *Time* magazine published a photo of Atatürk, I should say Mustafa Kemal, wearing the very same dagger in his belt. What a stroke of luck! He has such good business sense, your husband, but I don't mind him getting the better of me, truly. I'm a great admirer of your husband . . . and of his taste," said the Greek, looking at Adela as if he were mentally valuing an exquisite object.

But Adela was immune to flattery that night. She had spent the whole dinner being mechanically pleasant, a skill she had acquired over many years of tedious social obligations and could now exercise without mobilizing a single neuron: Yes . . . No . . . really? But how extraordinary! Adela was expert at

keeping a conversation going on autopilot with these rudi-
mentary but effective interjections and pursuing her own train
of thought while her face and gestures gave the impression
that she was fascinated by what her guests were saying.

"Really, Mr. Stephanopolous? Do tell me more! I'd love to
hear all about Mustafa Kemal and his red dagger."

The collector was only too happy to launch into a long
speech, during which in Adela's mind the founder of modern
Turkey and his youthful exploits were mixed with thoughts of
quite a different nature.

"As I'm sure you know, in 1912, when Mustafa was still a
boy . . ."

(Where was *her* boy, Carlos? Where could he be? wondered
Adela. During the meal he had served the tables farthest from
hers and she hadn't been able to catch his eye even once. But
the time for *digestifs* had come, and watching Karel and Chloe
move among the guests, offering them Cava, armagnac, and
malt whiskey, brushing against them as they went back and
forth, Adela hoped she could exploit the mingling to touch
Carlos surreptitiously. She wanted to stroke his arm as if by accident, caress the back that she would kiss later on, when the
dinner was over, when all these people have gone, she thought,
when there are no more faces to smile at or conversations to
pay attention to.)

"But that's incredible! Is that really how it happened, Mr.
Stephanopolous? How fascinating!"

"Exactly as I told you, my dear, and I'm delighted you appreciate the irony of it. If not for that incident, Mustafa Kemal
would never have come to be called Atatürk."

(Where are you? Where are you, my love? Come closer, I want to smell you, I want our bodies to touch in front of all these people, Teldi and his friends. A sweet foretaste of tomorrow, when I will be through with this life and we won't have to steal glances across a crowded room.)

"Metaphorically speaking, one might say our hero belonged to the tribe of dreamers," Stephanopolous was saying, encouraged by a "You don't say!" that Adela had thrown in to keep the conversation moving along. "But whether or not he was a dreamer, the fact is the young Mustafa played his cards so well that he was able to bring Turkey into the twentieth century. Although it did mean giving up certain things, traditional customs and so on . . ."

"How fascinating," Adela remarked adroitly, which was all the encouragement he needed to go on for another three minutes, allowing her to concentrate on looking for Carlos among the heads of her guests, wreathed in smoke. He wasn't there. For a moment she imagined him in the kitchen, hearing what she most feared Nestor would tell him. The thought made her wince with pain.

"Awful, isn't it?" said Stephanopolous, noting Mrs. Teldi's reaction to his account of one of the bloodier episodes in Turkish history.

(No, Adela, you needn't worry about that. The cook isn't likely to tell him tonight. And by tomorrow you will have talked with Carlos and told him everything he needs to know about your past. But . . . wouldn't it be better to silence that interfering cook for good?)

"And that, my dear, is where the dagger with the red handle

comes in. As I'm sure you'll appreciate, a dangerous situation like that called for expeditious, one might even say sanguinary, measures."

"Indeed, quite, absolutely, Mr. Stephanopolous," said Adela, on autopilot while the nonmechanical part of her mind thrilled at the sight of Carlos over near the door, making his way toward her across the crowded room with a trayful of tall glasses. She smiled inwardly.

What took you so long, my love?

~

MEANWHILE, CARLOS WAS thinking: There's Adela. At last I can be near her. And he made his way across the room, drawn as if by gravity, longing to touch her in the midst of the crowd, in front of everyone, as platonic lovers touch, as secret lovers thrill to the merest hint of a caress. Maybe I could even kiss her shoulder when I offer her a glass, he thought.

"Excuse me, madame. I didn't mean to . . ."

She smiled. She was so beautiful.

"Is this champagne or Cava?"

"Cava, madame. May I?"

And as he leaned forward, drawing closer still, his waiter's eye, accustomed to picking out singular features by which to identify people, noticed a green jade cameo that Adela was wearing as a brooch.

"Atatürk's objective was to show that Turkey was ready to enter the modern world, like any Western nation, but of course . . ."

(The gold setting, the green stone . . . My God, it's the cameo from the painting, the one the girl is holding. And, as if he were seeing Adela for the first time, Carlos searched for an explanation in her face.)

"Of course, daggers have come back into fashion now, and not just there, but right through the Muslim world. A remarkable development, as I'm sure you appreciate. And who could have predicted it? I certainly didn't. Did you?"

(It's her; it has to be. The Cava in the glasses began a weird dance to the rhythm of Carlos Garcia's trembling hand. The bubbles rose to the surface and burst, each exclaiming: My God, how is it possible? How can I have kissed her a thousand times and loved every inch of her body without realizing that she was the woman I had been searching for all along?)

Now Carlos couldn't stop looking at the stone, and the cameo's green gleam recalled other childhood memories: the silhouette of his grandmother Teresa playing solitaire in the yellow sitting room ("You're mistaken, young man, there's no woman in an armoire here. I don't know where you got that idea from"); himself as a child, his finger caressing the delicate curve along which, twenty or so years later, he would plant his kisses.

"No! No! The worst of all, my dear, was not the discovery in itself, however terrible it may seem, but the fact that, ironically, we have never really seen their faces. We look, but we don't see. It's absurd, but that's the way it is, you know, all the more so with Turkish women, who are obliged to wear a veil, however beautiful they are . . ."

(That was why it all seemed so familiar: the Lilies, which was so like Number 38, the platinum blond hair of the girl in the picture, just like Adela's hair, despite the difference in age . . .)

"Are you listening, my dear? You look tired."

"Not at all, Mr. Stephanopolous. Do go on, please."

The brooch on Adela's dress glowed, prompting a thousand questions. Yet urgent as those questions were, they would have to wait until the party was over. Then I'll be able to get it all straightened out, thought Carlos while the rocking glasses, like a drunken oracle, reminded him of something Nestor had said earlier that afternoon: "A word of advice, *cazzo* Carlitos. There are times in life when it's best not to ask questions, especially when you suspect you'd be better off not knowing the answers."

"And what, might I ask, is your problem, young man?"

Mr. Stephanopolous had interrupted his historical disquisition, surprised by the way Carlos was standing there, too close to Adela, as if he were participating in the conversation, a waiter with a trayful of glasses brazenly listening in on the guests.

"We have our drinks, young man, and no doubt you have other guests to attend to. So off you go."

At the sound of Stephanopolous's voice, Carlos snapped out of his reverie. He hardly dared look at Adela, as if he were frightened the others would guess his secret. Apologizing, he began to move away, but as he did, he noticed a miniature green scimitar in the dagger collector's buttonhole, facing Adela's green cameo like a reflection in a pond. Of course it might not be the same cameo. What if it was just a coincidence, another one of old Madame Longstaffe's tricks? They say there's always a catch to her prophecies.

Carlos walked away, trying not to look back, but his incredulity got the better of him. He stole a glimpse of Adela chatting with the knife collector, and even from a distance he could see the two pieces of jewelry, the cameo and the scimitar, face-to-face, precious and cold, like the insignia of an opulent world that for him was full of enigmas. You're such a hick, he said to himself. Maybe in the old days jewels were unique pieces, but now they're mass-produced. You idealize these rich people because they live in a world that is foreign to you, but there must be hundreds of green cameos and hundreds of green scimitars like the one that snooty Greek is wearing.

Carlos swung around. The glasses clinking on his tray, some full, others half empty, put an end to his reassuring reflections. Don't be a fool. It's her; it has to be. The resemblance is too strong. What I have to do now is find out what the link is between her and Number 38. I wonder if she knew my grandmother. Or my father? Nestor will be amazed when I tell him. It's weird. Like destiny was winking at me or something . . .

⸻

AT THAT VERY moment, Chloe was being subjected to a bit of winking, not by destiny but by Liau Chi, the collector of ghost stories.

"Come over here for a minute, young man," she said, and commandeered Chloe, steering her into a corner of the sitting room.

"What's your name? How old are you? What's your star sign? Aries? Or maybe Capricorn? Do you like ghost stories? Do you believe in reincarnation? Did you know that those who die young always find some way of coming back to earth and living out the part of their lives that destiny denied them?"

Uh-oh, off the planet, thought Chloe, trying to slip away. She was feeling hot under the tight collar of the waiter's uniform, and the madwoman from the East thought she was a guy and was trying to make a fucking pass at her, when all she wanted to do was look for her brother.

All through the meal, as she was serving the guests, Chloe kept trying to find Eddie's eyes in the various mirrors at the Lilies, the eyes she thought she had glimpsed for a moment in the bathroom mirror when she was getting dressed. She searched for them unsuccessfully in the tall mirrors of the dining room, a round mirror in the entrance hall, and any shiny surface she could find. Between dessert and coffee she even disappeared for a few minutes, bounding up the stairs to her room over the garage, hoping that she might be able to relive the experience of a few hours before.

Eddie, are you there?

The face looking back at her from all the mirrors was certainly similar to Eddie's, but the eyes were hers, as blue as ever.

What the fuck did you expect? You're losing it, girl. You're not going to find Eddie around here, so stop being an ass, she told herself. Yet on her way back to the party, she kept looking in all the mirrors, and in every one she was alone.

IN THE LIBRARY, Chloe stopped to stare into the mirror on the console beside the fireplace, trying to catch even the faintest glimpse of those dark eyes, but all she could see was the pale face of Liau Chi, expert in ghost lore.

"Don't think I'm going to let you slip away this time, now that I've found you again, young man. Are you listening to me? I have something very important to tell you, but before getting into astrology, I need another whiskey. So go and bring me one right away, will you?"

On the way to the kitchen, Chloe continued her futile search, peering into still more mirrors. She begged the mirror in the entrance hall: Please, let me see something, a shadow, even if it isn't real. And she lingered in front of the dark glass of the windows, hoping their vague, deceptive reflections, so conducive to illusion, might grant her what the other mirrors had refused.

"Psst . . . psst, Miss Trias."

Only one person in the world ever called her that. Still searching for her brother among the reflections, she recognized the face of Nestor Chaffino, who was standing at the swinging kitchen door, gesturing.

The cook retreated, then reappeared a moment later, beckoning with an air of urgency. It isn't good form for a cook to leave the kitchen, except for the ritual of greeting the guests and being congratulated on the meal. Nestor had just been through that formality, so now he had to stay at his post; but he needed help.

"Come here. It'll only take a second, then you can go on with what you were doing."

Chloe was happy to escape from the guests, a bunch of weirdos. It's like a madhouse here, she thought as she walked over to Nestor with her trayful of empty glasses.

"How can I help you, Nestor?"

They went into the kitchen together and Nestor pointed to the cool room, or rather to a very high shelf above its metal door.

"Some idiot had the bright idea of putting the detergent up there. Can you see it? Bring a chair over and get it down for me, will you."

Up she went. The metal door reflected the silhouette of a girl on a makeshift stepladder.

The unreachable shelf was filthy. Old rat-bait boxes, bottles of turpentine, and various cleaning products were stacked there in disarray, under a dense mat of spiderwebs that anyone would have thought twice about disturbing: it looked like the refuge of something sinister. Shifting a bottle, Chloe saw a scurrying multitude of those little black creatures she remembered from her childhood: when you touched them, they would roll up into balls. Thousands of tiny legs, and round, moist-looking carapaces running for cover in some dark corner while one, blinded by the light, boldly climbed up Chloe's hand, heading for the darkness of her cuff. But none of this, neither the musty smell nor the cold tickle on her skin, seemed to bother her, because on the way up to that shelf, when she glimpsed her reflection in the shiny surface of the Westinghouse cool room, for a fraction of a second Chloe thought she saw the dark flash of her brother's gaze. And she shut her eyes, trying to hold on to that vision.

"What *are* you doing, Chloe? Higher, just reach up and get it. What are you stopping there for, staring at yourself like an idiot? Come on, that's quite enough messing around. I haven't got all night."

But Chloe didn't move or dare open her eyes, because she knew that when she did, Eddie would have disappeared again forever, gone back to Neverland. The insect had climbed up to her shoulder now. The detergent Nestor wanted was just a few centimeters farther along on that filthy, slimy shelf, but in spite of her boss's impatience and the voice of Miss Liau Chi, who had just come into the kitchen looking for her ("Come back here, young man. I have something to tell you, something you'll be very interested to hear, I assure you"), she remained perfectly still until, finally, that absurd pose became impossible to maintain and she reached out and grasped what she had been asked to fetch. When she looked at herself in the mirror-like door of the cool room on the way down, she was forced to admit once again that it had all been a fantasy: her eyes were hopelessly, unequivocally blue.

"Come here, young man. We need to have a little chat, you and I," insisted Miss Liau Chi.

4

A DOOR SHUTS

THREE-THIRTY IN the morning and all the guests had finally gone home. Good-bye, Mr. Stephanopolous, we'll be in touch . . . Thank you, Mr. Teldi. Yes, see you soon. And thank you, Mrs. Teldi. It's been a pleasure to talk with a woman of your intelligence. I did enjoy our little chat about Atatürk. Your remarks were so penetrating . . . Good-bye, Monsieur Pitou. Thank you for coming . . . Good night, Miss Liau Chi . . .

The voices had faded away, the lights had gone out, and, all alone in the kitchen, Nestor supposed he was the only person in the house still awake. He always liked to take a moment to savor his culinary triumphs in solitude, like an artist reliving his moments of glory or a lover indulgently recalling each detail of an amorous encounter, sometimes enjoying the memory more than the experience itself. The texture of my lobster salad was just perfect, thought Nestor, glowing with pleasure. Absolutely spot on: not too hot, not too cold; not too hard, not too soft. When I looked out from the kitchen and saw the smooth motion of Ernesto Teldi's mustache, I knew it was superlative.

⤚

UPSTAIRS, AT THAT very moment, beads of cold sweat were gathering in Teldi's mustache. Suddenly, he sat up in bed. It wasn't the usual nightmares. Lying there unable to get to sleep, he had just come to a decision. The time has come, he said to himself. It has to be tonight. It isn't sensible to let this sort of thing drag on; I'll go and have it out with him right now. Ernesto Teldi looked at his watch and guessed that the cook would be sleeping in his room up in the attic, a little room tucked away up there where no one would hear anything. Just as well.

⤚

OH, MY SEA bass with potato and dill soufflé, thought Nestor Chaffino fondly, not up in his attic room but down in the kitchen still, with his elbows on the big Formica table that had played its modest part in his success. When I went out to be congratulated by the guests, Adela Teldi declared that never in her life had she tasted a dish of such simple sophistication. What a splendid way of putting it!

⤚

AT THAT VERY moment, Adela gently touched her lips, then reached out and did the same to Carlos, who was sleeping next to her, as if she were trying to pass on a secret that she had not dared to put into words. She had sworn that as soon as they were alone together, she would tell him everything that had happened in Buenos Aires, so he would hear it from her rather than Nestor, and yet when the party was finally over and they were alone in Carlos's little attic room, neither of them said a word. A couple of times she had felt that Carlos was on the point of asking her something, but when two bodies are so hungry for each other, words are out of place.

I'll tell him tomorrow, tomorrow, I promise, thought Adela between feverish kisses.

But when the fever had abated, and her well-preserved but middle-aged body lay still in Carlos's youthful embrace, Adela Teldi reconsidered. Love, she thought, is so complex, so delicate, this love at any rate . . . Perhaps it would be better not to put it to the test with confessions and secrets. I have to talk with that cook, buy his silence if necessary, beg him if I have to . . . There's no alternative, my dear, she said to herself, smiling. You have to make sure he keeps quiet, no matter the cost, whatever it takes. At your age you can't afford to let anyone spoil this chance of happiness . . . The ship has gone down, and you're clinging to a plank, holding on for dear life. Adela kissed her lover's forehead. He was sleeping the deep sleep of the young, which was lucky. He wouldn't be able to hear what happened when she went into Nestor's room down the corridor.

⌒

AND AS FOR my mousseline sauce, thought Nestor in the kitchen, sighing with an artist's pleasure and a lover's devotion, only sensitive and melancholic souls like Serafin Tous can fully appreciate that smooth, rounded flavor, with just the slightest hint of lemon. During his little speech to the guests, Nestor had smiled knowingly at Serafin as he mentioned the mousseline, and a look of tormented ecstasy had come over the judge's face. One needs to have a feminine sensibility to appreciate certain flavors, thought Nestor. I don't expect Mr. Tous's friends are aware of that side of his personality, and they probably wouldn't care for it. But his little secret is absolutely safe with me. Not just because we met at Freshman's and it would be unprofessional to pass on information about a colleague's clients, but also because I won't hear a word against a man who knows his mousseline sauce.

⁓

03:47, *CLICK* . . . 03:48. The phosphorescent numbers on Serafin Tous's alarm clock flipped over implacably, like the artful drip-drop of Chinese water torture, like the leaves of a calendar mercilessly marking the passage of time and the approach of a dreaded day. Unable to sleep, Serafin decided to get up. The night was black, conducive to melancholy, but also to wild thoughts. Where could that miserable individual be sleeping, he wondered. That slanderer, that gossiping cook. Serafin didn't know the house, but he imagined that the rooms for the domestic staff would be up in the attic, so he headed that way. He didn't switch on the light. He groped his way in the dark, so when he passed the armoire mirror, he was spared a surprising sight: in the eyes of this placid gentleman who wouldn't hurt a fly there was a gleam as hard and sharp as a stiletto.

⁓

AND WHAT ABOUT my splendid chocolate truffles! thought Nestor, going over it all again, like a lover remembering and reliving every move, every caress. Never have nuances of flavor been so masterfully blended, if I say so myself: vanilla, bitter chocolate, liqueur, a touch of ginger. That's the trick. The ginger is the secret ingredient that makes a really good chocolate truffle. Though of course only the cognoscenti can tell, the few who are capable of analyzing such a magnificent symphony of flavors. That's why I got so cross with young Chloe when she put two truffles in her mouth at once. Two truffles! "Let me tell you something, Miss Trias," I said to her. "Only a person possessed of two souls could appreciate the full range of flavors in two of Nestor Chaffino's truffles. Do you have any idea . . . ?" But she just said *Fuck that* or *Bullshit* or one of her other favorite expressions. With such a limited vocabulary, what kind of inner life can she have? That's the problem with the young these days, thought Nestor sadly. I bet right now her dreams are full of heavy-metal music or something equally brainless and vulgar.

⁓

BUT NESTOR WAS mistaken, for as it happened, Chloe Trias was dreaming of her boss's chocolate truffles in the room she was sharing with Karel over the garage. And like a sensitive soul—or, rather, two sensitive souls—she was savoring the memory of that hint of ginger and the sweet vanilla, summoning up the delicious aroma of the liqueur. Yet this sophisticated

gastronomical fantasy, which would have come as a great surprise to Nestor, did not last long. It was quickly displaced by
other dream fragments, in rapid and fluid succession, as often
happens when one is falling asleep. A couple of Pearl Jam songs
went through her mind, combined with an erotic memory fea-
turing the very tasty Karel Pligh, who was lying asleep beside
her. Then, in the garden of the Lilies, she saw a cockroach on a
doormat, reflected in a mirror, while Miss Liau Chi whispered
in her ear: "Do you believe in ghosts?" All this was quickly
swept away by a rush of other, equally incoherent images, but
after a couple of minutes of this turbulent dreaming, Chloe
woke up and lay there, tossing and turning, unable to get back
to sleep. Shit, she thought, now I'll probably be awake all night
like a fucking owl. Periodically, light from one of the lamps
shining on the facade of the Lilies burst into the room like the
beam of a lighthouse. While the room was briefly illuminated,
Chloe looked at Karel, then across at her pack, which was sitting on a chair, spilling its contents like a torn rag doll. The
room was plunged in darkness again, and Chloe remembered
how she had panicked before the dinner when she couldn't
find her maid's uniform. That was why her stuff was in such a
mess: T-shirts, a bikini, underwear . . . everything except the
case where she kept the framed photo of her brother. That red
case never left the bottom of her backpack, but the rest of her
things, lying scattered around the room, looked like ghosts
from one of Miss Liau Chi's books. Crazy old Chinese cow,
thought Chloe. She's supposed to hang out with ghosts and see
dead people and stuff, and she couldn't even tell I was a girl. As
if I looked like a fucking guy, she thought, before realizing

that in a way she had fooled herself, too: it was because she had dressed as a man that, for a few seconds, she thought she had seen Eddie's eyes in her reflection.

She tried to go back to sleep. Maybe tonight she'd be lucky and dream that her brother was coming to take her away to Neverland, like before. Come on, Eddie, come and play for a while, she said like a little girl, but instead, a pair of memories came to haunt her sleeplessness: the moleskin notebook Nestor always kept hidden in the pocket of his chef's jacket and the delicious flavor of his chocolate truffles. The truffles must have been put away in the Westinghouse cool room in the kitchen, she thought, the one that has a shiny metal door like a fun-house mirror.

Chloe kept tossing and turning, cursing her insomnia. She couldn't get to sleep, but each time she came close, pleasant thoughts began to stream through her mind, like the memory of Eddie's smile, the smile she thought she'd seen a few hours ago. And she could swear a voice was speaking to her, saying, Come on, Clo-Clo, come down; here I am. But she was wary. She was afraid of going down to the kitchen and being disappointed again. This time she wouldn't find her brother's eyes looking back from the cool-room door. He was just playing games with her again, like he used to when he was alive and she would ask him: "What are you writing, Eddie? It's a story with adventures and romance and crimes and stuff, isn't it? Can I read it?" And he would reply: "Not now, Clo-Clo. Later on, I promise."

But he was lying. There was no "later on," because her brother got it into his head that he had to live fast, since he wanted to be a writer and nothing worth writing about had happened to him yet. And in pursuit of that stupid fantasy, he had gone away forever and left her on her own.

Insomnia hatches strange ideas. Normally, Chloe wouldn't have thought of going down to the kitchen, much less looking for her brother's eyes in the cool room door. Chloe was a sensible girl at heart, and she wouldn't normally have risked another disappointment: having to admit that her brother was playing hide-and-seek with her. But insomnia is not sensible. Come on, Chloe, it said to her, a chocolate truffle is just what you need. It's well known that chocolate helps you go to sleep. Come on, don't be frightened. If you're scared, all you have to do is avoid looking at the door. It's a deceptive, distorting mirror, like the ones they have in amusement parks: it plays tricks on you, hurtful tricks sometimes, but you can just ignore it. Although, if you decide to be brave and look . . . who knows?

When the garden lamp shone into the room again, Chloe jumped to her feet. She was naked, and two items of clothing lay strewn on the chair: Choose me, said a T-shirt on which was written PIERCE MY TONGUE, NOT MY HEART. No, choose *me,* insisted the plain waiter's jacket, with its button-up collar, the jacket she had worn that night, pretending to be a boy. And, as if she were Alice in Wonderland again, Chloe hesitated before finally deciding on the jacket.

Ah, what the fuck's it matter, she thought as she put it on. I'm just going down to get a chocolate truffle, I'm not going to be looking at myself in any mirrors.

IT WAS FOUR in the morning. That was the time on each of
the characters' watches. The wall clock in the kitchen was
running slightly slow and still hadn't chimed. That old Festina
clock, clouded over with steam and smoke, looked down on
Nestor, who, suddenly realizing how late it was, roused himself from his pleasant reverie and, as if addressing a friend,
said: Okay, old mate, you've had a wonderful day, a tiring one
too, so it's time you toddled off to bed.

Which is what he was about to do when something caught
his eye.

"Oh sugar!" he exclaimed. He had forgotten to put the
boxes of leftover chocolate truffles back in the cool room. That
wasn't like him at all.

The kitchen clock struck four as Nestor opened the door of
the Westinghouse cool room.

ERNESTO TELDI'S WATCH was very quiet; it didn't even tick.
But it had a luminous face, which glowed in the dark as he
climbed the stairs, heading for Nestor's attic room. Serafin
Tous's Omega did not have this feature, so nothing, not even a
phosphorescent dot, revealed his whereabouts as he tiptoed in
the darkness, which was periodically illuminated by the beam
of the lamp sweeping across the facade of the Lilies, shining in
through one of the windows onto the stairs. Both Teldi and
Serafin waited for the darkness to return so that they could
move without being seen.

IT WAS FOUR A.M. on Adela's watch, too, but she had left it on Carlos's bedside table, beside the green cameo, so its luminous face hadn't witnessed her quick steps across the landing from Carlos's room to Nestor's. Nestor had been given the largest of the attic rooms: a very nice bedroom with two doors, one opening onto the stairs and the other leading to the rest of the servants' quarters. Adela Teldi came in through the second of these doors, a few minutes ahead of the other night visitors. She entered without knocking; in circumstances such as these, etiquette is inappropriate. What? she thought. No one here? She took a few steps in the dark, then the lamp beam shone into the room and revealed that it was empty, the bed untouched. Maybe he's in the bathroom, she thought, and sat down to wait. Two simultaneous noises made her start. It's him, he's coming. My God, what am I doing here? As Adela prepared herself, both doors opened at once and the silhouettes of two men entered stealthily. Yet neither shape was Nestor Chaffino, so when the light shone through the windows of the attic room again, three faces looked at one another in amazement, and, like a startled and out-of-tune choir, the voices of Adela, Ernesto Teldi, and Serafin Tous demanded in unison:

"What are *you* doing here?"

"What about you?"

"And you?"

⁓

OF THE CHARACTERS in this story, Karel Pligh was not the only music lover. He was not the only one who sang to express his state of mind. "C'est trop beau" is a pretty song. It's not a tarantella or a Neapolitan folk song, but when it came to choosing a tune to accompany a pleasant task, Nestor was no chauvinist; he didn't restrict himself to the repertoire of his beloved Italy. So the following scene unfolds to the tune of "C'est trop beau." Nestor was about to put the boxes of truffles away in the cool room. He had stacked ten boxes on the table and he was going into the Westinghouse to put them against the wall at the back, where they wouldn't get in the way. *"C'est trop beau notre aventure / c'est trop beau pour être heureux . . ."* The light from the kitchen did not reach far into the dark interior, where the frozen bodies of game animals were dimly visible—rabbits or hares, maybe even a small deer—but Nestor preferred not to investigate further. *"C'est trop beau pour que ça dure / plus longtemps qu'un soir d'été."* He had forgotten the rest of the words, so he continued whistling the tune and amused himself with this joyful rendition for a few seconds before going back out to get the rest of the boxes. Just a few seconds: the space of a breath, but some breaths last an eternity.

⌇

WHEN CHLOE CAME into the kitchen, she stopped in her tracks for a moment. Then she saw that the door of the cool room was open and heard a happy whistle emerging from within. As she approached she could hear noises, as if someone were in there moving things around. But it was a different sound that attracted her, drawing her toward the shiny metal surface. It seemed that the trick mirror was speaking to her: "Here I am, Clo-Clo. Come over here, don't be a coward. Come on."

The whistle from the cool room sounded joyful. How could anyone extinguish such a happy, innocent whistle? But that's silly. Chloe wasn't going to kill anyone; she just didn't want to miss her chance again. She was convinced that Eddie had told her to come downstairs and that he would be looking at her from the other side of the mirror. So, to see Eddie's eyes in her reflection, Chloe had to move the door. Not shut it, just give it a bit of a push. You're not going to trick me this time, are you, Eddie? You'll be there when I look, won't you? And sure enough, when she dared to look, for a moment Chloe saw her brother's unmistakable dark eyes in her own reflection. She couldn't help reaching out toward those eyes, which seemed to be smiling and asking for a kiss. And as she leaned against the cold surface, the door swung shut with a *click*.

"Bloody brilliant, but it *can't* be true," said Nestor, since incredulity often precedes fear, and then: "But for the love of God, I can't have been in here more than two minutes, three at the most, stacking away these boxes of frozen chocolate truffles."

The following minutes went by in a blur, both inside and outside the cool room. A blur for Nestor, who started beating on the door with his hands and then his feet. Holy Virgin of Loreto, Merciful Mother of God, Santa Maria Goretti, and Don Bosco . . . I forgot to pull down the bolt so the door couldn't swing shut. Meanwhile, outside, Chloe was thinking: There must be a way. There has to be a way I can make Eddie stay longer, instead of playing this cruel hide-and-seek. What can I do to make you stay forever? What game do you want to play?

⁓

LET'S SEE. I have to keep calm and think straight. Who could help me? Who's left in the house? wondered Nestor on the other side of the metal door. There's Karel and Carlos, and then four others I'm not so sure about: Ernesto and Adela Teldi, young Chloe Trias, and of course Serafin Tous. Nestor called out their names:

"Tous! Teldi! Trias!"

But the cold was gradually becoming unbearable, making his teeth chatter, so his tongue stumbled over the Ts and all that came out was an indistinct stuttering.

⁓

CHLOE TRIAS WAS holding her hands over her ears. I heard you, I heard you, just be quiet, please, she said, not out loud or in her usual tone of voice but mentally, the way she talked to her brother. She had to do it silently like that, it was crucial, otherwise her imaginary world might evaporate. So with that mute voice in her head, she begged the prisoner to wait a moment. Just a moment, Nestor. I can't open the door now. You have to understand—he'd disappear forever. And Chloe couldn't let that happen; it would be too stupid to let him go away again like on that afternoon when he set off in search of emotions, barely twenty-two years old, the age she would reach very soon.

This time the magic of the mirror promised to be more generous and lasting, so to make the most of it, she decided to replay what had happened on that last afternoon, in the hope of changing the ending. Tell me a story, she begged, as she had done years before, adding something she should have said then but hadn't: Don't go. Please, please don't go. Stay with me. And this time her brother's dark eyes seemed to be smiling at her, although he said nothing. Or maybe he *was* saying something. Staring into his eyes, her eyes, Chloe could see a kind of anger in them, like the rage welling up in her, and she refused to believe that death could snatch away a young life just like that, with all its promises unfulfilled. What happens to all those dreams and plans canceled by death? They can't simply disappear. They must go somewhere.

⁓

THE BANGING ON the other side of the door interrupted Chloe's speculations and reminded her of the chef. He's such a bore, she thought. Just shut up, unless you want me to leave you in there for good. Maybe you could work this one out for me: Is there a way of fulfilling a destiny that death has cut short?

But Chloe was talking to herself, so no one could hear or help her, least of all Nestor, who could feel the cold gradually numbing his will and his mind, dulling all his senses. Which is why he had come up with an original form of insulation, to stop the icy torment creeping into his skull. Somehow, he needed to block off all his bodily orifices, to stop the ache driving him crazy. Santa Madonna de Alexandria. He had managed to get his moleskin notebook from the pocket of his jacket, the little book in which he had recorded a wealth of trade secrets: so many little indiscretions jotted down in his tiny hand. Don't give up, Nestor. You have to stop your brain freezing. The paper will block out the cold and keep your mind from seizing up. That's all you can do for the moment. And destroy an irreplaceable collection of dessert recipes? Worse still, you'd be destroying all the secret details of those . . . little indiscretions. Now, there's proof your neurons are freezing up, you old fool. What use is all that to you now? Come on, it's going to be all right. Remember what the witch said: "You have nothing to fear until four *T*s conspire against you." And that's impossible, so don't give up. Keep banging on the door. Someone's bound to hear.

~

CHLOE WAS ABOUT to open the door.

Okay, okay, for fuck's sake, she said to herself. So I have to risk losing Eddie again because of some old fool. Doesn't he realize that as soon as the mirror moves, Eddie's eyes will disappear? You'll go away, won't you, Eddie? Like you always do, leaving me on my own. You'll say you have to go off somewhere to look for some stupid story like you did that afternoon, and I won't be able to stop you. That's what ghosts do, isn't it? They repeat what they did on the last day of their life? Over and over, forever. That's what Miss Liau Chi was telling me, something like that. Or was it that people who die young find a way of coming back to finish off the destiny that death cut short? Now Chloe dearly wished she had paid more attention to what Liau Chi had said, though it had sounded like bullshit at the time. She wished she could turn back the clock, rewind and listen to the ghost lady's mad theories again, but all she could hear was Nestor's banging and his muffled shouts.

He was kicking now. And she was confused: it wasn't a ghost; it was coming from inside, and the door was shaking, so the image blurred and she could hardly see her brother's eyes.

"Nothing's going to happen to me," said Nestor, trying to convince himself, just a few centimeters away in the darkest and iciest of hells. I'll come through this; I know. I just have to stay calm until someone hears me. And someone will, because somewhere here, near the door, thought the cook, feeling around in the dark, there's an alarm bell, and with all this banging I must have pressed the button. And when they hear it, one of them is bound to come and save me: Teldi, Tous, Trias, T . . .

If I could turn back the clock, find an explanation . . . sooner or later, people who die young come back to accomplish their destiny . . . the things they left unfinished. All these confused thoughts seemed to be swimming on the dark surface of the shiny door, which shook as Nestor thumped it, while Chloe stared at the blurry image until it all seemed to come clear, as if a brilliant solution were written there, in unequivocal letters, for her to read.

And now that she knew exactly what to do next, she burst out laughing.

Laughter. On the other side of the door, Nestor clearly
heard someone laughing. My God, there's someone out there,
and that means it wasn't an accident, he thought, launching
into a panicky deduction. That's when he noticed the three
names beginning with T (and counting two Teldis, that made
four Ts). Madame Longstaffe's words came back to him: "Nestor
has nothing to fear until . . ."

. . . And they're all here, the four of them together, just as the
witch foresaw, no doubt about it, he thought with the lucidity
of those who are about to die. Teldi, Teldi, Tous, Trias: four Ts.
Why didn't I see it before? I'm such an idiot. The cold felt
thick and heavy, pressing in from all sides, filling his lungs. In
his mouth it had the bitter taste of poison. He wanted to let
go. There was no point struggling now, but the cold had not
yet extinguished the last flicker of reason in his mind. Wait a
minute, hold on; there's something that doesn't make sense.
Why would those four want to hurt you? You of all people:
you've always been a model of discretion. You've never med-
dled with other people's lives.

Absurdly, he could feel a sneeze coming on, rising and rising: *Achoo!* The paper he had stuffed in his ears felt as if it were
exploding in his head. All those little indiscretions, those little
secrets, trying to escape, he thought with a shudder. Of course,
that's it, *cazzo.* You know their shameful secrets: an adulterous
affair that led to a death . . . cries in the night . . . an unspeakable desire . . . Adela Teldi, Ernesto Teldi, Serafin Tous . . . they
all seem so respectable, but you know what they're ashamed of.
And that's enough to get you locked in a cool room with someone laughing on the other side of the door.

The cold kept pressing in, turning Nestor's fingers into claws gripping the notebook. Those claws would never straighten out again, nor would his legs, which had turned to ice and lost all feeling, so Nestor hardly noticed when they buckled and let his rigid trunk drop to the floor of the cool room. His mind, however, felt as if it were boiling, and with the blind hope of the dying, he thought: Hang on, it'll be all right. It can't happen like this. Listen, it can't, because the prophecy hasn't been completely fulfilled. I know shameful secrets about three of them, not about all four. I know Ernesto's story, and Adela's and Serafin's, but the fourth *T,* Chloe, what can she have against me? She hasn't done anything shameful, as far as I know, so why would she join the conspiracy?

Another laugh. On the other side of the door, Chloe laughed again, but under her breath, so it sounded to Nestor like a sort of fizzing, or a whisper, like a series of *TTTTTTTTTT*s promising that all would be well.

"There are only three *T*s, three *T*s, three *T*s . . ." he said, repeating himself like a frightened child. Good old Madame Longstaffe made it perfectly clear: my time has not yet come, so I'll get out of this pinch. Hang in there a bit longer, old mate, just a bit longer. The door will open. Hang on.

And then Nestor Chaffino heard the lifesaving *click.*

You see? I told you it would be all right in the end. Madame Longstaffe may be a crooked old witch, but even crooked prophesies are bound by the laws of fate, and there were only three secrets this time.

Every muscle in my body is frozen, thought the cook as he heard the door begin to open. Holy Mary, Mother of God,

Santa Gemma, and Don Bosco, I can't move a finger, but my brain is still working perfectly. It's okay. It's over now. A *click*, and then another *click*.

Not a moment too soon; just when the cold was getting to me, filling my head with stupid thoughts and fears.

5

A RAY OF SUNLIGHT ON
NESTOR CHAFFINO'S BODY BAG

A SERENDIPITOUS ACCIDENT, thought Ernesto Teldi, alone in his room at the Lilies. Several hours had passed since they had all gathered around Nestor's body in the kitchen. The police had spoken with each person present after dusting the door of the Westinghouse cool room for finger-prints, which, as one might have guessed, was next to useless given the number of prints they found. Nestor's for a start, brown from the chocolate, then those of Carlos, Karel, and Chloe (lots of Chloe's), and finally a smaller number of prints left by Adela, Serafin, and Ernesto. "It's what you'd expect in this sort of case," said the detective, scribbling in his notebook. "You were all in the kitchen yesterday. Now, what we need to know is whether any of you saw anything suspicious that might help us in our investigation."

But they all remained silent, because the only thing that

might have been considered suspicious, that is, the sheet of paper Nestor had been clutching, on which was written:

especially delicious with cappucci
lso be served with a raspberry coul
which prevents the mering
not to be confused with frozen chocolate
but rather with iced lemon

was sleeping innocently between the pages of the chef's copy of Brillat-Savarin, while Karel, the only one of them who might have remembered that piece of paper and linked it with the death of his friend, was not trying to solve the mystery but admiring the serene beauty of Chloe's face. Somehow that morning she seemed more mature, as if she had suddenly grown out of the PIERCE MY TONGUE, NOT MY HEART T-shirt she had just put on.

The kitchen was empty again. The police and the magistrate had finished their investigation, concluding that the death was due to a household accident, an unfortunate bit of carelessness. "There's nothing more we can do here. They can take the body away now." Looking out of his bedroom window, Teldi was dazzled by the unseasonably strong sun reflected off the shiny plastic body bag in which Nestor was being transported. He watched the bag proceed toward the garden gate, carried on a stretcher by two men in green coats. Resting on the dead man's feet (or perhaps on his head) was a bunch of flowers that had been cut and gathered at Ernesto Teldi's request. A naïve observer interpreting this as a kind gesture on the part of a thoughtful employer would not, in fact, have been too far from the truth. If it was not kindness exactly that prompted Teldi to have the bouquet made up, it was at least a kind of elegance: when an enemy abandons the field, or, better still, has the good manners to die before one is obliged to kill him, the very least one can do is send him off with a tribute.

Roses, wisteria, petunias . . . a simple but elegant bouquet, he thought, watching the flowers bob up and down on the mortal remains of his enemy. He even found the scene rather moving. It had a certain grandeur that reminded him of his treasured works of art, and in particular his most recent acquisition.

He moved away from the window, reached into his pocket, took out the love letter he had bought from Monsieur Pitou the previous evening, and examined it. There could be no doubt: it was definitely Oscar Wilde's handwriting, his signature, his particular way of writing the letter *C*. All the signs were there, clear as day. How could I ever have thought, even for a moment, that it was a fake? he wondered, genuinely surprised. Because now that Nestor was dead, Ernesto Teldi could hardly even remember the inexplicable and uncharacteristic attack of insecurity he had suffered the previous evening, when he had started to panic, imagining that his colleagues might be trying to cheat him. Him of all people! How absurd! Who would dare? Teldi was a highly reputed collector and so he would remain until his dying day. His credentials were impeccable . . . The insecurity he had felt seemed remote to him now, as remote as the possibility that his reputation could have been threatened by that cook, who was now being carried off in a body bag as if he were wrapped in foil. All that worrying, the cold sweats, the terrible thoughts that had passed through his mind for a couple of hours; it all seemed like a bad dream. As distant and harmless as the screams he heard each night in his sleep.

How neatly it has all worked out, thought Teldi with a smile. Had he believed in such things, he might have attributed his good fortune to the helping hand of a sardonic god with a fine aesthetic sensibility. But Ernesto Teldi didn't believe in gods, not even sardonic ones with aesthetic sensibilities; he believed only in himself, and that was why he had the bouquet made up, to congratulate Nestor, and himself, on such a happy (and sensible) ending.

The funeral procession was already approaching the gate of the property. Ernesto slipped Oscar Wilde's letter lovingly back into his pocket, giving it a little pat. Life had to go on and things were looking up: tomorrow he'd be flying to Switzerland for a meeting of collectors at the Thyssens' house. Next week he was off to London to do a difficult valuation (who else could they rely on?), and next month the Gulbenkian Foundation would be rendering him a well-deserved little tribute. Life is sweet, thought Ernesto, unable to resist the cliché, and he was so absorbed in his pleasant meditation that at first he didn't hear the knocking at the door.

⁓

"THERE'S A MAN downstairs who would like to talk with you," said Karel Pligh when Teldi finally opened the door.

But Teldi was still imagining delicious projects and triumphs, so rather than rushing down, he gazed over the boy's head, appreciating the tasteful décor of the stairwell. It really was quite charming: the curtains gave off a subtle fragrance of lavender, while the yellow walls of the landing provided the ideal backdrop for a set of beautiful still-life paintings. Perfect, just perfect.

"What is it about, young man?" he asked, returning (how dreary!) to mundane matters for a moment. "Don't tell me there are more policemen, I'm thoroughly sick of men in uniforms."

But Karel Pligh said he didn't think it was a policeman.

"He must be about seventy, an ordinary-looking man, and he's insisting on seeing you today. Of course I didn't let him in just like that. I told him to wait at the door, so he wrote this note (it was very hard for him—his fingers are all twisted), and he said he was sure that when you read it, you'd want to see him immediately."

Karel was not familiar with Teldi's refined ways, so he had not used the little mail tray to deliver the note. He was holding it in his hand, and his fingernails were not quite as clean as the collector might have wished. But Ernesto didn't notice these details, nor did he pay any attention to what Karel told him about the stranger's appearance, because as soon as he saw the writing on that card, he was mesmerized by the green, scribbly letters that seemed to be peering back at him like a row of parrots on a wire.

IT WAS NOT by chance that the rooms occupied by Carlos and Adela at the Lilies were one above the other. Yet the walls and floors were so thick that no sound filtered through, making it impossible even to guess what was going on up- or downstairs. Had it not been so, Adela and Carlos would have been surprised to discover that while Nestor's body was going out through the gate of the Lilies for the last time, they were simultaneously performing the same actions in their respective rooms, like a pair of dancers following the same choreography.

At the same moment both came to their windows to bid the cook a last good-bye and then leaned pensively on the sill. Yet although their movements were the same, their motives were quite different. Carlos was moved by sorrow, Adela by relief, one might almost say gratitude.

Suddenly a ray of sunlight struck the body bag and the reflection was so dazzlingly bright that Adela had to step back. Take a good look, Adela, she said to herself. Don't turn away. There goes the last obstacle to your happiness. Take a good hard look, the way you looked at his lifeless face in the kitchen before, to make sure that his lips were sealed for good, to be certain that his eyes could never witness your foolish passion again. For better or worse, you're free: the contents of that frozen brain no longer pose any threat to you. However terrible secrets are, they die with the people who keep them. So take a good look, Adela, and thank your lucky stars. This is the first day of the rest of your life.

GOOD-BYE, MY friend, thought Carlos, standing at the window of his attic room, watching the shiny bag as it was carried away, containing a body that had once been Nestor Chaffino. But no longer, because the corpse of a friend is already a stranger. So Carlos had discovered, observing Nestor's face that morning. And as the hours went by, he noticed other changes that confirmed his theory about the transformation of corpses: before long, he could hardly find a trace of his friend in that gray remnant. The head seemed to have shrunk, as if death were an overzealous Jivaro tribesman. Carlos preferred not to kiss the wretched mask—it seemed so alien to Nestor. The death of his father had taught him that memories keep better if they are not associated with the vision of a dead body. The less one looks at the dead the better, because it is hard to erase what the eyes have registered, and those who have spent hours looking at the lifeless face of a loved one often find that image superimposing itself on their fondest memories of the departed. There is no such danger, however, in paying one's respects to an anonymous, shiny body bag. Good-bye, Nestor; good-bye, my friend. And now, if you'll excuse me, I have to start gathering my things.

Even after a death, the living have their chores to do, so Carlos turned from the window to start packing. He looked around at the room he had shared with Adela last night. It didn't feel like his room at all, but why should it? The only things in it that belonged to him were two shirts, a waiter's uniform, and a pair of jeans. Even the objects on the bedside table were not his but hers. Sitting on the unmade bed, Carlos stretched out his hand to pick up the watch Adela had left behind and lifted it to his lips. A lover's belongings are passion's strongest and most faithful allies, often more faithful than their owners. *Tick-tick,* said the clockwork, beating like a heart. Everything will be all right, *tick-tick.* And Carlos put the watch back where he had found it: yes, it would all work out in the end.

Then his fingers encountered the green cameo, which Adela had left behind along with her watch. Carlos had not noticed it before, as it was hidden by various other objects. It was beautiful, it was hers, but somehow he was not inclined to kiss it, perhaps because cameos do not beat like hearts.

⟶

IN A FEW hours' time I'll leave all this behind me, thought Adela, sitting on her unmade bed like Carlos upstairs. Beside her was an old wooden box she had just taken out of the armoire. She opened it. Adela was not a romantic. Throughout her life she had been careful to keep sentimentality out of her love affairs. It's far more sensible; it saves you pain. So for years she had not examined the contents of that box, in which she had piled up letters, passionate words, declarations of love, souvenirs, photos . . . the memories of many, many years. Adela preferred not to look at them, since each letter, each object, represented a piece of her life that was gone forever and each reminded her that the years had fled like her looks, and that she was no longer the woman who had inspired those beautiful words. Beautiful and dead, Adela. All you have is the future. Love while you can. But first . . .

Before leaving it all behind, the Lilies and her memories, Adela had one last thing to tie up. She sat down at the little table in front of the window to write a farewell letter to her husband. A rather nineteenth-century way of doing things, cowardly too, but without doubt the simplest solution. An unwritten but long-standing rule of their marriage enjoined both Ernesto and Adela to avoid all embarrassing displays of emotion, particularly the distasteful and inconvenient sort of scene that would go with announcing one's departure after twenty-something years of convenient cohabitation. So she wrote:

The Lilies, 29th of March

Dear Ernesto

(Then she paused, searching for the right words.)

CARLOS, however, had no difficult letters to write or old memories to say good-bye to. His attention was focused on relics of a much more recent past: the objects Adela had left behind the previous night. What should I do with this? Should I put it in the case with her clothes? Should I take it myself? They had agreed not to leave together. They would meet up later, in Madrid, after a few days, when things had settled down a bit. At the Phoenix Hotel perhaps. That would be wonderful: they could start again where it all began. Carlos looked at his watch and then at Adela's: there was five minutes' difference between the two. No doubt hers was showing the correct time. It was getting late. He picked up the few things that were left, and, last of all, the cameo.

⁓

Dear Ernesto,

I don't know how to begin this letter. You will probably think I have gone mad, or, worse still, that I have turned out to be just as stupid as those deluded, romantic women we used to make fun of.

Adela stopped again, suddenly conscious of her thumbs. A superstitious fear made her check for Hecate's symptom, which always warned her when something bad was about to happen, but she could feel nothing. Relax. Everything is all right. The cook is dead. No one can go delving into your past now.

⁓

AS HE PICKED up the cameo and put it in his pocket, Carlos realized that, since the moment he had seen it pinned to Adela's dress, he hadn't given it another thought. But that was hardly surprising; so much had happened since then, such terrible things. Before putting it away, he wrapped it in his handkerchief. It had an odd glow, but there was no reason to interpret that as a bad omen, he thought. And besides, he should have been grateful, really, because today, or maybe in a few days' time, when they were reunited forever at the Phoenix Hotel, he would be able to ask Adela and find out how that cameo had forged such a beautiful link between them long before they met. "You tell me where you got that cameo, and I'll tell you a story you won't believe." That's what he would say to her, and they would probably end up having a good laugh about the invisible threads that for years had been drawing them toward each other. Even if Adela's cameo isn't the same as the one in the picture, thought Carlos, it's such an odd coincidence; it's enough to make you believe in Madame Longstaffe's prophecies. But it *is* the same cameo. It has to be. I'm sure of it.

⌒

AS IF SENSING the danger, Adela Teldi's fingers tightened on the pen and began to tingle. Without realizing it, she wrote, "By the pricking of my thumbs, something wicked this way comes," in her letter to Ernesto, and then had to cross it out, because it had nothing to do with what she wanted to tell him. Come on, Adela, just forget about those stupid premonitions. You're never going to finish the letter this way, and it's getting late.

⌒

. . . ADELA'S BLOND HAIR, so much like his grandmother's . . . the resemblance between the Lilies and Number 38 . . . a portrait kept in an armoire for years, and the blue eyes of a girl who must have been Adela . . . Carlos had thrust the cameo to the bottom of his pocket, but he couldn't stop thinking about it. He had gathered all his things and was walking across the landing. As he passed the door of Nestor's room (Good-bye, my friend), the thoughts that were troubling him crystallized as questions: Why was the picture of Adela banished from the yellow room? Why did his grandmother forbid his father to enter Number 38? Why had his mother, Soledad, died in Buenos Aires, of all places? And why hadn't he recognized Adela as the girl in the picture when he had been looking for her in every woman he saw?

⁓

SOMETHING WICKED this way comes . . . Now that Carlos had left his room, Adela could hear him walking across the landing upstairs. The steps were young and curious and full of dangerous questions: Who is this woman? What exactly happened? Where and when? Of course she could not actually decipher or even guess what those steps were asking, but her witch's thumbs knew. The prickling was painful now, and it continued until, suddenly, the steps upstairs came to a halt. Who are you? Why? How did it happen? Twinge after twinge as Adela tried to guess why the steps that had sounded so resolute and dangerous a moment before had stopped.

Since Adela was not possessed of Madame Longstaffe's extraordinary powers, which would have been particularly handy for understanding this scene, she would never know that as Carlos went past the door of Nestor's room, his mind a welter of ever more clamorous suspicions, something the cook had said the previous afternoon came back to him. He had already remembered it once, on seeing Adela in the salon of the Lilies, wearing that cameo from the painting: "One day you'll realize, *cazzo* Carlitos" (it was as if Nestor were there, whispering in his ear) "that there are times in life when it's best not to ask questions, especially when you suspect you'd be better off not knowing the answers."

"... SO GOOD-BYE, ERNESTO, I don't expect you to understand," wrote Adela. She was writing fluently, her fingers relaxed now, not a trace of that premonitory prickling. The pen flew over the paper, finishing off the highly conventional, bourgeois farewell letter to her husband: "I'm sorry, believe me. I don't regret a moment of the years we have spent together and I hope you won't either. I wish you all the best and I bid you good-bye with . . ." As she was finishing this sentence, Adela raised her head, as if defiantly, and looked out the window, but being shortsighted, she did not see the object falling from the floor above.

So she would never know that on her last day at the Lilies, just before she walked out and left it all behind, upstairs in Nestor's room Carlos had decided to get rid of the green cameo so that its lustrous sphere, bulging with troublesome questions, would disappear among the various shades of green in the garden of the Lilies. And there it remains to this day, among the leaves and branches, if anyone should care to confirm the veracity of this story.

FROM HIS WINDOW, Serafin Tous also saw Nestor's body taken away, but he didn't have flowers cut, like Ernesto Teldi, nor did he pause to watch the sun sparkling on the shiny body bag, as both Adela and Carlos had done. Rather than observe the goings-on in the garden, the mild-mannered magistrate preferred to busy himself packing his bags. Serafin Tous was intending to leave that day. Nice house, the Lilies, but not the sort of place in which he was inclined to linger—too many unpleasant associations.

Fastidiously, he began to fold his clothes, starting with the trousers, following the method his late wife had taught him, so that they would be impeccable when he got home. He took them from the hangers, checked the alignment of the creases, then packed them away: the blue on the gray and the beige on the blue. But as he was folding the beige pair, he realized that there was still a very noticeable sherry stain at the crotch. That was from yesterday, when Nestor had appeared on the terrace and given him a shock. A silly little accident, nothing serious . . . But it is remarkable, he reflected, how accidents can happen, and just at the right time too, occasionally. He was no longer thinking about his mishap on the terrace but about another, much more serious, and for him much more fortunate, household accident: the door of the cool room happening to swing shut while that bothersome cook was inside. It couldn't have come at a better time, thought Serafin. He realized that death by freezing was no trifling matter, of course not, but he couldn't help wanting to shout: Thank God for household accidents!

Serafin Tous proceeded to pack away his shirts. First he put them into the very practical and handsome covers he had brought with him (one of his late wife's ideas), which he then smoothed and laid in the bottom of the suitcase: there, excellent. Nora would have been proud of him. Household accidents are quite unpredictable, thought Serafin, who was beginning to find this line of thought most reassuring. And they happen all the time, much more often than people think, all sorts of accidents, from disasters to little slipups, often just silly things. Anyone can give himself an electric shock with a toaster or start a fire with a panful of hot oil, say. It can happen to anyone, anyone at all. And yet, as Serafin Tous admired his perfect shirts, he felt a little thrill of pleasure, as if the sight of them so neatly piled had revealed something to him. Suddenly it seemed there was something different, unique, about the accident that had set him free. Something, but what? Serafin didn't know quite how to put it: the way it had happened, the place, the circumstances . . . there was something curiously domestic and benevolent about it . . . motherly, you could almost say. Yes, that was it.

The mild-mannered magistrate was counting his pairs of socks now: five of them, each folded in two, each bearing a discreet little label on which the name of their owner, Serafin Tous, was written in navy blue, black, or bloodred. It was another of his late wife's practical ideas, to prevent the pairs from getting mixed up in the wash or lost in hotels. Among many other things, Nora was a superlative housekeeper, he thought proudly. There wasn't a stain she couldn't remove or a household mishap she couldn't set right, such was her skill. Serafin always admired the way she directed those invisible but indispensable operations that transform married life into an idyll. With Nora, everything in the house seemed to run itself. Her organization was perfect: no detail was neglected, the meals were always done to a turn and delicious, and it all seemed to happen effortlessly. There was never an unpleasant cooking smell in the house, never an object out of place, and Nora herself had the rare virtue of being unobtrusive. It's only now that I really notice you, my dear, said husband to wife, now that you are gone, now that I need you, my treasure. The people we really miss are those who quietly filled our lives with pleasure, not the noisy fools we couldn't help noticing when they were alive.

Serafin Tous had gone into the bathroom to gather his toiletries, and as he packed them away—the impeccably clean razor, the tube of toothpaste rolled up from the bottom, just like Nora used to do it, to save him the trouble—an idea began to take shape in his mind. He found himself marveling once again at the neat, domestic way in which all his problems had been tidied up. Domestic and practical at the same time, he thought. It bore the mark of a woman's touch or, rather, the delicate touch of a ghost, because there was something about this accident that reminded him of Nora. So as he put his razor and his other toiletries away, Serafin wondered if the souls in the next life could shut the doors of earthly cool rooms, and finding in favor of this conjecture, he couldn't help exclaiming: "It was you, Nora, wasn't it, my darling?"

⁓

AS THE BODY of Nestor Chaffino was being carried through the garden to the gate of the Lilies, Chloe was sitting in front of the window at a makeshift desk with a look of girlish concentration, as if she were preparing to note down all her observations like some sort of record keeper. A little black moleskin notebook lay open to her left, and she was holding a pencil, which every now and then she raised to her lips. Now the pencil stopped halfway, as if she were trying to work out some particularly difficult problem.

An observer of human behavior watching her at that moment through the window would have been able to see how, behind the elaborately neat desk, the room was a complete mess, with the contents of Chloe's backpack spilled on the bed and her clothes scattered all over the place, while among the rumpled sheets lay the red case containing the photograph of her brother, Eddie. Yet if that same busybody had happened to be in the bedroom just a few minutes earlier, he would have witnessed an even odder scene. He would have seen Chloe striding up and down the room like a child throwing a tantrum, leafing through the notebook, then rummaging around in her backpack until she found the photo of her brother, as if she wanted to confront one object with the other, absolutely furious, as if those objects, photo and notebook, were to blame for a betrayal or, worse still, a pointless murder.

But there was no curious observer looking in through the windows of the Lilies, just a cockroach on the mat outside the front door, wiggling its antennae knowingly, as if it understood the quirks of human psychology. But who can really understand what makes a capricious girl like Chloe tick? Or how she might come to believe that she could modify the destiny of someone who died before his time. Or why she might think that sooner or later he would return to this world to complete the life he left unfinished. Few can fathom such irrational thoughts, but that doesn't stop them from existing and explaining why Nestor was now inside a shiny body bag on the way to the cemetery while Chloe observed his departure with a smile.

"And you got what you deserved, old fool," she said. Put me back in the same situation and I'd do exactly the same thing again, every time, she thought, relishing each detail of what had happened in the kitchen the previous night, like a triumphant artist or the perpetrator of a perfect crime.

With her pencil still suspended in midair, as if she were choosing which part of the perverse story to relate to her nonexistent readers, Chloe decided to leave aside what had happened in the small hours of that morning, when she had heard Nestor whistling in the cool room. She preferred to evoke what she felt a little later on, looking into her brother's dark gaze reflected in the mirror, searching for an idea, a message, some way of making him stay close to her. Chloe remembered how gradually she came to the conclusion that the only way to revive the memory of the dead was by fulfilling the desires they had when they were alive. A simple, obvious idea that gathered force as she stared at herself in the mirror. On the last day of his life, Eddie had gone off on a motorcycle because he had this crazy idea that to be a writer he had to "live fast, have tons of experiences, kill someone, fuck hundreds of girls, whatever, Clo-Clo, you wouldn't understand, you're too young."

And when she had asked him what would happen if it turned out he didn't have the guts to do any of those terrible things that were supposed to give him the experiences he was looking for, he replied: "Well then, Clo-Clo, I'll just have to steal someone else's story, won't I." That's what he had said, her brother Eddie, but he didn't carry out his plan; instead, he went away forever, leaving it all unfinished.

But she was here now, young Chloe, little Clo-Clo, the same age as Eddie when he died, ready and willing to do all those things he would have done if he'd had time. She hadn't planned what had happened the previous night at the Lilies, nor did she have any grudge against the chef, with his pointy mustache and his little notebook full of the scandals and secrets he'd been privy to, or so he said: a treasure chest, in other words, of real-life stories, cruel and perfect, better by far than anything a writer could invent.

"Okay, I'm opening the door, you old fool, it's okay," she had said. But when she finally opened the door to help Nestor, there he was on the floor holding that little book, as if he were offering it to her, while her brother looked on. All Chloe could think about was helping Eddie fulfill his dream. That's why she snatched the book from the cook's outstretched hand: that's where they were, all those stories of love and crime that Eddie would have loved to write.

The opportunity had presented itself; exploiting it was easy. Easy to find a justification for what she had just done, to shut the door again, pretend not to hear, dream of Eddie, wait for the cold to silence the cook's cries forever, and then go up to her room as if nothing had happened . . . it had all been very easy. And now she realized that she, the little sister, had succeeded where her brother had failed, because now she would be able to fulfill the destiny that death had snatched away from him. "Those who die young always find a way to come back to this world and finish off their destiny." That's what Miss Liau Chi had said to her, and she believed it. Wasn't she holding the proof in her hands: the very thing he had gone looking for the day he died?

Little Indiscretions, that was the title Nestor had given to the collection of anecdotes he was writing. It was bound to be full of really juicy gossip, terrible, shameful secrets: exactly what she needed to live out Eddie's crazy idea of writing books about other people's lives.

So, the previous night, without checking the contents of the notebook, Chloe had gone off to sleep peacefully, pretending that nothing had happened. And she believed it—she had fooled herself. It's the best way to fool others, after all.

SITTING IN FRONT of the window now, Chloe Trias remembered all this as well as something far worse, which had happened just a few minutes earlier, when she opened up her treasure chest and discovered what the chef had really written in his moleskin notebook. What the fuck?!

She couldn't believe her bad luck. She read the sentences over and over, stunned: "The secret of a chocolate mousse . . . the trick for making a perfect *île flottante* . . ." Jesus fucking Christ! "The scandalous flavor of a mango sorbet . . ."

She looked out of the window. The funeral procession was approaching the garden gate now. The bright sunshine seemed to be mocking her as she tried to spot Nestor's body. She wanted to shout something obscene at that lying, cheating cook. She even opened the window. But then she stopped. There's no point abusing the dead, so she went back to leafing through the notebook, as if she were hoping a magic spell might grant her the power to find something she hadn't noticed before. But all she could see were Nestor's culinary indiscretions, written down in that neat, rounded hand of his, stubbornly occupying the pages. A pointless murder, another broken dream.

KAREL WOULD BE coming to get her soon. It was nearly time to leave the Lilies. She would have to pick up her clothes and stuff them into her backpack. Another chapter of her life would come to an end and she would be alone again. As usual, she thought. And yet, as she was about to stand up, something outside caught her eye and made her stop. She sat there watching a ray of sunlight shining on Nestor Chaffino's body bag, the same ray the other characters in this story had seen from their respective windows. The way the plastic of the bag reflected the sunlight reminded her of all those mirrors and their sparkling reflections, and suddenly she was laughing again, as happy as she had been staring at the closed door of the Westinghouse, as if her brother's dark gaze had returned to her eyes. Life had not been kind to her, true: stealing what she loved, deceiving her and laying traps. And it was true that luck had just played the cruelest trick of all: substituting recipes for the stories she was going to use to live out a dream. And yet despite all this, she smiled as she said good-bye to Nestor's body bag, because she had just realized that there might still be a way of beating destiny. She had a story that no one could ever take away. The story of a little or perhaps a not so little indiscretion: her own story, what had happened to her at the Lilies. And realizing what she had, like a boy with a head full of dreams who has just completed the first twenty-one years of a long, ambitious life, Chloe began to tear out all the pages on which Nestor had written. Nestor's culinary secrets were scattered in a flurry of paper—after-dinner petits fours, ginger truffles, ice creams and sorbets—until only blank pages were left and the title page, which read:

LITTLE INDISCRETIONS

Once she had removed all traces of cookery, underneath the title inscribed in Nestor Chaffino's tiny, round hand, Chloe noted down the first lines of a story. She would work out how it ended later on. This is how it began:

> His mustache was stiffer than ever, so stiff a fly could have stepped out to the end, like a prisoner walking the plank on a pirate ship.

She stopped to take a breath and think about what to say in the next sentence of *Little Indiscretions,* a novel by Eddie Trias. And as she continued her draft:

> Except that flies can't survive in a cool room at twenty below zero, and neither could the owner of the blond, frozen mustache: Nestor Chaffino, chef and pastry cook, renowned for his masterful way with a chocolate fondant.

Chloe discovered that with a real death and a couple of basic ideas, it's not so hard to spin a story of passion, secrets, and malice, because lies can be perfectly convincing if they contain an element of truth.

So where do I go from here? she wondered, before writing:

And that's how he was found hours later: eyes wide open in astonishment, but with a certain dignity still in his bearing. True, his fingernails were scratching at the door, but there was a dishcloth tucked into the string of his apron as usual, though looking smart is hardly a major preoccupation when the door of a 1980s-model Westinghouse cool room, two meters by one and a half, has just shut automatically behind you with a *click*.

⁓

BUT AS SHE drafted the first paragraphs of *Little Indiscretions,* unbeknownst to Chloe, on the doormat of the Lilies a cockroach was wiggling its antennae.

CARMEN POSADAS is the daughter of a Uruguayan diplomat and has lived in many capital cities, including Moscow, Buenos Aires, and London. She is a prizewinning children's author and co-writer for film and television. *Little Indiscretions* was first published as *Pequeñas Infamias*; it won the coveted Planeta Prize in 1998 and has since gone on to sell more than half a million copies worldwide. She is the author of *The Last Resort,* also published by Random House, and her books have been translated into fifteen languages. Carmen Posadas lives in Madrid.

ABOUT THE TYPE

This book was set in Granjon, a modern recutting of a typeface produced under the direction of George W. Jones, who based Granjon's design upon the letterforms of Claude Garamond (1480–1561). The name was given to the typeface as a tribute to the typographic designer Robert Granjon.